SOMEWHERE IN THE CROWD

SOMEWHERE IN THE CROWD

KATRINA LOGAN

HODDER

First published in Great Britain in 2023 by Hodder & Stoughton
An Hachette UK company

1

A CIP catalogue record for this title is available from the British Library

Paperback ISBN 978 1 399 71890 5
eBook ISBN 978 1 399 71891 2

Typeset in Plantin light by Manipal Technologies Limited

Printed and bound in Great Britain by Clays Ltd, Elcograf S.p.A.

Hodder & Stoughton policy is to use papers that are natural, renewable
and recyclable products and made from wood grown in sustainable forests.
The logging and manufacturing processes are expected to conform to the
environmental regulations of the country of origin.

Hodder & Stoughton Ltd
Carmelite House
50 Victoria Embankment
London EC4Y 0DZ

www.hodder.co.uk

For the dreamers

PROLOGUE

Brighton, UK

1974

Saturday 6 April

There she was again.

Tom had noticed her earlier. He'd seen her outside, before they were all ushered into the Brighton Dome to start taking their seats for the show. She'd drawn his attention straight away. Among all the people milling around near the entrance in their smart dark jackets and overcoats, she was standing there in a bright yellow dress. He couldn't help but smile as he spotted her.

He's on the same row as her now, up on the left-hand side of the balcony area. From what he can make out, she's here with her parents, too. Tom's father works as a producer for BBC Radio Brighton, which is why they got tickets to this year's Eurovision Song Contest. Tom knows he's lucky to be in the live audience. As soon as the orchestra struck up the introductory music moments ago, he felt a huge rush of excitement to be here. And then, as he joined in the applause for the host, Katie Boyle, who appeared on the stage in a bright flamingo pink outfit, he happened to glance along his row, and there she was a few seats along: the girl in the yellow dress.

She's petite – she can't be more than five foot four – with unruly soft brown curls that fall past her shoulders and an untidy fringe that serves to highlight her large eyes and delicate features.

He tries to focus on the show as the first act takes to the stage, but Finland's entry fails to hold his complete attention, and he continues to steal glances at her as she listens to the music. He cheers along with the rest of the audience when Olivia Newton-John glides to centre stage to represent the United Kingdom, smiling to himself when he sees the girl in the yellow dress nodding her head along to the catchy chorus of "Long Live Love".

At first, he can't put his finger on what it is that's so mesmerising about her, but it gradually dawns on him that it's the fact she's so enraptured by the show: leaning forwards in her seat as each act takes to the stage, her eyes bright with curiosity; lifting her hands high above her head to clap when the musicians take their bows. Everyone else in the audience here – the sea of men in their stiff black ties; the women with their perfectly coiffed curls and high-neck dresses – seems composed and restrained in comparison to her. Tom has always been shy and reserved, plagued by insecurities, but she seems to exude the confidence and self-assuredness that he wishes he had.

When it's Sweden's turn, Tom tears his eyes away from her so that he can look at whatever it is that's making her giggle so much: the conductor has marched into the room wearing a full-on Napoleon costume. Tom chuckles, his eyebrows lifting in surprise as he takes in the bright, glitzy, colourful outfits of the band representing Sweden: ABBA. Standing by the curtain to the back of the stage as they wait for their performance to begin, one of the female singers is wearing some kind of bright blue satin catsuit with knee-high silver glitter platform boots – and the male guitarist is wearing matching boots.

'What *do* they look like?' a man in the row in front of Tom whispers disapprovingly.

Tom bristles with irritation at his comment. He thinks they look … *fantastic*.

The lights dim on the audience, the band strikes up and the two singers bound to the front of the stage, wide grins across their faces, a burst of infectious energy.

They start singing "Waterloo", and it's as though the whole room lights up.

It's fun and energetic and upbeat and *brilliant*. Tom is captivated by the performance, unable to stop his foot tapping, his shoulders bopping, barely noticing he's moved forwards to the edge of his seat. If he wasn't in an auditorium surrounded by an audience and he was all alone, he'd be up on his feet and dancing, and that's saying something – Tom never dances. But there's something about this song that makes him feel so light and happy, as though everything is going to be okay.

When it comes to an end and ABBA take their bows, Tom forgets himself. He jumps to his feet, clapping and cheering. He hears his mother next to him gasp at his reaction and she tugs on his jacket, insisting he sit back down. He should be mortified at his surprising and out-of-character behaviour and sink back into his chair, cheeks blushing at the embarrassment of making a spectacle of himself. But he's not.

And that's because he's not the only one on his feet.

The girl in the yellow dress is standing and whooping, too. Suddenly noticing that she's not alone in her enthusiastic response, she turns to look at him.

Their eyes meet.

She beams at him and laughs, lifting her hands up high above her head to clap as she holds his eye contact, delighted to be sharing this moment of pure sparkling joy with someone else. As her dad instructs her to sit back down, she offers Tom a shrug, as though the two of them have tried their best; as though they're in this together.

As though he's the only one here who gets it.

Tom slowly sits back down. A few moments later, full of hope and hardly daring to breathe, he glances her way again. She's looking at him, too. She smiles.

The rest of the show is a blur.

CHAPTER ONE

Oslo, Norway

2010

Saturday 29 May

Millie is here. She's finally *here*.

Standing in the middle of the roaring crowd, she can't quite believe it, but it's really happening. She's in Oslo at the Grand Final of Eurovision. After years of faithfully watching the contest at home with her grandparents, Millie is at the show in person, surrounded by fans from all over the world. It's even more incredible than she imagined. There is an electric atmosphere in the arena as the audience waits for it to start. Everyone is cheering, whooping and proudly waving flags, all of them with huge smiles on their faces – this evening is like no other. It really is a bubble of pure happiness.

And this year, she gets to be a part of it.

'I can tell you're having a moment right now,' laughs James, Millie's best friend from school who has joined the trip with her and her grandparents. He nudges her arm. 'This is incredible, right?'

'Right.' Millie beams up at him. 'I'm so glad you're here with me.'

He grins at her, the red glitter brushed across his cheeks shimmering in the lights, his eyes twinkling behind the round glasses he's desperate to replace, but that his parents won't let him because glasses aren't cheap. James hates them, raging about them 'ruining his vibe', but in Millie's opinion, he can easily carry them off – with his tight black curls, intense dark brown eyes and strong jaw, James is handsome and his style is effortlessly cool.

Tonight, he has come dressed for the occasion. He's ditched his signature style of buttoned-up chequered shirts and skinny jeans in favour of a velvet shirt in cobalt blue, which he discovered after rummaging through the local charity-shop rails, and slim trousers with an iridescent purple sheen that he bought a couple of weeks ago from a kooky menswear shop in Brighton where the owner also tried to persuade him to buy a pink satin top hat. Millie could tell that James was tempted, until he saw the price. Instead, his accessories for the night are the Union Jack flag draped round his shoulders and matching glitter streaked across his face.

He tried to convince Millie that she could be a little more daring with her Eurovision Grand Final outfit – he caught her stroking the material of a silver metallic puff-sleeve midi dress in that charity shop, but when he suggested she try it on, she dropped the fabric from her fingers like it was burning hot and told him not to be so silly, blushing furiously and turning away.

She can't pull off a dress like that, no matter what James tells her. The kind of person who wears those dresses is the sort who walks into a room and instantly commands attention; someone with excellent posture and a cool demeanour, who can convey their coveted approval or dreaded discontent with just one look; someone who people clamour to talk to and impress.

Millie is not one of those people.

Already petite in stature, her tendency to hunch makes her seem even smaller. She mostly goes unnoticed in a crowd and prefers to stick to plain, dark outfit colours that aid her in blending in. It is Eurovision, though, so she has made a bit of an effort tonight, wearing a dark belted dress patterned with little white stars all over it, tights and black boots. She's straightened her shoulder-length hair – she inherited her dark wayward curls from her grandma – and done her best at applying some mascara, blush, and the plum lipstick she'd felt rushed into buying from Boots after applying a couple of testers to the back of her hand and noticing the shop assistant glancing at her. She became paranoid that the assistant might laugh about her with her colleagues afterwards, wondering why she thought those lipsticks might possibly suit her, and so wanted to get out of there quickly.

'I'm in the audience of the Grand Final of Eurovision in Oslo – this is a once-in-a-lifetime experience!' James responds ecstatically. 'I wouldn't miss it!'

He turns to address Millie's grandma standing next to him. 'Thanks again for letting me come, Julie.'

'James, you're a member of the family,' she smiles, gripping his arm. 'And you've been coming to our house to watch Eurovision for a long time now! We wouldn't dream of being here without you. Isn't that right, Tom?'

Millie's grandpa nods. 'Absolutely.'

'Besides, it's hardly much fun for a seventeen-year-old to go on a trip to Oslo with just her boring grandparents,' Julie remarks, raising her eyebrows at Millie. 'I'm sure we're cramping your style!'

'No way,' Millie says, frowning at her. 'We're here *because* of you!'

Julie chuckles, looping her arm through her husband's. Tom pats her hand affectionately. Julie and Tom first met in the audience of Eurovision – when the UK hosted it in Brighton, in 1974 – and so the song contest will always hold a special place in their hearts.

'Do you remember the first time I came to one of your famous Eurovision parties?' James says to them, his eyes widening. 'How old were we, Millie? Thirteen?'

'Twelve,' she corrects.

'It was the best night,' James claims, smiling at the memory. 'You kept going on at school about the big parties your grandparents hosted every year and I was waiting for you to invite me – I'm pretty sure I ended up inviting myself.'

'You did,' Millie confirms. 'But only because I was too nervous to ask you to come! I wasn't sure if you even knew what Eurovision was. You were my only friend at school – I was worried the party might scare you away forever.'

'A valid concern, to be fair. Julie's costumes can be *blinding*. Many would run away in fear,' Tom teases.

Julie gasps, slapping her husband playfully on the hand as he chuckles at his own joke. 'Eurovision is all about being loud and colourful, thank you very much. And as far as I know, no one has been scared off by our parties – if anything, they're growing in numbers every year. Last time, I was worried we wouldn't fit everyone in the house!'

'It did start spilling into the street,' Millie reminds her.

'Oh yes. We had to round everybody up. Luckily, our neighbours didn't mind,' Julie recalls. 'I think that might have been something to do with them joining in with the party themselves. Even Barry from next door came over – remember, I encouraged him to go fetch his ukulele and play it for everyone? It was fantastic to see him get so involved! He's usually such a closed book, bless him.'

'It would have been more fantastic if he had known more than one song,' Tom mutters, sharing a smile with Millie. 'I'm all for a good rendition of "Baa Baa Black Sheep", but it got a little much after the sixth performance.'

The first memory Millie has of Eurovision is being at one of her grandparents' annual parties to celebrate the contest when she was six years old. She remembers coming down the stairs in a dark red party dress that she was obsessed with at the time and the house was filled with guests wearing extravagant outfits, each of them sporting the colours of a different country. Everyone who comes to her grandparents' Eurovision parties knows that you don't go half-heartedly and that night was no exception. The TV was on in the sitting room, blaring out the performances at full volume, filling the house with music as people bopped away, spinning each other round, her recollection of it a blurry haze of colours, lights and an atmosphere of elation.

It felt like she'd stepped into a whole new world.

She was hooked from then on, although it would have been difficult for Millie to grow up without being a fan of Eurovision. Her grandparents are devoted to it and, as she was raised by them, it feels like it runs in her blood. As soon as she was old enough, she was helping her grandparents plan their annual extravaganza in its honour, its place in the family calendar as highly anticipated as Christmas – for everyone, that is, except for Millie's mum, Aggie. She can't stand it and finds her parents' love of it embarrassing and infuriating – she makes no effort at hiding her disdain for the whole thing and has never attended the parties.

Millie would rather Aggie didn't come, to be honest. She'd only bring the mood down with her sneers and snide comments. A workaholic who lives in London and seems to only visit them in Brighton when it suits her busy travel schedule, Aggie looks down her nose at anything fun and joyful.

As far as Millie is concerned, her mum is welcome to keep her distance.

'Your Eurovision parties are *legendary*,' James enthusiastically confirms to Julie and Tom, before addressing Millie. 'If anything, inviting myself to that party cemented our friendship. I had watched Eurovision before, but I had no idea it could be celebrated in that way. It usually went unnoticed in my household. That first party I went to at yours was the night I fell in love with Eurovision and everything it stands for. I owe your family a lot. Thank you for bringing it into my life.'

Julie shares a warm smile with Tom.

'And to think, right now I could have been stuck at home working and missing out on being here!' James continues, looking horrified at the thought. 'I'm so glad you persuaded my parents that it would be a good idea for us to come this weekend, Julie.'

'Well, I can appreciate they thought it was a little reckless coming to Oslo so close to your exams,' she reasons. 'But the brain needs a break from revision every now and then. This will refresh you! You'll return ready to tackle anything.'

'As long as I get the grades I need,' he says, holding up his hands and crossing his fingers.

'Of course you will,' Millie reassures him. 'You've worked harder than anyone in our year. I've barely seen you recently, you've been so buried away in your books. There's still plenty of time when we get home for you to revise.'

'The University of Brighton will be lucky to have you,' Tom adds, his eyes twinkling at James. 'A fierce young journalist in the making!'

'A fierce young *music* journalist,' James emphasises with a wide grin. 'But you're right, it's important to give myself a break from revision and I can't think of anywhere I'd rather be. I mean, look at this' – he gestures to the audience surrounding them. 'Where else do you get *this*? A room full of eccentricity, authenticity, acceptance and joy. No one is a stranger in this arena. We're all in it together, no judgement, no barriers.'

Millie looks at the three women in the row in front of her with the Greek flag painted across their faces chatting animatedly to the man next to them, who has an Irish flag draped over his shoulders and green glitter sprayed all over his grey scraggly beard. Meanwhile, a Norwegian group of lads nearby have struck up conversation with a British couple, asking them where they think the UK will place this year. They laugh heartily at their response and wish them luck. It really is a remarkable atmosphere.

If only Millie could freeze time and stay here in this moment forever: standing in the middle of the Eurovision audience where it doesn't matter who or what you are.

All that matters is you're happy.

Millie closes her eyes and takes a deep breath in.

'What are you doing?' James asks her. 'Are you having another moment?'

She nods, keeping her eyes shut. 'I read somewhere that if you want to hold on to the memory of a specific moment, you should close your eyes and breathe deeply – it makes time stand still.'

'Then I'll join you,' James declares, and she hears him inhale loudly next to her.

They stand next to each other in silence as the audience continues to chant around them, despite the contest being yet to begin. Loud cheers ripple through the crowd, causing Millie's body to tingle with the excitement of what's to come.

She never wants to forget this feeling.

'Do you think I might have a chance with Alexander Rybak?' James asks suddenly.

Opening her eyes, Millie bursts out laughing. 'So much for creating a moment of calm reflection to create a memory!'

'My mind wandered,' James admits with a shrug. 'Alexander Rybak is hot *and* he's musically talented. He's a catch.'

'Not to mention he's won Eurovision,' Millie adds with a smile, 'which is fairly impressive.'

'That is quite the achievement.' James nods. 'If only we could find a way to meet. The man of my dreams is backstage right now. I feel so close to him, and yet so far. What if we persuaded someone to let us into the green room?'

'I hate to dash your dreams, James, but even if we made it backstage, I'm not sure you and Alexander would work out. He's straight. I think he might have a girlfriend.'

'Reality is always so crushing,' he sighs wistfully. 'Still, we could be best friends. Maybe he could let me have a go on his violin.'

'You don't play the violin.'

'I know, but I have a feeling I'd be a natural.'

Suddenly, the lights dim and the audience is bathed in a wash of purple. A ripple of gasps floods through the crowd, turning quickly into cheers and screams, a sea of waving flags lifted high in the air. Millie feels a rush of adrenaline like never before, as James squeals next to her, grabbing her hand and squeezing it tight. They gaze up at the twinkling blue lights dotted around the ceiling like stars, before images of Eurovision fans from all across the world are projected onto the huge screen hanging above the stage at the front.

The crowd erupts with thunderous applause when the screen glows red and a spotlight comes up on Alexander Rybak, standing alone centre stage in his trademark white shirt and black waistcoat, holding a violin in his left hand.

James gasps.

The arena now awash in a red hue, Alexander launches into his opening performance of 'Fairytale', the song that won him first place last year. Along with the rest of the audience, James and Millie belt out the lyrics, forgetting any inhibitions as they dance around wildly. Julie happily sways next to them, while Tom chuckles away at his family's enthusiasm, his arms folded across his chest, nodding his head in time to the music, which is as far as he'll go when it comes to dancing.

'I need to meet him!' James cries above the noise when Alexander's performance comes to an end. 'We *have* to get backstage.'

Millie laughs in response, but does a double-take when she realises that James is still staring hopefully at her, wide-eyed.

'You're not serious,' she checks.

He nods. 'I am.'

'James, we can't … we can't go backstage!'

'Why not?'

'Because they won't just let anyone wander backstage!' she points out, aghast. 'This is the Grand Final of Eurovision. We have tickets to be here in the audience. We don't know anyone involved in the competition!'

'They don't know that,' he says with a shrug. 'Come on, Millie, what's the harm in trying?'

'There is no chance we're going to get in! It will be a waste of time. Why can't we just enjoy being in the audience? We're here to see the show.'

'We're here for a Eurovision adventure!' he counters. 'Think about it this way – in years to come, when we're old and boring, what would you rather tell people: that you once stood in the audience of the Grand Final of Eurovision, *or* that you managed to blag your way backstage and meet all the acts?!'

'You forgot the other outcome: that we *missed* the Grand Final of Eurovision because we tried to get backstage and instead got kicked out.' Millie gives James a stern look. 'You can't really be serious about this.'

In response, he reaches over to tap Julie on the arm.

'Julie, what would you say if I told you that Millie and I were going to try our luck at getting backstage tonight?'

She places a hand on her heart. 'How wonderful! I think that's a fantastic idea!'

James gives Millie a triumphant look.

'We won't get in!' Millie cries, dismayed.

'You don't know that,' Julie says.

Millie holds up her hands. 'Am I the only one here who thinks that this is absurd? We're never going to get past security! It will never work!'

'You sound just like your grandfather at the *Strictly Come Dancing* live tour,' Julie sighs, putting her hands on her hips. 'I wanted to hang around the stage door, but Mr Grump wasn't having any of it. Now we'll never know what Len Goodman is like in real life.'

'Mr Grump had sat through a lot of dancing by that point and very much wanted to get home,' Tom grumbles next to her.

'The point is, you won't know until you try,' James announces, Julie nodding in agreement. 'If you ask me, this feels like one of those big life moments.'

Millie raises her eyebrows. 'What, us being kicked out of an arena?'

'Us taking a chance,' James corrects. 'Come on, Millie, imagine if it works! Imagine if we get to see behind the scenes of Eurovision!'

'You have officially lost the plot,' she sighs, but his pleading eyes are difficult to ignore.

As outrageous as his idea is, part of her is tempted to give in – she has to admit that some of her best, most treasured memories are thanks to James's fun, spontaneous streak.

'OK, how about we stay and watch some of the performances here,' James pitches, catching on to her relenting. 'Then we try to sneak backstage later. A compromise! Best of both worlds!'

Millie bites her lip.

'Come on, Millie,' James urges, grinning like he knows he's got her. 'Take a chance.'

CHAPTER TWO

Noah has been watching the blue-haired girl attempting to argue her way backstage for a few minutes now and it has been thoroughly entertaining.

The stony-faced doorman has been standing in front of her this entire time with his arms crossed, entirely unaffected by her various methods to talk her way in.

She started by just trying to waltz past him, as though she was meant to be there. He stopped her immediately and said something in Norwegian – when it was clear she didn't understand, he repeated himself in English, asking to see her pass. Responding in flawless English with a German accent, she proceeded to act as though she'd lost it, claiming to be part of the German Eurovision team. He told her that he couldn't let her through, but she persisted, telling him that she'd left her pass in her luxury hotel room and she could go back and get it; however, she was *really* needed backstage and so if he wouldn't mind just this once letting her off …

'Sorry, but you need a pass,' the doorman says gruffly as she continues to argue.

'You must recognise me! You must have seen me coming through here before!' she claims, throwing her hands up in the air. 'Do I really have to go all the way back to my hotel?'

'No pass, no access,' he states.

She sighs. 'OK, I'm embarrassed to say this, because it is not very cool, but …' – she pauses for dramatic effect, glances around and then lowers her voice to continue – 'I'm a celebrity.'

The doorman doesn't say anything.

'I am Ingrid Vogel?' she says, looking at him expectantly. '*The* Ingrid Vogel.'

When he doesn't react, she brushes it aside with a wave of her hand.

'Don't worry about it, I'm a big star in Germany. Anyway, if I could go through …'

The doorman holds out his arm to stop her passing him.

'You need a pass,' he emphasises, the corner of his lips twitching into a mocking smile as he adds, 'even if you are a *celebrity*.'

She purses her lips, narrowing her eyes at him. 'If you don't let me through, you're going to regret it. I should be behind that stage with the German Eurovision team. You are stopping me from being where I should be and I am NOT happy about it.'

Until now, Noah has managed to suppress his sniggering while spectating, but at that moment, he can't help but let a bubble of laughter escape from his throat. Hearing him, she glances over furiously, then whirls back to argue with the doorman.

Noah had been about to make his own attempt to blag his way backstage before this Ingrid Vogel brazenly over-took him as he was approaching the door and got straight to work – he had thought it best to stand aside for a while, out of the doorman's line of sight, to watch how she got on before he stepped up to have a go.

Whether or not he gets backstage at the Eurovision Grand Final is not a big deal to him. He doesn't care either way. He's here as a matter of chance. Noah didn't mean for his visit to Oslo to coincide with the song contest. In fact, he'd been wondering why the terrible hostel he was staying in was so expensive, but knows now he was lucky to find accommodation at all – the whole city is filled with visitors from all over the continent, here to support their nation. It's not like he hasn't heard of Eurovision – it has a big following in Australia – but he doesn't have any personal interest in it. In his opinion, it seems weird and wacky, and, no offence to Europe, but the music is pretty terrible.

A girl he met in his hostel was bragging last night that she had a contact on the Spanish team and she'd be able to get people in backstage – Noah thought it sounded fun. He'd been exploring the city on his own when she'd texted earlier to say she'd got a group of them in and if he wanted to join, he needed to come to the arena straight away.

That was a few hours ago now – he hadn't exactly come running – and he's wondering if he's missed his window. He'd sent her a message to let her know he's here, but is yet to hear back and is growing tired of hanging around.

As Ingrid Vogel continues to explain to the doorman why she should be allowed through, when it's blatantly clear by now that she's a crazed fan and absolutely shouldn't, Noah smiles to himself and checks some of the shots he got today on the screen of the Canon EOS 5D Mark II camera hanging round his neck – a gift he'd bought himself two years ago when photography first piqued his interest. He rarely goes anywhere without it.

His phone buzzes in his pocket and he reaches for it, hoping it might be the go-ahead he needs to get in. But he deflates when he sees it's a message from Charlotte, his sister. He doesn't bother to read the text, putting his phone away. What is she doing texting him at this time? It's early in Melbourne. Typical. She'll be at her desk already, no doubt.

He feels a pang of guilt at ignoring her, though. She's been messaging him every now and then to check in, but their conversations are stilted and Noah's useless at replying. When he left for his year of travelling, they weren't exactly on good terms.

'I'm only looking out for you,' Charlotte had said, watching him pack the day before his flight to London. 'I think it's great that you're heading off to see the world, but make the most of it. Don't laze around and do nothing with the year. Get some good experience.'

She was standing in the doorway of his bedroom, wearing a red designer gown, about to leave for a charity gala, hosted by their family. Her long blonde hair was swept away from her face in an elegant up-do, complemented by diamond drop earrings, and her blue eyes were accentuated by smoky black eye make-up.

The good looks of the Pearce family were as renowned as their fortune. Their father had built up a successful property empire before marrying their mother, a former model with a fashion and skincare line under her belt. They were a remarkably glamorous pairing and their children were as beautiful as everyone expected them to be.

'I haven't even left yet and you're already lecturing me about wasting my time,' Noah retorted, searching for a pair of shoes under his bed.

'I also just said that I think it's great you flying off,' she replied defensively, leaning on his doorframe. 'And don't forget that I was the one who encouraged you to take a year out before taking your university place.'

'Yeah, on a business and commerce course I don't even want to do,' he mumbled.

Her eyes fell to the floor. 'Noah, that course will provide you with an excellent foundation to get a good job at the end of it.'

He paused what he was doing to give her a look. 'You sound like him.'

She glanced up. 'What?'

'You sound like Dad,' he emphasised, returning to his packing. 'He doesn't need you spouting his opinion, too. He's very happy to tell me to my face exactly what he thinks.'

'Come on.' She sighed. 'You really think photography is a serious career?'

'For lots of people, yeah, it is. And not that any of you have noticed, but I happen to be good at it.'

'I know you're good at it! Mum won't shut up about how good you are at it. Maybe one day, you can have a go at making it as a photographer and you'll have everyone's support on that, but with a business degree, you have something sensible to fall back on.'

Noah snorted. 'Charlotte, don't say shit you don't mean.'

'How was I—'

'We both know Dad will never – *never* – support a career in photography,' he said, looking her right in the eye. She swallowed. 'You were there when he made it perfectly clear that if I consider anything in the arts, then I won't have a penny to my name. He'd kick me out.'

'He wouldn't kick you out,' she said quietly, but she didn't sound convinced.

'I'm surprised he's letting me escape for the year,' Noah said begrudgingly, squishing a few t-shirts into his bag

20

and pressing down on them as hard as possible. 'If he had it his way, I'd already be in a suit, my own opinions squashed out, no independent thinking allowed, learning the ropes from dear old Dad. But I suppose he already has you for that.'

Charlotte's eyes filled with tears. 'That's unfair, Noah. And not very fucking nice.'

Noah hesitated. 'Sorry. I didn't mean it.'

'Yes, you did,' she fired back.

Since then, Noah hasn't been able to shake away the guilt he felt at the look on her face before she turned her back on him and walked away, leaving for the gala without saying goodbye.

He really should text her back at some point.

'OK, how much?'

Noah snaps his head up at blue-haired Ingrid's latest statement. She's now waving cash under the doorman's nose.

'How much?' she repeats, holding the notes aloft. 'Don't pretend that you're above this. I'm sure we can work out a way of coming to an agreement.'

Uh oh. She's taken it too far. It's time for Noah to step in.

Clearing his throat, he marches towards the door and then comes to an abrupt halt right in front of her.

'Oh my god,' he says, his eyes widening as he looks her up and down. 'Are you … are you *Ingrid Vogel*?'

She blinks at him. 'Huh?'

'Wow! I am freaking out!' Noah exclaims, running a hand through his hair. 'Ingrid Vogel! I am a HUGE fan!'

The doorman looks surprised by this turn of events. Ingrid looks utterly thrown, but decides to play along.

'R-really?' she says, as Noah nods vigorously.

'I am big into the German music scene; you have a huge fan base in Australia,' he explains, holding up his camera. 'Hey, can I get a photo of you? I'm one of the official photographers here at Eurovision.'

'Uh … OK. Yes, sure. Anything for a fan,' she says.

He lifts his lens and she obligingly strikes a pose, hands on her lips, pouting, as he takes the photo.

'Perfect, thank you.' He hesitates, pointing at the backstage door. 'Are you heading in? We can go in together. I'd love to chat to you about your future projects. Maybe you could do a shoot for the … uh … publication I work for. After this Eurovision gig, of course.'

'Yes, we can talk once we're backstage,' she says.

'Cool.' Noah looks at the doorman expectantly. 'Thanks, if you wouldn't mind—'

His breezy attempt to pass him is quickly stopped as the doorman blocks his path.

'I need to see your press pass,' he insists.

'Sure,' Noah nods, feeling round his neck as though the lanyard should be hanging there. He acts confused that it's not. 'Hang on, it will be here in my pocket.' He does a good job of searching his jeans. 'Oh no. It must be in my jacket.'

The doorman raises his eyebrows.

'I put my pass in my jacket and I left that through there earlier during the rehearsals,' Noah explains, nodding to the door. 'If you let me in, I can go get it for you.'

The doorman sighs. 'No.'

'OK, no problem, I'll call my colleague who is backstage at the moment and she can come here with it,' Noah shrugs casually.

He takes out his phone and calls the girl from the hostel, who still hasn't got back to him. She doesn't pick up.

22

'She'll be busy working,' he explains, trying her again. 'But I'm not lying, she'll come prove to you that we have every right to be backstage.'

'Sure,' the doorman says sarcastically.

The phone goes to voicemail. If only Noah could remember her name at least, that might help his case, but unfortunately she's saved in his phone as 'Oslo Hostel Person'.

His enthusiasm flagging, Noah is about to have one last attempt at persuading the doorman to let them through when he's distracted by a guy with red glitter streaked across his cheeks flouncing past him, followed by an embarrassed-looking girl.

With a fantastic air of confidence, the glitter boy heads determinedly for the door, gliding past the doorman as though he hasn't noticed him.

'Wait!' the doorman says, turning to stop him as he reaches for the handle. 'I need to see your pass.'

'Oh, I'm so sorry, of course,' he says in an English accent, with an apologetic titter. He begins searching his pockets before his expression turns from calm to confusion. He sighs, shakes his head and then looks up at the doorman with a hopeful smile. 'Oh dear, I must have left it in my hotel.'

Noah tries and fails to suppress a smile at the doorman's utterly fed-up eyeroll.

'None of you are getting through! Now, PLEASE, return to your seats or I will throw you out of this arena,' he bellows.

'But, we really have left our passes—' the British boy begins hopefully, astounded by such a dramatic reaction.

'*That's it!*'

Losing his patience, the doorman ushers them away from the backstage door with a thunderous expression. Instructing them to 'KEEP MOVING', he rounds the four of them up and directs them towards the first door that they come to leading to the arena seating.

He flings it open and hisses, 'Back to your seats and don't even *think* about trying to get backstage again tonight or I really will throw you out. Got it?'

Before any of them can protest, he shoos them in and slams the door firmly behind them. Noah gapes at the huge audience extending out in front of him, everyone up on their feet dancing along to an upbeat pop song in a language he doesn't recognise. He turns to address the others, specifically the boy and his pretty companion.

'Sorry about that,' Noah grimaces. 'Before you arrived, we' – he gestures to Ingrid and himself – 'were also trying to get backstage using the exact same excuse of leaving our pass somewhere. I think we may have riled him up a lot by the time you arrived.'

'Ah, that makes sense.' The boy nods. 'Oh well, it was always a long shot!'

'Guess we'll just go back to our seats?' the British girl suggests, looking a little relieved at the outcome. Noah assumes that it wasn't her initial idea to try to blag their way backstage.

'I don't have one!' Ingrid admits, beaming at them. 'I may not have managed to get backstage, but that security guard has just got me free entry to the Eurovision Grand Final!'

'Me too,' Noah realises, before noticing a nearby member of staff giving them a strange look. 'Although we probably shouldn't linger here by the exit. I think we're going to be moved any minute.'

'Where shall we go?' Ingrid asks, panicked, looking around her. 'I don't want to be kicked out now that I've managed to get in!'

'Why don't you come with us?' suggests the British boy, looking to his companion, who nods in agreement. 'You can squeeze in next to us, no one will notice.'

Ingrid gasps. 'Are … are you sure?'

'Yes! This is Eurovision!' He shrugs. 'Everyone is welcome, right?'

'Right!' Ingrid replies, squealing and throwing her arms around him, making him laugh. 'Thank you so, so much! I'm Ingrid.'

'James,' he replies with a wide grin at her. 'And this is Millie.'

'Hi,' Millie says, smiling up at them and giving a small wave.

'And I'm Noah. Nice to meet you.' He glances at the member of staff, who is now approaching them with a confused expression. 'We should probably make a move.'

'Come with us,' James announces, leading the way back to their seats. 'And if anyone asks, we can pretend we're all very good friends.'

'I won't be pretending. You're saving me from being kicked out of Eurovision,' Ingrid says, skipping along next to him, her eyes twinkling as she takes in all the lights. 'As of right now, you're my favourite people in the world!'

* * *

'Hang on,' Millie says, putting her drink down on the table as she stares at Ingrid in shock. 'You're saying you travelled all the way here from Berlin with your boyfriend, Anton, and he cheated on you *today*?'

Ingrid nods. 'Sadly, yes. That is exactly what happened.'

Millie is shocked. James reaches over to give Ingrid a sympathetic pat on the arm. After having a wonderful night watching the Grand Final together, the four of them have ended up at a random karaoke bar in the centre of town. Julie and Tom happily welcomed Ingrid and Noah to their row, and when the Final came to an end and Noah suggested continuing the night elsewhere, Millie's grandparents strongly encouraged they go have fun with their new friends.

'Anton knows how much I love Eurovision,' Ingrid continues, slurring her words slightly, while a karaoke enthusiast belts out a Britney Spears song in the background. 'So when I said we should come to Oslo for the weekend, even though we didn't have tickets, he said it sounded fun! Then we got here, I left the hostel for a few hours while he "works on his songwriting"' – she uses her fingers to do air quotes, rolling her eyes – 'and when I got back to the hostel, he was in bed with a very pretty Spanish girl.'

'That is … brutal,' Noah comments, shaking his head.

'So harsh,' James agrees.

'She didn't speak a word of German and looked very confused when I walked in and started shouting at him,' Ingrid says, pausing to take a large swig of her beer. 'She obviously didn't know he had a girlfriend. Anton explained that they had just met and had communicated their attraction through body language.'

'Eugh.' Millie frowns. 'That's horrible!'

'I thought he loved me,' Ingrid sighs, before she takes a deep breath in and rolls back her shoulders. 'But you know what? I don't want to ruin tonight by talking more about *Anton*. I marched out of that hostel determined to have a fun adventure without him. That's why I was trying to get backstage. I don't know how I ended up at the arena, but I did. My feet took me there. I wasn't going to let him ruin my Eurovision weekend!'

'Good for you!' James cheers. 'He doesn't deserve any more airtime. I've only just met you, Ingrid, and I know for a FACT that you are much too good for Anton.'

'You're right, I am! Screw him! You know what we should be talking about instead? Eurovision! And how it brings people together.' She points at each of them individually. 'Look at us. We never would have met. And now we will be friends for life!'

Noah chuckles. 'If you say so.'

'I do say so!' Ingrid confirms, slamming her glass down on the table.

'Oh my god, we *have* to stay in touch,' James insists eagerly. 'You can visit us in England!'

'You will come to Germany!' Ingrid suddenly gasps, putting her hand on her chest. 'Wait! I have the BEST idea: why don't we all promise to meet at Eurovision in Germany next year?'

'Ingrid, you are a GENIUS!' James exclaims. 'It will be our friendship meet cute – four strangers who met at Eurovision, reuniting every year to celebrate together.'

'*We're* not strangers,' Millie corrects him, but he rolls his eyes at her.

'It sounds better if we are,' he says haughtily.

'Yes, James. It will be our story,' Ingrid nods, her eyes flashing determinedly at the others before picking up her glass again. 'Whichever German city is chosen for the Grand Final next year, we will meet there. Yes?'

'I'm in!' James declares, holding up his glass and nudging Millie in the ribs.

'All right,' she says, following suit, before glancing at Noah. 'Although it might be trickier for the non-Europeans among us to come all the way to Germany. That would be a very expensive trip from Australia, especially after a year of backpacking.'

'That's true,' Ingrid says, her eyes widening at Noah. 'We'll all have to chip in to pay for your ticket!'

'No, no,' he laughs, with a wave of his hand. 'Don't worry, I'll be there.'

'You can find me on Facebook; you'll always remember my name: THE Ingrid Vogel,' she says, winking at him. 'We will find a way to raise the funds to get you back to Europe. You have to come, for the good of such a great story!'

'You're absolutely right. For the good of the story, I will be there,' Noah says, sharing a conspiratorial smile with Millie. 'I promise.'

Ingrid whoops in excitement, punching the air. 'Yes, I love this! Eurovision Germany 2011, we will reunite!'

'Now that's decided, time for some more karaoke!' James cries happily.

Noah and Millie both groan in unison. Ingrid cheers, grabbing James's hand and rushing through the crowd to select what song they'll put on next, as someone else up on the stage massacres a Celine Dion ballad. Millie takes a sip of her drink, nervous to be left in the company of Noah – he's intimidatingly good looking with his scruffy blonde hair, stunning blue eyes and chiselled jaw. And his Australian accent is undeniably sexy, as James whispered in her ear when they left the arena.

'So, you're travelling around Europe for a whole year?' Millie asks, trying not to stare while admiring his perfect side profile. 'That's really cool.'

'Yeah,' he says, nodding as he turns to face her. 'It's pretty awesome so far.'

'I'd love to do something like that,' she says wistfully. 'But I'm not sure I'd last very long away from home.'

'You'd be fine.'

She shrugs. 'I don't exactly have an adventurous spirit.'

'You won't know until you try,' he tells her. 'You might discover yours once you've taken the risk and set out. I've only just started my travels and I can tell you, it's the *best*. There's so much to see and do. It sounds stupid, but you feel so free.'

'Yeah? OK, maybe I could save up once I've got a job and then just … fly off one day,' she chuckles. 'Is that what you've done?'

'Sorry?'

'Did you work and save up to fund your year out? Or are you planning on getting work as you travel around?'

He frowns. 'Oh … um … yeah.'

'Well, that's seriously admirable of you,' she declares, although she's not sure which option he was agreeing with. 'To have that kind of motivation to earn enough to go after what you want. Good for you.'

Shifting in his seat, Noah takes a glug of his drink. Millie suddenly worries that she's talking a bit too seriously. She's only just met this guy and she's telling him she admires his *motivation* to save up the money to go travelling? She needs to chill out.

'Have you been to England yet?' Millie asks hurriedly, trying to sound less intense.

He brightens at the question, his demeanour relaxing again. 'Yeah, a few weeks ago. It was my first time there.'

'Really? What did you think?'

'I think the weather sucks,' he says, a grin slowly spreading across his face as he looks at her. 'But the people are amazing.'

She blushes furiously, glancing away, unable to take the intensity of his piercing blue eyes. He *can't* be flirting with her. She shouldn't get her hopes up.

'I … I'm glad we made a good impression,' she manages to say, flustered and tripping over her words, as he watches her curiously, completely at ease in comparison. 'I'd love to visit Australia one day.'

Noah surprises her by frowning in response. 'Yeah, it's … great.'

She chuckles. 'You don't sound very convincing.'

'Sorry,' he says with a wave of his hand. 'I left under a bit of a cloud. My family … it's complicated.'

'Oh.' Millie bites her lip, feeling terrible for laughing. 'Sorry. I didn't mean to—'

'No, no, it's fine.'

She watches as he takes a swig of his drink, his brow furrowed. First, she scares him by congratulating him on his motivation and now it would seem she's bummed him out by reminding him of bad times back home. Bloody hell. She *really* needs to improve when it comes to talking to guys.

'I don't exactly have the easiest family, either,' she offers.

He looks confused. 'Your grandparents? You seemed so close back at the arena.'

'Sorry, I mean with my mum,' she explains. 'I'm really close with my grandparents. They raised me. My mum had me very young, after she left school. I was, you know, not exactly planned.'

Noah nods.

'Anyway, we're so different, me and her,' Millie continues hurriedly. 'We don't get on at all. She's very successful

– she works for Credit Suisse and travels a lot internationally – and it's like she can't understand that I don't have the same … drive that she does. She was *furious* when I told her I wasn't going to university. She said I was throwing away all these opportunities that she never got, blah blah blah. We had a huge fight about it. She definitely hasn't forgiven me.'

'At least you had the courage to stand up to her and tell her what you want,' Noah says, looking impressed.

'I don't *feel* courageous. I feel like a failure and I haven't even left school yet. She makes it so obvious I'm not meeting any of her expectations and—'

'That's *exactly* how it is with my dad!' Noah confides, leaning forward, his eyes widening at her. 'I feel like a constant let-down.'

She smiles sadly at him. 'Yeah, same. Whenever she visits, we argue. She doesn't seem to know how to talk about anything that isn't … serious life stuff. We never chat or laugh together or anything like that.'

'You could be talking about my dad right now,' Noah says. 'He's so formal. Sometimes I just want him to be Dad – not my life coach.'

She stares at him in disbelief. 'Same with my mum!'

'Nice to meet someone who understands.'

'Yeah,' she smiles, 'it is.'

He mirrors her smile, nodding slowly. Her cheeks grow hot again under his gaze. They don't say anything for a few moments.

Eventually, he clears his throat.

'We should take a leaf out of Ingrid's book,' he declares. 'We shouldn't be talking about stuff like this. This is a great night, let's not bring it down with this kind of chat.'

'You're right. Sorry.'

'I'll admit something I've been thinking all night,' he says, folding his arms across his chest and flashing her a mischievous grin. 'I don't get Eurovision.'

'*What?*'

'What is it about this event that is such a big deal?' he questions with a shrug. 'Why do people love it so much?'

'What's *not* to love about it?' she responds. 'It's wonderful!'

'Yeah, but you're just saying that because obviously your grandparents enjoy it, right?'

'That's an understatement,' she smiles. 'They met at a Eurovision Grand Final. They named their child after Agnetha Fältskog.'

He stares at her blankly. 'Who?'

'She was a member of ABBA. But anyway, I'm not defending Eurovision because my grandparents are fans. I genuinely love it.'

'But it's just a song contest.'

'It is SO much more than that,' she insists.

'OK, explain it to me.'

'As Ingrid pointed out, it brings people together. Do you know how rare that is? For people from different cultures and backgrounds to come together without any kind of bad feeling or real rivalry, just support and happiness?' She leans forwards across the table as she speaks. 'In fact, unity is pretty much the best thing about Eurovision, because it's not just about celebrating different countries and cultures, it's about celebrating differences … *end of*. It's fun, diverse, inclusive – everyone should feel safe at Eurovision, no matter who you are. It welcomes everybody and all expressions. It's a completely surreal escape from the world. It's about liberty and acceptance and love; it's …' She stops, suddenly aware that she's been rambling. Her cheeks flushing, she looks down at the table and draws herself back.

'Sorry,' she mumbles, shaking her head in embarrassment. 'I didn't mean to go on.'

'No, no, it was interesting,' Noah insists. 'I liked what you were saying. You've convinced me.'

'Yeah?'

'Liberty, acceptance and love. Powerful stuff. I'll declare it now: I'm officially a Eurovision fan,' he says, reaching over to nudge her arm.

At his touch, a shudder goes down her spine. Someone like Noah shouldn't notice someone like her. He's gorgeous and self-assured. She would never have a chance with him in a million years and she knows she'll never see him again after tonight. The promise Ingrid convinced them to make was an empty, drunken one – they all know that, or if they don't right now, they certainly will acknowledge it in the morning.

Noah is that perfect guy you meet and then spend the rest of your life wondering whatever happened to him.

'I mean it,' Noah asserts, when Millie laughs at his declaration. 'I'm a Eurovision fan for life. You heard it here first.'

'All right, in that case we'll definitely meet next year at the Final.'

'Yes, we will.' He grins at her. 'Just you wait and see.'

CHAPTER THREE

Brighton, UK

2011

Thursday 12 May

'Millie, you're not wearing your hat. Again.'

Millie winces at Jeff's authoritative voice behind her, and turns round to face him. His eyebrows raised, he's got his hands on his hips, looking at her in the same weary way a headteacher would while scolding a particularly bothersome student.

'This is the second time this week I've had to remind you of the staff dress code here at Beebee's Buns,' he says, shaking his head in disappointment. 'If I have to do it a third time, you'll get a formal warning. Do you want to get a warning, Millie?'

'No,' Millie admits. 'I don't.'

'I didn't think so. Here.' He holds out her hat that she left tucked underneath the counter earlier. 'Put it on.'

She looks down at the offending hat in his hand. It's huge and in the shape of a cupcake. If that wasn't bad enough, it also has 'GREAT BUNS!' in bold yellow letters printed across the front. She reluctantly takes it from him and places it on her head.

Jeff waits for her to adjust it slightly so it's straight.

'There you go, not so hard.' He gives her a thumbs-up. 'You've got this.'

She offers him a weak smile before resorting to a scowl as soon as he turns his back to head into his office. Millie has been working at Beebee's Buns for almost eleven months now, all the while under the tyrannical management of smarmy, arrogant Jeff, who waltzes about the café on a serious power trip, even though he can't be more than a year older than her. He's tall and slender with a mop of curly fair hair and a thin line of barely visible blonde hair growing on his upper lip, his obstinate attempt at growing a moustache. If she didn't know him, Millie would assume he was still at school – a nasal-voiced pompous prefect of some sort. But by a horrible twist of fate, he's her boss and she's had to put up with his self-importance for much too long now.

Heaving a sigh, Millie turns to greet a group of customers who have come bustling through the door, the old-fashioned bell hanging above it announcing their entrance. It's three young women and as they examine the cupcakes and pastries on offer, Millie plasters a smile on her face.

'Welcome to Beebee's Buns,' she says on auto-pilot. 'What can I get for you today?'

One of the group, who has been peering at the hot drinks listed on the board above Millie's head, lowers her eyes to her face. They widen in recognition.

'Oh my god!' she exclaims with a gasp. '*Millie?*'

Millie realises in horror that it's Tara Herring. They were in the same class at school. It's only been a year since they left but Tara looks different, much more grown up in her loose white shirt, skinny jeans and heeled boots, her dark brown ringlets swept up from her face in a loose up-do, wearing barely there eye make-up and striking red lipstick.

Millie glances over at Tara's two companions and recognises Ferne Edgar, another former classmate, as well, but thankfully the reunion stops there. Millie's whole face burns hot as they take in her appearance.

Oh god. The hat.

If ever there was a time that Millie wanted to be swallowed into the ground, now would be it.

'Oh, wow, hi Tara! And Ferne! S-so great to see you!' she stammers, praying that the foundation she applied that morning before work is doing a good job at hiding how red she must be right now.

'And you,' Tara replies, still looking a bit shocked. 'How … how are you?'

'Great, thanks! Really good. You?'

'Yeah, good,' she says, before gesturing to Ferne. 'We're both home from uni for a few days before end-of-year exams, so thought we'd meet up. Nice to be back in Brighton.'

'Cool.' Millie nods. 'How is uni?'

'Amazing,' Tara says, breaking into a wide smile. 'It's the best; *so* much fun. I'm at Leeds and Ferne is at Durham.' She gestures to the third girl. 'This is my mate, Imogen. We're in Halls together and she's never been to Brighton before, so I invited her down to show her the sights.'

Imogen gives Millie a small wave.

'Great,' Millie says. 'Must be nice to be home.'

'Yeah, nothing's changed,' Tara shrugs.

Millie masks the personal sting she feels at the innocent comment with a fixed smile.

'So, how long have you worked here?' Ferne asks curiously.

'Oh … um … a bit.'

'I think I remember you getting the job here last summer,' Tara recalls. 'When we left school, you mentioned it.'

'Right.' Millie laughs nervously. 'Wow. Almost a whole year. Time flies, I guess!'

'Are you going to uni this September or …?' Ferne trails off, not sure how to end the question.

'No, I'm not … I'm not going to university. I thought it would be good to get out in the world, get stuck into a job,' Millie explains, tapping her fingers on the counter. 'I'm still working out what I want to do long term.'

'Sure,' Ferne says, her eyes flickering up to the hat. 'And you're still living at home?'

'Yes, with my grandparents.'

'Ah, that's nice.' She gives Millie a warm smile. 'Must be nice to have homecooked food all the time!'

'Exactly. Anyway,' Millie says brightly, desperate to get them out of here as quickly as humanly possible to put a stop to this torture, 'what can I get you?'

They order three lattes and a couple of cupcakes, standing in a huddle to chat. As she carefully places two cupcakes in a takeaway cardboard box and tends to their coffees, Millie overhears their detailed descriptions of their 'great' new friends, the 'amazing' nights out, the 'interesting' societies they've joined outside of their course.

It feels like forever, but she finally applies the lids to their coffee cups and slides them across the counter.

'There you go,' she says, as Ferne pays with her card.

'Thanks, Millie.' Tara smiles. 'Really nice to see you again.'

'And you. Enjoy your day!'

'See you,' Ferne says, holding open the door for the others. 'Bye!'

They file out the door and as soon as it's closed behind them, Millie's smile fades. Through the window, she watches them stroll away down the street giggling together and tries not to imagine their conversation that likely comes at her expense. She's wearing a *cupcake hat* for goodness' sake. Alone on the shop floor, Millie buries her head in her hands, groaning loudly, before attempting to distract herself by cleaning the coffee machine so that Jeff doesn't have anything to complain about when he eventually emerges from his office.

Tara's remark rings in her ears: *Nothing's changed*.

It feels painfully true for Millie. She does have a boyfriend now, though. She's comforted at the thought. Louis. She should have found a way to weave him into conversation with Tara and Ferne so they could have at least been impressed that, in spite of the stupid cupcake hat she's still wearing a year later, she'd managed to land herself a boyfriend – they met when he came in as a customer a few weeks ago. Thankfully, Jeff was ill that day and she wasn't wearing the hat. She doubts Louis would have asked for her number if she had been.

Louis is a skateboarder, which is very sexy in Millie's opinion. She's watched him at the local skate park and he's really good. He wears baggy jeans and large t-shirts, and styles his light brown hair into a sweeping fringe across his forehead. Thanks to Louis, Millie's started listening to indie rock music, which she wasn't really into before, but now she loves it. In fact, they're meeting tonight and going to a really cool club down by the beach. She's excited to see him, albeit apprehensive about meeting the group of friends they're going with. She hopes she doesn't embarrass him. She's determined to look the part in her new denim mini skirt that she's going to wear with a red and black chequered shirt, black boots and heavy black eyeliner. The bell rings above the door again signalling the arrival of a much more welcome customer. She beams at James as he shuts the door behind him. He looks great in black jeans and denim shirt, and his new thick-rimmed rectangular glasses.

'Am I glad to see you,' Millie says, leaning on the counter, her shoulders slumping forwards as he approaches.

'Uh oh, bad day?' he asks, before lowering his voice to add, 'Is Jeff here?'

She nods towards the office door and James gives her a sympathetic look.

'Would it help if I said that you look absolutely adorable in that hat?' he offers.

'No, because we both know you're lying.'

'Excuse you, I speak the truth. No one on this planet should be able to pull off a giant cupcake stuck on their head, but somehow you make it look not so offensive,' he argues. 'You look cute.'

'Yeah, well, I didn't feel cute when Ferne Edgar and Tara Herring wandered in just now, home from their respective universities.'

James grimaces. 'I can't imagine that was too fun. Although, they were always nice, weren't they? I mean, as far as people we went to school with, it could have been worse.'

'It doesn't matter how nice you are, you're still going to judge the hat.'

'Did you chat?' he asks, eyeing up the brownies on display.

'Briefly. They are having the *best* time at uni.' She lowers her head to rest it on the counter. 'I felt like such an idiot.'

'You are not an idiot!' James insists, coming to lean on the surface next to her. 'Why do you feel like that?'

'I'm wearing a hat that says "Great Buns" on it,' she groans, lifting her head.

James can't help but laugh. 'And you pull it off.'

Millie groans.

'Look,' James says, giving her a stern look, 'this job isn't forever. You're still working out what you want to do! Who cares what they think anyway? You don't know them, they're not your friends. All that matters is what *I* think, and I think there is no one else in the world who can look as sexy as you do in that hat.'

She rests her chin in the palm of her hand. 'Really?'

'Really,' he says, reaching over to tuck some loose strands of her hair back into the brim of the hat. 'Now, stop sulking and make me one of your delicious coffees, because I need the caffeine. I have an essay to finish tonight.'

'You still haven't finished it?' Millie says, grabbing him a cup. 'I thought you were working on that last night.'

'I was, and then I got a call from one of my course friends persuading me to come to a '90s-music-themed quiz at the Students' Union. I tried to be strong but I cracked eventually,' he admits with a sly smile. 'It was a fun night out, but I'm suffering for it because I have this essay hanging over my head and all I want to do is pack for Germany.' He claps his hands excitedly. 'You ready for our trip?'

She adds the last finishing touches to his coffee and passes it to him. 'I've been counting down the days. This time tomorrow we'll be in Düsseldorf!'

They squeal in unison.

'Eurovision here we come!' James announces. 'It is going to be the best.'

'I wish we had tickets to the Grand Final, though.' Millie rings James's coffee through the till – with her discount applied, of course. 'Imagine how good that would have been.'

'We're lucky we got tickets to the rehearsals,' James points out. 'And that your grandparents were happy to pay for your plane ticket and my parents paid for mine. Us paupers should be very grateful we're able to go at all.'

'You're right. I can't wait.' Millie glances up at the clock at the wall, willing time to go faster. 'Just half an hour more and I am officially off for the weekend.'

'Are you spending tonight packing?' James enquires.

'I told you I'm going to this indie night with Louis and his mates.'

'Oh yeah.' James nods, taking a sip of his coffee.

Millie gives him a look. 'What?'

'I didn't say anything,' he says innocently.

She puts a hand on her hip. 'You're thinking something. I can tell. You have a very open-book face.'

'I wasn't thinking anything! Enjoy tonight, but don't be hungover tomorrow – there's nothing worse on a plane,' he advises, heading to the door.

'See you tomorrow,' she calls out after him. 'Don't be late.'

'For Eurovision?' He puts on a mock-insulted voice, flashing her a smile over his shoulder as he exits the café. 'Never.'

* * *

James tried to like Louis. He really did. When they met last week, he was determined to warm to this guy that his best friend had become so obsessed with, but after an evening of listening to him spend the entirely evening describing his skating tricks, he was forced to come to the conclusion that Louis, as far as James can tell, is a bit of a prick.

Sure, he can see the aesthetic appeal – Louis has that sexy skater boy look down – but he was bemused to watch Millie hanging off every word of his self-obsessed mono-logue. She showed up that night in a black Arctic Monkeys tour t-shirt – a band James could state with certainty that she'd never seen live – with ripped black jeans and the heaviest eye make-up he'd ever seen her wear. James was all for her experimenting with her style and she looked great, but it was as though she was trying to morph into what Louis expected his girlfriend to look like.

Millie's lack of confidence can be so frustrating – he can see that she's convinced herself she's lucky for *anyone* to be interested in her. And Louis is lapping up the attention rather than reciprocating it.

But if Millie is happy, then James is happy. At least Louis is getting her out her house and she's not spending every night watching TV with her grandparents, which she'd got into a bit of a habit of doing recently up until she met him.

That's why he really wants this weekend in Germany to go well – so that Millie can blow off some steam. He hates how unhappy she is at that job, but the only person who can change that is Millie and whenever he asks her if she's applied for anything new or thought about speaking to a career advisor, she's brushed off his questions and told him that she still doesn't know, but she's got time to work it out.

The unknown is scary. James knows that. He can under-stand why Millie isn't quite ready for it yet, but he couldn't feel more different about the future. The University of Brighton was the best decision he made and he's loving his course, but it's making him even more excited about forg-ing his career as a world-renowned music journalist. He's going to interview the best bands out there, feature the next big things, review albums before anyone else is allowed to listen to them: that's his destiny and he won't settle for any-thing else.

He's already something of a name on campus; his course mates have been relying on him to introduce them to the Brighton music scene and he's been happy to take them to the best places for live music and gigs. The only drawback of his carefully constructed new image as someone with impeccably cool taste is that he just can't bring himself to admit how much he loves Eurovision – he nearly let slip where he was going this weekend, but he couldn't face the thought of his new friends judging him.

Fishing out his house keys from his pocket, he hesitates when he hears raised voices coming from inside. It's his par-ents – they're having a blazing row. Again. He overheard them arguing earlier this week, but as soon as he came in, they fell silent and pretended like everything was fine. They never normally fight. He tries to make out what they're say-ing, but they must be in the kitchen towards the back of the house because their voices are muffled and he can't hear them properly.

Turning the key in the lock, he pushes open the front door and the voices stop instantly. He kicks off his shoes and clears his throat.

'Hey, I'm home!'

'Hi darling,' his mum trills from the kitchen. 'How was your lecture?'

'Good thanks,' he responds, padding down the hallway towards them.

He finds his mum standing by the sink, leaning on the surface with a fixed smile on her face. Her eyes are red. She's been crying. His dad is sitting at the kitchen table, hugging his arms across his chest, attempting a smile, but the worried creases embedded across his forehead are giving him away. James looks from one to the other.

'What's going on?' he asks slowly.

'Nothing,' his mum insists, turning to fill up the kettle. 'Would you like a cup of tea?'

'I just bought a coffee.'

'How is Millie?'

'I heard you arguing,' James says, knowing his mum is doing her best to distract him. 'Is everything all right?'

'Of course everything's all right,' she says, her expression softening. 'We were having a little disagreement, that's all.'

'Nothing for you to worry about,' his dad adds.

'What were you disagreeing on?'

'Oh, some house things,' his mum says with a wave of her hand. 'Don't you have that essay to finish tonight? I know you wanted to hand it in before you leave tomorrow. Don't let us distract you; you get on with it and we can order a nice takeaway tonight to celebrate you hitting your deadline!'

Relenting, James nods. He doesn't want to force them to tell him what they were fighting over and as long as they're okay, then maybe he doesn't need to know. He really does want to finish this essay before his flight tomorrow, too, and he still needs to pack. So, he heads upstairs to his room and sets himself up at his desk, ready to work.

But a while later, he hears them sniping at each other downstairs in hushed voices. He can't shake the feeling that maybe this is something bigger than they're letting on. Maybe he should be worried about something. He tries to concentrate on work, but he's too distracted. He reaches for his phone and calls Millie for some comfort. It goes to voicemail and he sighs, hanging up. She'll be out with Louis by now.

Leaning back in his chair, he rubs his forehead. He's only a few hundred words from the end of his essay. He can do this. He just has to work out the best way to conclude it. But he also needs a break; he's spent a long time staring at his screen and his back is aching. He decides that he can pack for tomorrow and, at the same time, think up a good ending.

Jumping to his feet, he grabs his bag and starts rooting through his wardrobe for appropriate Eurovision outfits. He wants to go as colourful as possible. After laying out some options, he realises it would be sensible to get his passport ready now so he doesn't forget it. He opens the drawer of his bedside table and rustles around all the random things he's thrown in there to find his passport buried at the bottom. As he does so, a pot of red glitter catches his eye. He smiles, picking it up. He remembers smearing Vaseline across his cheeks last year and sticking this glitter all over it.

A memory flashes across his mind: toasting Eurovision with Millie and two strangers in that odd karaoke bar they ended up in after the Grand Final. He smiles to himself thinking about that random night. The blue-haired German girl – Ingrid, he remembers – and he's pretty sure the Aussie was Noah. Very fun, but unbelievably random.

'Guess that's Eurovision for you,' James says out loud to his empty room.

Throwing the red pot of glitter in his washbag just in case, he lets out a long heavy sigh before hauling himself back to his desk to finish the essay.

Tomorrow can't come soon enough.

CHAPTER FOUR

Düsseldorf, Germany

2011

Friday 13 May

Noah quickly lifts his camera, adjusts the lens and takes the picture.

Inspecting the screen to make sure he got the shot of a man with the Norwegian flag painted across his face strolling hand in hand with his partner, he smiles to himself. Perfect. He puts his camera carefully back down on the table and returns to enjoying his coffee.

He's been sitting in the Arrivals terminal of Düsseldorf Airport for half an hour now, ever since he collected his luggage and came through passport control. He had planned on going straight to the hostel he'd booked as soon as he landed and then exploring the city, but when he realised that this was a prime spot to capture Eurovision fans arriving in their droves, he thought there was no harm in hanging around for a bit to get some photographs of them in their outrageous outfits. The Grand Final isn't until tomorrow, but already people are dressed up. All of it is still baffling to Noah – it makes for some great photos, though. Relaxing, he takes another sip of his coffee. There is no rush. Nowhere he needs to be.

A young woman with auburn hair approaches him and says something in German.

'Uh, sorry,' he says with an apologetic smile. 'English?'

'Can I take this chair?' she asks, switching to excellent English, and gesturing to the seat on the opposite side of his table. 'Or is it for someone?'

'No, no, you can take it,' he confirms.

'Thank you.'

She carries the chair to a nearby table where another girl is waiting for her and Noah notices the two of them exchange some words before they look back at him, both smiling coyly. He smiles back. They giggle, returning to their conversation. He's only been in Germany for an hour or so and he already gets the feeling he's going to like it here.

For the last few months, Noah has been staying in the French Alps, where he spent the winter skiing and making the most of the lively *après-ski* scene. When he first arrived at the ski resort Avoriaz in December, he met a ski instructor named Harriet – he'd originally planned on spending just a couple of weeks skiing there over Christmas before travelling around France a bit and then heading back to Australia, but Harriet told him all about her incredible life skiing in the winter and biking in the summer, free from the humdrum nine-to-five routine. Just a few days in the company of Harriet and her fellow resort colleagues was enough for Noah to contact the University of Melbourne and ask to defer his place another year. University in February suddenly seemed stifling.

The university said yes. Of course they did. He's Noah Pearce.

That part was easy.

The hard part was telling his parents he wasn't coming home. He didn't bother contacting his dad – instead, he waited until he knew he wouldn't be at home and called his mum to talk her through his decision. She was very upset at first, but he brought her round to his way of thinking with a carefully constructed list of arguments: this experience was making him a more rounded person; he was meeting so many interesting people from all different walks of life; he would still be going to university, but starting with an expanded mind; these opportunities were keeping him active, relieving any stress and anxiety about his future; he was happy.

By the end of the call, she sounded almost pleased about his decision.

He asked her to tell his dad. It was cowardly, but necessary. His father would only shout down the phone at him and that wasn't good for their already fragile relationship.

'He'll cut you off if you don't get a job,' Charlotte warned over the phone when they spoke in January. 'You got a free ride last year, but you need to start showing some responsibility and working. Are there any in the ski resort you can apply for?'

'Loads. Don't worry, I'm already on it. I've got some contacts here who are very keen for me to stay, so they've promised they can find me something,' Noah assured her, grinning at Harriet and running his fingers down her bare back as she lay next to him in bed. 'Anyway, I have to go deliver my CV to a few places, so I'll speak to you later.'

'Yeah sure,' she sighed, hanging up.

His fling with Harriet was mutually casual, but she did help him get a job in one of the bars that hosted great *après* nights. Noah learnt two things very quickly: one, working behind the bar was perfect for meeting women and enjoying casual hook-ups, and two, he was a terrible barman. He lasted a couple of weeks there before he got tired of it – he quit just before he was fired. He hadn't found another job for the rest of the season, but it didn't matter, he didn't really need one. No one seemed to be checking his accounts.

He'd been watching French TV one evening when Eurovision was mentioned. He'd sat up straight and decided that instant to go to Düsseldorf for the Grand Final. As the snow melted, he'd been wondering where to travel to next and he *had* made a promise, albeit a drunken one, last year to be there.

Why the hell shouldn't he go? He'd never been to Düsseldorf and he was all about making spontaneous decisions and seeing where they might lead.

He didn't care about Eurovision, but maybe, by some stroke of luck, he'd see *her* again. That British girl, Millie.

He had booked his flight straight away.

Noah finishes the last of his coffee. Standing up and pushing his chair in, he flashes another smile at the two women, who glance up at him as he leaves, and then throws his bag over his shoulder to head towards the taxi rank. As he's crossing the terminal, he notices clusters of Eurovision fans walking in the same direction and he hurries out of their way to one side, lifting his camera eagerly. Another flight must have just landed.

He chuckles as he gets a picture of a group of women in their fifties, all wearing matching Union Jack suits, and then secures a shot of a young man strolling along behind them wearing silver leggings and a gold sequin jacket, carrying his bag in one hand and a pompom in another. Noah keeps his camera poised, pleased that he stuck around for this latest surge of Eurovision arrivals. His eye up against the viewfinder of the camera, he moves the lens across the sea of blurred faces moving through the terminal until he stops at a familiar one.

It's her.

As he lowers his camera in amazement, Millie happens to look his way. She stops dead in her tracks as their eyes meet, then her entire face lights up. He beams at her.

Noah doesn't usually believe in fate.

But it's difficult to describe this moment in any other way.

* * *

Saturday 14 May

James opens his eyes and groans, pulling the duvet over his head.

Why did he drink tequila last night? WHY? He blames Noah. He kept insisting on buying those rounds of shots after they met up with him. Noah must have spent a fortune at that bar. James may be in a terrible way this morning, but surely Noah will be feeling worse when he remembers the bill he racked up on his card – he hardly let Millie and James pay for a thing, even though they kept trying.

Maybe bars in Switzerland pay their staff really well. Wait … was that where Noah said he'd been recently? Or was it the French Alps? James can't remember and, to be honest, right now he doesn't care. He needs a coffee. And to get out of this tiny box hostel room that he and Millie are holed up in.

He manages to push himself up, whimpering and reaching for the bottle of water he bought at the airport yesterday. Taking a good few glugs, he peers over at Millie. She's fast asleep and he doesn't want to wake her. She had more to drink than she usually does – James suspects it was a mixture of nerves and excitement at being around Noah.

He'd suspected last year that there was a spark between them, and last night they definitely had a connection that was adorable to witness, even if it did make James a third wheel. He noticed that whenever Noah told a funny story about his travels, he didn't fail to glance over at Millie to check she was laughing. And Millie blushed almost every time Noah asked her a question.

Did Louis come up in conversation last night? James rubs his head. He can't remember that he did. *Oh well*.

Stretching, James reaches for the jeans and t-shirt he was wearing yesterday and throws them on along with his hoodie, deciding to shower when he gets back. He just about manages to make his way to the shared bathroom and brush his teeth, but it takes a lot of effort and he has to grip the sink for a few seconds afterwards to muster the energy to go back to the hostel room and get his wallet, sunglasses and phone. He double-checks that Millie is still asleep and then creeps out the room, texting her to say he's popped out for coffees, in case she wakes up while he's gone.

Stepping out of the front door of reception, James squints into the light and quickly shoves on his prescription sunglasses as the brightness sends the searing pain in his head into overdrive. He remembers a café round the corner at the end of the street they're on and sets off. As he walks, appreciating the fresh air, he notices a family strolling on the pavement on the other side of the road. The kids have the Slovenian flag painted on their cheeks. James smiles. Today is the day of the Grand Final and there is a sense of excitement in the air. Once he's had his coffee and some food, and the hangover has ebbed, he's sure he'll feel more enthusiastic about it. Last night was great, though.

It was so lucky that they bumped into Noah at the airport. While Millie inhaled sharply at the sight of him standing in Arrivals, James let out a loud cry of excitement, causing everyone to look his way as he went running over to Noah to give him a giant hug. Thankfully, Noah reciprocated the greeting, gushing about how he'd hoped he might see them again, but he'd never really believed he would.

'What are the *chances*?' Noah kept saying in disbelief.

Once he told them he was travelling on his own, they insisted that they get his number so they could all meet up after the Jury Rehearsal, which, they had to explain to him, is the rehearsal the night before the live show. That's what Millie and James had managed to get tickets for – they're much cheaper than those to the Grand Final.

The Jury Rehearsal was great fun and afterwards they went to meet Noah in a bar he'd been hanging out in. They'd expected it to be some dive in the middle of nowhere, but Noah had picked somewhere quite fancy and they arrived to find him waiting with a bunch of new friends Noah had spent the afternoon making and two cocktails already ordered for them. The cocktails were delicious and it was a great night, but were the two rounds of tequila shots absolutely necessary? *No.* He will have to make sure that Noah doesn't get carried away again tonight. They said they'd meet up later to watch the Final together.

As James turns the corner at the end of the road, someone walks straight into him carrying a tray of four large coffees.

James yelps as hot liquid spills all over his hoodie. The man carrying the tray gasps and then cries something repeatedly in a different language.

'Oh, bloody hell,' James says, stepping back to stare down the front of his jumper and survey the damage. The coffee is everywhere, dripping onto his jeans.

'I am so sorry!' the man says on realising James is English, clapping his hand round his mouth and staring at James's front in horror. 'So sorry! Oh god!'

If it had been a different time in a different outfit, James might have cared. But he is really hungover and this is just an old hoodie anyway, and it's not like he's going anywhere important. So, he bursts out laughing.

The man looks startled at James's reaction.

'It's fine,' James smiles, swiping down the front of his hoodie with his hand. 'Don't worry about it.'

'But the coffee … it's everywhere! I'm so sorry!'

'Honestly, it's not your fault. And this jumper is really old, it's not a big deal.'

'Are you sure you're not hurt? It didn't burn you?'

'No, it's a thick hoodie,' James assures him. 'Honestly, please don't worry.'

'I will pay for it to be cleaned,' he insists.

James snorts. 'It's only coffee, I can throw it in the wash. Seriously, no harm done.'

'I should have been looking where I was going.'

'Me too,' James says.

'And not going so fast round the corner.'

'Me too.'

They both break into smiles. In the haze of his hang-over and the chaos of the coffee spillage, James hadn't really taken him in, but now that he does, he realises that this guy is *hot*. With a mop of untamed brown hair and dark stubble that threatens to mask his sharp cheekbones, he's about James's height, but much more broad-shouldered, wearing a black fitted t-shirt that shows off his toned arms.

Suddenly James is very aware of his own appearance.

And the fact that he hasn't showered.

Not to mention he now has a large dark brown stain all down his front.

Bollocks.

'Were … were you going to get coffee by any chance?' the man asks, gesturing to the café behind him. 'Because if so, I would like to buy you one. I have to go back there anyway to replace the drinks I just threw over you, so …'

He looks at James hopefully.

'Actually, I was,' James confesses. 'But you really don't need to buy me one.'

'Please,' he says, holding up his hands. 'I insist.'

James hesitates, feeling bad when it really wasn't anyone's fault. It was an accident.

'Classic British politeness,' the man continues, rolling his eyes at James's torn expression. 'Just accept the coffee.'

'All right, thank you,' James chuckles, before holding out his hand. 'I'm James, by the way.'

'Zachary,' he replies, shaking it. 'You're from London?'

'Brighton. It's south of London, by the sea. Where are you from?'

'Geneva, Switzerland,' Zachary tells him. 'My dad is English though; he's from Sussex.'

'That explains your perfect English.'

There's no queue at the café, so Zachary heads straight to the counter and, in German, orders six coffees.

Taking off his sunglasses, James listens in awe. 'You speak German as well?'

'And French and a little Italian,' Zachary admits with a modest smile. 'But apparently my Italian accent is shit.'

'Well, I feel embarrassed. I speak exactly one language. English,' James sighs. 'Look, let me pay for one of the coffees at least; you shouldn't have to buy my friend one, too. That wasn't part of our deal.'

'It's fine,' Zachary says with a wave of his hand. 'I'm putting it on my company card anyway. Expenses.'

'OK, well, thanks. Do you live here in Düsseldorf, then?'

'No, in Switzerland, but I'm here for work.'

'What is it that you do?' James asks curiously.

'I work for Eurovision,' he replies breezily.

James's jaw drops to the floor. 'WHAT?'

Zachary laughs. 'You like Eurovision?'

'That's why I'm here in Düsseldorf!' James exclaims.

'I thought you might be, but I didn't want to assume,' Zachary says, passing James his two coffees once they're ready.

'What do you do for Eurovision? Oh my god.' James places a hand on his chest. 'I actually feel a bit starstruck.'

Zachary chuckles. 'I work on the official Eurovision marketing team at the European Broadcasting Union. It's based in Geneva.'

'Right! I knew that!'

'Yeah, I'm lucky. I love my job. You're a big fan, then?' Zachary checks, picking up the tray of his four replacement coffees and strolling out with him.

'*Huge* fan,' James confirms. 'I love it.'

'That's always nice to hear. Are you going to the Grand Final tonight?'

'No, we didn't get tickets.'

'We?'

'I came here with my friend, Millie. She's as obsessed with Eurovision as I am. Her grandparents first met in the audience of Eurovision in 1974.'

'You're kidding,' Zachary says, stopping to smile at him. 'That's really sweet.'

'Yeah, it is. So we always watch it together. This year we got tickets to the Jury Rehearsal, which was amazing, hence why I'm so hungover ...' – he pauses as Zachary laughs, pleased that he's managed to slip in a reason for his bedraggled appearance – 'and tonight we're meeting up with another friend and going to find a bar somewhere to watch it. Apparently there's lots of places playing it, so it should be fun.'

James finds himself lingering on the corner as they reach the turning for the hotel, unwilling to leave Zachary's company. There's a strangely comfortable silence between them – but maybe the other man is just being polite, waiting for James to say goodbye so he can get to work.

'Thanks for the coffee,' James says brightly. 'This will sort my headache out, so I owe you one. And my friend Millie will be very grateful to you, too, for hers. So ... yeah ... thanks.'

'Sorry again about spilling coffee on your clothes.'

'Don't be. It was ... nice to chat.'

Zachary smiles warmly at him. 'It was.'

'Yeah. Bye, Zachary.'

'Bye, James.'

James lifts one of the coffee cups up, as though giving him a cheers, and then turns, walking away from him, wishing he had had the courage to ask for his number.

'James!'

He spins round, his breath caught in his throat.

'Y-yes?' he says, as Zachary catches up to him.

'Buying you coffee doesn't feel like a big enough apology,' Zachary begins. 'Especially when I didn't even pay for them, the EBU did.'

'I've told you, it's really not—'

'What if I get you and your two friends into the Grand Final tonight?'

James blinks at him. '*Huh?*'

'If you'd like to come, that is,' Zachary says, raising his eyebrows at him. 'I feel it's the least I could do since I ruined your clothes.'

James is too stunned to speak. Zachary scrutinises his expression.

'What do you think?' Zachary prompts.

'I think … I've never been happier to have a drink thrown all over me.'

Zachary throws his head back and laughs, a proper belly laugh, and James thinks it might just be the sexiest laugh he's ever heard.

* * *

Ingrid throws her hands up in the air, cheering as Azerbaijan's act takes to the stage. The singing duo, Ell & Nikki, launch into their song and it's such a lovely melody that all of Ingrid's group starts swaying together, arms round each other's shoulders. She's here at the Grand Final in Esprit Arena with some fellow students from her college music course – in truth, none of them could really afford the tickets, but they splashed out on them anyway. How often is the Eurovision Grand Final going to be hosted in their own country? They *had* to be here. And wow, is it worth it. Germany can put on a show – the stage has a ginormous LED-screen backdrop and the entire arena has been turned into an alternate, magical world of lights.

Even Ingrid has to admit that, this year, the Eurovision set threatens to steal the show from the performers themselves. She had no idea that such imaginative and striking staging could blow your mind like this.

She closes her eyes as she sways to the music, a thrill running through her as Johanna, standing next to her, moves her hand down to the small of Ingrid's back. Ingrid's crush on Johanna began the moment they met in class, but it's only recently that she's come to learn her feelings have been reciprocated. They kissed two weeks ago on a night out in Berlin, after Ingrid performed a couple of songs to a meagre audience composed mainly of her friends in a bar, and haven't spent a night apart since.

Up until she and Johanna got together, Ingrid had been openly complaining about being at college, wondering if she was wasting time studying music when she should be out there performing it. What's the use of being holed up in a classroom? She should be booking gigs or using her time to write the perfect song to enter into Eurovision next year. She *knows* that she is going to make it as a singer, it's only a matter of time – it is pretty obvious that she's one of the best on her course. She has what it takes and she's growing impatient. She needs the right person to walk in while she's playing a gig and notice her. She needs to expand her audience on her YouTube channel. She needs to find the time to write meaningful, memorable songs. There's so much to do and college is getting in the way.

But now she's with Johanna, she supposes it's not all bad.

As she opens her eyes at the conclusion of the song and the lights come up on the audience, she notices someone step into the walkway to her right as they leave their seat. She recognises her immediately.

'*Millie?*' she whispers in disbelief, before repeating her name at the top of her lungs as she breaks free from her group and runs towards her. 'MILLIE!'

Millie stops, looking round in confusion until she's almost knocked sideways, enveloped in Ingrid's arms. It takes Millie a moment to recognise her as Ingrid pulls away – then her mouth drops to the floor. Last year she had blue hair – now it's nearer her natural dark brown except the tips are dyed pink. (She's actually thinking of going darker when she gets back to Berlin and putting purple streaks through it.)

'Ingrid, it's you!' Millie gasps. 'Oh my god!'

'You're here! You're actually here!' Ingrid exclaims.

'Not just me,' Millie tells her, pointing to the seats she's just exited.

Noah and James are standing next to each other, now looking as shocked as Millie as they spin round on hearing the commotion. With a squeal from Ingrid, the two of them emerge from their row to greet her, laughing their heads off.

'I can't believe this,' Ingrid cries, holding James's arm and shaking it. 'We're here. We're all here! I can't believe we all made it!'

'Unbelievable,' Noah says, shaking his head.

Ingrid beams at him. 'We kept our promise! We all got tickets to the Grand Final!'

'Actually, we didn't,' James corrects. 'It's a long story involving spilt coffee, but it doesn't matter. The point is, we found each other again. My brain feels like it might explode from how the stars have aligned for this moment.'

One of the Eurovision staff interrupts them to ask them to return to their seats as they shouldn't be lurking in the walkway. Ingrid promises him they will in a moment, before hurriedly addressing the other three.

'Let's meet after the show for another night out together. Yes?'

'Yes,' Millie grins at her. 'Of course.'

'And now that we've done this once, we have to do it always, for evermore,' Ingrid gushes. 'We will make a pact to meet every year at Eurovision. The four of us. It's fate, I'm certain of it!'

'Excuse me' – Noah gets the attention of the usher and passes him his camera – 'would you mind taking a photo of us four? Thank you.' Noah turns and shrugs at the others. 'I don't know about you, but it feels like we have to capture this moment.'

They all agree and huddle together to smile at the camera.

'You know, this could only happen at Eurovision,' Ingrid says after the photo's been taken, her eyes glistening. 'Our lives from all over the world, colliding. It is magical. Meant to be.'

Noah laughs. 'You really are a dreamer, aren't you, Ingrid?'

'We're all dreamers here, Noah,' Ingrid calls out over her shoulder as she's ushered back to her seat. 'Everyone in this arena is a dreamer. Even you.'

CHAPTER FIVE

Copenhagen, Denmark

2014

Thursday 8 May

'Come back to bed,' Noah encourages, propping himself up on his elbows.

Clara smiles playfully from the dressing table at which she's perched on a white cushioned stool, brushing her hair.

'I can't,' she says. 'I have to work, remember?'

'Cancel it.'

She lifts her eyebrows. 'Cancel a *Vogue* photoshoot? Sure. That's a sensible plan.'

'I'll make it worth your while.'

'That I don't doubt. But still, I have to go. You're sweet, though.'

As she studies her reflection in the mirror, Noah reaches for his camera that's sitting on the bedside table, turns the lens to get her in focus and takes the picture. She hears the click and catches his eye in the mirror, before spinning on the stool and striking a pose.

He shakes his head, returning the camera to its perch on the table. 'You know I'm only interested in the candid moments.'

She sighs, her shoulders slumping. 'Fine.'

She stands up and wanders through to the bathroom in her purple lace underwear, Noah watching her until she disappears through the door. He rests his head back down on the soft, plush pillows of the luxury hotel and grins, taking a moment to appreciate how great life is right now.

He's been dating up-and-coming Danish model, Clara, for a few months. They met on a spiritual retreat in Greece and, hitting it off straight away, Noah decided to accompany her to the various locations she was sent to by her agency for photoshoots. She's obviously beautiful and sexy, but Noah also likes how driven and calm she is. Nothing seems to faze her and she's on a certain career trajectory that she can't be distracted from, which gives her an independence that is particularly attractive to Noah after dating a string of women who wouldn't seem to leave his side, and didn't seem to appreciate that he's too young for anything serious.

He didn't love getting a glass of Champagne thrown in his face in the middle of a restaurant in Paris after he checked with Camille that she too was seeing other people. And he can still feel the sting of Stephanie's palm making contact with his left cheek when she came to surprise him in Thailand, only to find him distracted by Kylie, the American tourist he'd met there.

But Clara gets the relaxed nature of their relationship. They're enjoying themselves and seeing where it goes. No pressure, no responsibilities, plenty of fun.

Which, as far as Noah is concerned, is how life should be.

'Tell me again why you're so intent on getting involved with Eurovision this weekend?' Clara calls out from the bathroom.

Noah laughs softly. 'I've told you. I meet friends at Eurovision every year. I have done the past four years.'

'It's ridiculous.'

'Eurovision? Sure. But it's our tradition.'

Clara pokes her head round the door as she moisturises her face. 'Do you know how beautiful Copenhagen is? There is so much to do here, so many amazing restaurants to go to and sights to see … and you're going to spend the next few days celebrating Eurovision. It makes no sense, Noah.'

'You're a snob.'

'Yes. So are you.' She folds her arms, leaning against the doorframe. 'I cannot imagine someone like you enjoying Eurovision.'

'Who says I enjoy it?' he retorts, making a face. 'I like seeing my friends.'

'Your Eurovision friends.'

'Yes.'

She watches him curiously. 'If you like them so much, why don't you see them the rest of the year? Why only once a year at Eurovision?'

He pauses. 'I don't know. We made a pact and we stick to it.'

She tilts her head, putting on a teasing baby voice. 'Adorable.'

Laughing, he picks up a pillow and throws it across the room at her. She disappears back into the bathroom. She's right, though. As someone who's not exactly a diehard fan of Eurovision, it is a bit strange that Noah has stuck to the pact, meeting Millie, James and Ingrid every year in whichever city the contest is being hosted. He doesn't like to admit it to himself, but deep down, he knows why he keeps coming back.

For Millie.

There's something about her. In between their annual gathering, he and Millie do message each other every now and then. It has become a habit that whenever he's feeling a bit low about something, he'll contact her. They've stuck mainly to the occasional message, but there have been a few phone calls – it's always been him calling her and only when he's had too many drinks. She happily entertains his calls, though, laughing at his pathetic reason for getting in touch – 'I just met a guy named Benny! Like that ABBA fella! I had to call to tell you' – and she'll ask him about his travels and listen to his anecdotes, then he'll ask her how life is in Brighton, and they'll talk until Noah is distracted and has to go.

There aren't many people that Noah really trusts, but Millie is one of them. Every year, he considers telling her and Ingrid and James about his family background – but he always bottles it. It feels as if he's left it too long, now. He's surprised they haven't discovered who he is without his help, but then again, why would they feel the need to google him? And he's not on social media, which helps. He doesn't want them to change their opinion of him and he's scared that if they knew the full story, they would. When people find out who Noah really is, they always see him differently. They can't help it. It's just the way it is.

When they first met, Millie said she admired him for being sufficiently motivated to earn enough money to go travelling and he's never forgotten how good it made him feel that she thought that about him. No one had ever admired him before. He liked the idea of her seeing him that way.

He doesn't want Millie to think less of him.

As he lies in bed thinking about seeing Millie in two days, his phone starts ringing. He quickly reaches for it, thinking for a moment it might be her, but when he checks the caller ID, he groans, tossing it to the side.

'Who was that?' Clara asks, emerging from the bathroom with her skin prepped and ready, and moving over to her suitcase to get some clothes.

'No one.'

Clara gives him a look. 'A woman?'

'Why? Would you be jealous if it was?' he asks with a teasing smile. When she rolls her eyes, he sighs and adds, 'It was a woman. My sister.'

'Ah.' She pulls out a pair of high-waisted shorts and a t-shirt from her bag. 'You never talk to me about your family.'

'Nothing to say. So, what time will you be done with your shoot today?' he asks, keen to move the conversation along.

'You know I don't know the answer to that,' she replies, buttoning her shorts and throwing on her t-shirt. 'It depends on how well it goes.'

'If you finish early enough then you can take me to one of these amazing Copenhagen restaurants you keep bragging about,' he suggests, sitting up and propping up the pillows before slumping back into them. 'What shall I do to keep me busy until then? I'm going to be bored.'

She pouts, crawling across the bed towards him. 'Poor baby. No work to do. Life must be very hard for you.'

'Oh, it's the worst,' he says, reaching out for her. 'You have no idea.'

As she moves to straddle him, Noah's phone rings again and, without bothering to look to see who it is, his hand locates where it's buried in the duvet and throws it off the bed. The phone clatters on the floor, the sound of the ringing drowned out by Clara's infectious giggles as Noah picks her up and flips her onto her back, kissing her deeply.

* * *

Saturday 10 May

'You and Noah might finally happen tonight.'

Millie snaps her head up so fast at James's remark that she feels a twinge in her neck.

'What do you mean?' She frowns. 'There is no "me and Noah".'

'*Please*.' James swings his legs up on the bed and checks his phone. 'You two have always had a little something. Every year, Ingrid and I wonder if it's going to happen.'

Millie blushes, mortified. 'You and Ingrid *talk* about this?'

He shrugs. 'Of course. This year could be THE year.'

'OK, stop. Firstly, it wouldn't happen anyway because … well, obvious reasons. And secondly, even if there was any chance, he has a girlfriend, remember?'

'Clara?' James wrinkles his nose. 'He's not serious about her. He's not serious about anyone.'

With a sinking heart, Millie realises that James is right – and that's exactly why there won't ever be a 'her and Noah'. He's made it very clear that he doesn't want any commitments, whether in his personal or professional life, and he seems to live by that – Millie can't keep up with what he's doing or who he's with – while she needs someone she can rely on.

But that still doesn't stop her heart fluttering whenever he texts her out of the blue.

'What did you mean by "obvious reasons"?' James interrupts her thoughts.

'Sorry?'

'You said it won't happen between you and Noah "for obvious reasons". What did you mean?' he asks, looking confused.

'Oh,' she says, standing up from the edge of his bed and going to check her reflection in the long mirror that is hanging on the inside of the wardrobe in their hostel room. 'Noah is like … you know.'

'I really *don't* know,' James emphasises. 'That's why I've asked you the question.'

She sighs, irritated at having to say it out loud in case it sounds like she's fishing for a compliment. 'He's way out of my league.'

James bristles. 'Come off it.'

'Have you seen the kind of women he dates? They're always *stunning*. Which makes sense because he's … he's …'

She trails off.

'Carved by angels?' James offers with dramatic flair.

Millie bursts out laughing. 'Sure, let's go with that. Very poetic. Noah is carved by angels. He'd never be interested in someone like me.'

'What is *wrong* with you?!' James cries, outraged on her behalf. 'You are gorgeous. Noah would be lucky to catch your eye. I mean that, Millie, even though I know you don't believe me. And today you look particularly HOT.'

With a grateful smile, Millie shakes her head. Obviously what James is saying regarding her and Noah simply isn't true, but she loves him for saying it all the same. She has taken extra care over her appearance today in anticipation of seeing him, despite the fact that he has a girlfriend and he's never given Millie any hope that something might happen between them.

She turns slightly to check how this dress looks from various angles. It's new – a yellow mini dress inspired by a photo taken at the Eurovision Grand Final in 1974 of her grandma that Tom keeps on his bedside table. Millie bought it this week to go with a pair of Julie's silver ankle boots that she remembers admiring as a child.

'Is borrowing shoes from your grandma tragic?' Millie had asked James before the trip.

'When your grandma is Julie, it's *inspired*,' he'd assured her. 'Vintage, baby.'

Millie nervously examines her figure, adjusting the capped shoulders slightly, fretting over how her arms look, before picking up her eye-liner pencil and applying a little more to the bottom line of her lashes. When it comes to Eurovision, bold make-up is almost compulsory, and she's gone for a really smoky-eye look and fake lashes – she perfected heavy eye-liner back when she was dating Louis. With the silver shadow and pretty gemstones she's carefully stuck at the corners of her lashes, even she has to admit that her eyes really stand out.

For the first time in ages, she smiles at her reflection. She's slowly had to rebuild her confidence since the major hit it took when Louis broke up with her a couple of years ago – it took her a long time to recover from the discovery of just how many girls he'd cheated on her with, emotionally and physically.

He was in the shower one day when she saw a message pop up on his phone from a girl and, already full of doubt and suspicions, she'd glanced at the first line that read: 'lying here, thinking of you ...'

Her stomach twisting in a knot, she'd felt physically sick as she read that message in full and then, having already taken the plunge into his private texts, scrolled down to be confronted by a whole host of them from various women.

He'd strolled into the bedroom topless, his towel round his waist, his hair plastered across his forehead, and stopped dead still when he saw her holding his phone, tears running freely down her cheeks.

The truth is, they should have broken up long before then. But Millie wanted to believe in what they had and was desperate to convince herself that she was enough for him. The messages confirmed all her worst suspicions – she had never been cool enough to date Louis. She wore a cupcake hat at work, lived with her grandparents and loved Eurovision. No amount of ripped black shorts and t-shirts with 'THE ROLLING STONES' branded across the front could change that.

After the break-up, she withdrew into herself, paranoid that any girl who walked into Beebee's Buns wearing distressed denim and a beanie might have been one of Louis's flings, terrified that they were on their phones messaging him things like: 'Lol, your ex has a giant cupcake on her head. What did you see in her again?'

She knew she was being stupid, but she couldn't help it. Her mind would jump to these weird scenarios and then she'd be convinced there was truth in them. It was easy to let herself become consumed by her insecurities.

But James was there to pull her up – after months of her hiding away in the comfort of home, he started to persuade her to join nights out with him and his university friends, and slowly but surely she began to find herself again. Her eyes began to open to the flaws in her relationship with

Louis, and the anguish that she'd woken up feeling every morning after his betrayal started to fade away, until one morning, she woke up and it was gone.

She's been happy enjoying her single life and now she needs to make a change to her professional one. Yesterday, when Jeff informed her that, despite her experience, he still wasn't sure she was 'management material', she made a promise to herself: in a year's time, when she'd next meet up with Ingrid and Noah, she'd tell them that she was no longer working at Beebee's Buns. She'd have a different job, a new career path.

Looking in the mirror now, she lifts her chin.

'YES!' James cries suddenly, making her jump.

'What? What is it?'

'Zachary has replied,' he announces, leaping to his feet and shimmying his shoulders. 'He's invited us to a Eurovision afterparty tonight. Oh my *god*. This is going to be the best night EVER. You need to help me pick an outfit!'

'You already look amazing,' Millie grins, watching him jump up and down on the spot. 'He's really invited us to a Eurovision afterparty?'

'Yes, he has.' James holds out his phone so she can inspect the message on the screen. 'Millie, do you think this could be the night that it finally happens for *both* of us? You and Noah, and me and Zachary!'

'There is no "me and Noah"!' Millie emphasises, rolling her eyes. 'You and Zachary on the other hand …'

She shoots him an impish smile and James swoons.

Millie would love if James and Zachary got together tonight. James deserves something good when everything at home is so rubbish for him at the moment. His parents are in the middle of a horrible divorce – his dad had an

71

affair with his colleague, which was shocking enough for James to get his head round, but even worse, James also discovered that it wasn't the first time. His parents had kept his dad's previous affair three years earlier secret from him, having decided to work through it.

Since the truth came out, James's relationship with his dad has deteriorated – he can't forgive him for tearing their family apart. James has been such a rock for his mum and Millie knows that it hasn't been an easy time for him, so this weekend is a good excuse for him to let loose. A fun night with Zachary is exactly what he needs.

'Come on, text Zachary back and tell him we'll come to the afterparty,' she encourages, grinning at his elated expression.

'I can't seem too eager! I have to play it a bit cool and give it at least leave five minutes before replying,' he insists.

Millie giggles as James stands in the middle of the room, closes his eyes and clasps his hands together.

'Please, please, please Eurovision gods,' he whispers. 'Please can he like me back.'

'You know he does,' Millie insists, as he opens his eyes to study the message from Zachary yet again. 'You two have been flirting for three years. I really thought last year in Sweden when we met up with him at that bar it was going to happen, but then …'

She trails off, pressing her lips together as she tries to suppress a laugh. James narrows his eyes at her.

'Yes, thank you, Millie. None of us needs reminding of what happened last year.'

'I did tell you to slow down on the schnapps.'

'How was I to know it was so strong?' he retorts grumpily, before burying his face in his hands and peeping at her through his fingers. 'You promise Zachary didn't see me being sick outside that bar?'

She holds her hands up. 'I swear to you. It was only me and Noah who had the pleasure of witnessing that incident.'

'Poor Noah having to carry me up the stairs of that hostel.' James grimaces at the memory. 'That will *not* happen again this year. I will keep my head and NOT have to be taken home by a hunky straight Australian.'

'Hopefully this year you'll be taken home by hunky Zachary,' Millie teases, raising her eyebrows. 'No schnapps allowed.'

'No schnapps allowed,' James repeats solemnly, before breaking into a smile. 'Did I tell you what your grandpa said to me the other day? I was saying how I had yet to find the kind of spark I'd felt with Zachary with anyone else and he replied that he'd met the love of his life at Eurovision and maybe I had too.'

Millie feels a warmth in her stomach at her grandpa saying that. He isn't much of a talker and he certainly refrains from speaking about any kind of emotion if he can help it, but beneath that reserved exterior, he's a real romantic.

'And you know your grandma always says love is in the air at Eurovision,' James reminds her. 'She says it's something to do with all the sequins.'

'Yes,' Millie giggles. 'It's a very odd theory, but, in her head, apparently a room full of sequins equates to a room full of love.'

'I'm telling you, Millie,' James continues brazenly, 'I've dated a few guys and none of them have come close to Zachary. Tonight is the night for us, I can feel it in my bones.'

He starts dancing around the room in excitement.

'Shall we play some ABBA?' he suggests, leaping through the air. 'I feel like we should play some ABBA! Put on "Dancing Queen"! Or "Gimme Gimme Gimme"!'

'At once,' she replies, scrolling through the playlists on her phone.

'You know what I'm ready for, Millie?' James says, dancing over to her.

She presses play on "Dancing Queen" before looking up at him. 'What?'

'I'm ready to dance, I'm ready to jive,' he answers, grabbing her hands and pulling her to her feet to twirl her around the room, making her shriek with laughter. 'And I'm ready to have the time of my life.'

CHAPTER SIX

'Ingrid Vogel, you are a true dreamer,' Noah announces, putting his arm around her and squeezing her shoulders after they've found a free table to huddle around at the Eurovision afterparty venue. 'And thank goodness for people like you. You are proof, if proof was ever needed, that dreams really do come true.'

'Just like the winner today,' Ingrid grins. 'Conchita Wurst is an inspiration.'

'Yes!' James cries, slapping his hand enthusiastically against the table. 'The right person won Eurovision today. I hope they play her song again tonight.'

'They've already played it three times,' Millie says. 'I don't think a fourth time is out of the question.'

'I will be playing "Rise Like a Phoenix" on repeat for the next few weeks at least,' James declares.

'And next year, there will be people standing at the Eurovision afterparty in Austria talking about how they will be playing Ingrid's hit song for weeks to come!' Noah says.

'Just because I've got an agent doesn't mean I'll be entering Eurovision next year,' Ingrid says. 'But I hope one day I will be!'

'I *know* you will be. Congratulations on signing to an agent. What a huge achievement.' Noah reaches for his glass and holds it aloft. 'To Ingrid!'

'To Ingrid,' James and Millie chorus, knocking their glasses against his.

Ingrid smiles modestly.

'Tell us how it happened,' Millie insists. 'Did you write a song and send it off to loads of talent agencies? Did you have to play an open mic night? In my head, you're the girl in *Coyote Ugly*. I have no idea how this stuff actually works.'

'Actually, you're not far off,' Ingrid laughs. 'I secured a set at a bar in Berlin that's known for emerging artists, but I wasn't playing any of my own songs. I was performing covers – I really got everyone up on their feet, you know? It was a great atmosphere.'

'I bet you have the most amazing stage presence,' James says, engrossed in the story. 'Wait. Don't tell me – there was a talent agent in the crowd.'

Ingrid smiles, nodding slowly. 'There was a talent agent in the crowd.'

'Oh my god, it is LITERALLY a scene from a movie,' James cries, causing Noah and Millie to burst out laughing.

'His name is Emil,' Ingrid tells them. 'I actually noticed him during the performance because he wasn't singing along like everyone else or getting involved. He was sitting there at a table in the corner with another guy and both of them were in suits. They looked so serious. I thought they were being arseholes, because they had very stern expressions the whole way through my set and neither of them clapped at the end like everyone else. Instead they huddled together and talked in low voices – they looked like two spies passing on information in a busy bar.'

'But they were talking about *you*,' Millie squeals.

'I guess so,' Ingrid says, looking as though she still can't quite believe it. 'I started packing up my guitar after the set and I didn't even notice Emil had approached until I turned around and he was there, standing right behind me. From his serious expression, I thought he was coming over to tell me how bad I was. I was ready to punch him in the face.'

'Now that would have been a great start to your story of getting an agent,' James notes. 'Imagine telling future interviewers that one.'

'It certainly would be memorable,' Noah agrees.

'I'm glad you didn't punch him in the face,' laughs Millie. 'Did he give you his card?'

'He asked me if I had representation,' Ingrid says. 'I was so confused I had to ask him to repeat himself, I wasn't sure I'd heard right. When I said no, he told me his name was Emil Fischer and he was a talent agent who would be interested in talking to me. I was in shock but I managed to hold it together to say I'd be very interested, and that's when he gave me his card and asked me to call his office the next day to set up a meeting. I had to miss one of my college classes to take the meeting, but obviously it's worth it.'

'Obviously,' Noah grins, looking at her in amazement. 'So what happens now?'

'We're in the middle of creating an EP – a few songs that we can send off to record labels,' Ingrid tells them, beaming with excitement. 'It's been a bit of a slow process because … well, songwriting doesn't come that easily to me, to be honest. I've always been more of a singer than a songwriter, but I have to be both if I'm going to get signed. Emil is helping me a lot, though. We've been working on my music together; he's dedicated a lot of time outside of his office hours to help me, going over and beyond what an agent needs to do – he's been … *amazing*.'

Millie raises her eyebrows. 'Uh oh.'

'What?' Ingrid asks innocently.

'I know that look,' Millie claims, shaking her finger at Ingrid. 'You're *falling* for him!'

'He's my agent!'

'He's more than that,' James counters with a mischievous grin. 'Millie's right, it's written all over your face. Come on, tell us what he's like.'

'Who? Emil?' Ingrid shrugs. 'He's nice! In his late thirties, good looking. He dresses really well – he has these expensive tailored suits, you know? He looks … smart. Successful. And he's incredibly talented. He knows the music industry so well and he has all these ideas to make sure my music is commercial enough to sell. I'm so lucky to have him guiding me.'

'Oh god, she's in love,' James teases, his eyes widening. 'Look at her, all bashful!'

'Shut up!' she cries, throwing a napkin at him, but unable to stop a wide smile spreading across her face. 'I respect him as a professional colleague.'

'Sure, sure, course you do,' James says, nudging her. 'So, what's he like in bed?'

'James!' Millie cries, slapping his shoulder playfully. 'You can't ask that!'

'We're friends, of course I can,' he protests, before turning to Ingrid. 'Look me in the eye and tell me you're not sleeping with him.'

Ingrid sighs, giving in. 'Fine. We've been together a few weeks now. But it's *serious*. We're serious about each other.'

'Always the romantic,' Noah comments, smiling at her before putting on a wistful voice to add, 'I can picture how this happened: long nights writing music together, gazing into each other's eyes as you play sweet melodies …'

'Oh god,' Ingrid laughs, burying her face in her hands.

'It really is playing out like a movie,' he chuckles.

'Honestly, he's wonderful,' she insists, flustered. 'I wish he was here so you could all meet him.'

'He does sound pretty amazing,' Millie remarks. 'Good looking, smart, successful.'

'He'll be even more dreamy if he lands you a big, lucrative record deal,' James says.

'Exactly.' Ingrid nods sharply. 'Obviously, Emil and I … it's great. But the most important thing is the music and getting signed. I am going to work my arse off.'

'There is no doubt that you'll make it,' Noah says firmly. 'Hey, this is really cool. I'm going to be friends with a popstar.'

'Not just any popstar, either,' Millie adds. 'But one who will be representing Germany in Eurovision someday!'

'OK, slow down, I haven't even got a record deal yet,' Ingrid tells them, holding up her hands. 'One thing at a time. But I will say this: I really …' – she pauses to take a deep breath, the others watching her expectantly – 'I really hope that I do make it and that I don't let anybody down. I want this to be real.'

Throwing an arm around her, Millie rests her head against Ingrid's. 'It is real. This isn't a dream any more. You believed in yourself and, because of that, things are happening for you. You deserve it.'

Ingrid closes her eyes and smiles. There's a flash of light and the two women start. Noah lowers his camera with an apologetic smile.

'That was a good moment to capture,' he explains. 'Millie can use it as proof that we were once friends when Ingrid no longer remembers our names because she's an international superstar. Also, sorry to change the subject but' – he nods to someone standing behind them, a grin spreading across his face – 'I had to get photographic evidence of that outfit. I don't think I've ever seen anything like it.'

Following his eyeline, the others turn to admire a woman wearing a striking sequin dress with twinkling lights wound around it. Ingrid's jaw drops to the floor.

'Where can I get one?' she whispers jealously.

'How would you wash it?' Millie asks.

James bursts out laughing. 'And so we witness the very different workings of your brains. OK, who wants to help me get another round of drinks?'

'My turn!' Ingrid claims, looping her arm through his and dragging him to the bar.

While they're gone, Millie spots Charlotte's name flashing up on Noah's phone that he's carelessly left out on the table among the glasses. He's too busy examining his camera screen to notice.

'Your phone is ringing again,' she points out.

He declines the call. 'It's my sister. It's fine, I'll call her tomorrow.'

'That's the second time she's called tonight. Sorry, I don't mean to be nosy,' Millie adds. 'It's only that I noticed you ignore her call earlier, too. Are you sure it's not important if she's ringing you twice in one night?'

'Yeah, I'm sure. She's been messaging me, too. I haven't checked in with the family in a while, that's all,' he explains, sliding his phone back into his pocket. 'Mum will be nagging her to get in touch. She always seems to call at inconvenient times.'

'I guess it's difficult with the time difference.'

'True. I'll call when I have the time to speak to her properly. There wouldn't be any point in answering now when we're at a party. She knows I'm fine: I messaged her this morning to say I was alive.'

'When we last spoke on the phone, you mentioned that things between you and your family were still … difficult.'

'Really?' Noah frowns. 'I don't remember telling you that.'

'I'm not sure you were entirely yourself,' Millie admits. 'You were camping somewhere and I think you'd ingested one or two interesting concoctions.'

'Ah.' He winces, embarrassed. 'Sorry about that.'

'Don't be,' Millie insists. 'It was nice to talk to you about your family.'

He shifts uncomfortably. 'What did I tell you?'

'You said that it's hard not to be able to be honest and that it was complicated.'

'Did I bore you with specifics?' he asks anxiously.

She shakes her head. 'Not really. I know things aren't easy with your dad. I figured that's what you were referring to. Anyway, we don't have to talk about it if you don't want, it's really none of my business. I just wanted to make sure you're OK. I know it's been a while since you've been home to Australia …'

'Four years,' he says. 'Time has gone very quickly.'

'They must miss you.' She pauses before carefully adding, 'Noah, if you haven't been able to fly back to Australia to see them because it's so expensive, you would say, wouldn't you? Because we could maybe all chip in to loan you the money if you needed—'

Noah looks horrified. 'What? No!'

'I know you might not be able to save up much, travelling around and getting work as you go,' she says hurriedly, 'and I would hate for you to feel that you can't—'

81

'Millie,' he interrupts firmly, 'that is really kind of you, but money is not the reason I haven't gone back. Yes, flights are expensive but … I … I'm sure I could save up enough if I wanted to. But I don't.'

She nods, watching him carefully. 'OK. I don't mean to stick my nose in your business and I know you have other friends and your girlfriend who you'd probably go to first for that kind of thing, but I want to make sure …' – she hesitates, thinking of the right way to put this – 'I want you to know that we're here if you need us.'

Running a hand through his hair, he looks at her in amazement. 'Millie …'

He exhales, his shoulders slumping forward, before his expression softens.

'You really are amazing, did you know that?' he continues, making her blush. 'Thank you. For the offer. That was really sweet of you to check.'

She smiles modestly, shrugging.

'The reason I don't want to go back to Australia is my dad,' Noah emphasises. 'To say he disapproves of my lifestyle would be an understatement. He doesn't get that people our age like to travel and see the world, rather than be squished into a suit and trapped in a mind-numbing job.'

'Have you talked to him about how serious you are about photography?'

Noah hesitates, appearing taken aback by her question. 'What do you mean?'

'Anyone can see that it's your passion,' she points out. 'You're really good at it. You have a talent and, if you love it, then you should trust your gut and think about pursuing it as a career. I figured that's what you were thinking long term.'

'I … I couldn't do that,' Noah frowns.

'Why not?'

'Because it's a hobby.'

'It's an art,' Millie corrects, looking at him in confusion.

'Maybe a long time ago, I considered it as a career. You know, when I was young and naïve. But I couldn't do it properly. I don't really know anything about it.'

'That's easily remedied,' she says simply. 'You can take photography courses and learn about the craft. Aren't you dating a model at the moment? She must know photographers, probably very successful ones if they're heading up fashion shoots for glossy magazines. Why don't you ask her to put you in touch with one of them? They might be able to take you under their wing, give you some experience.' She tilts her head at him. 'Don't let what your dad thinks of you get in the way of what you love doing. If anything, it would feel really good to prove him wrong. You have a talent, Noah – you don't have to waste it simply because your dad doesn't approve of it.'

Noah stares at her, unsure what to say.

'What?' she asks, her eyebrows knitting together in concern. 'I hope I haven't overstepped the mark. I didn't mean to say anything that—'

'No, it's not … it's not that,' he assures her quietly, reaching out and putting his hand over hers. She shivers, a lump forming in her throat. His hand is warm and strong and comforting. 'It's nice to have someone believe in me, that's all. I think … I think you might be the only one who does.'

She lifts her eyes to meet his. A small crease forms between his eyebrows as he looks at her intently, as though he's grappling with something.

She wishes she could read his mind.

He wishes he could kiss her.

Just when he thinks he might, she drops her eyes back to the table and the spell is broken. He removes his hand from hers and she suddenly feels vulnerable without it there. She had to fight every urge in her body not to throw herself at him then.

He has a girlfriend, her brain reminded her. *Even if he kissed you back today, he'd drop you tomorrow.*

Resting her arms on the table, she looks out across the party in the hope that the room full of celebration will distract her from Noah.

There's another flash of light.

She spins back to see Noah has taken a photo of her.

'I wasn't smiling,' she says, bewildered.

'You were deep in thought,' he replies, lowering the camera again. 'You looked beautiful.'

Millie swallows the lump in her throat. Gazing at her in deep concentration, Noah opens his mouth as though he's about to say something when Ingrid returns abruptly to the table.

'We've lost James,' she announces.

'What?' Millie asks, frowning. 'What do you mean, "lost" him?'

Ingrid winks at her. 'I mean that we have lost him for the night, because someone else came to find him.'

* * *

When James wakes up to see Zachary lying next to him fast asleep, he scrunches up his eyes and breaks into a smile so broad it hurts his jaw. It wasn't a dream.

Last night might just have been the best of James's life. When Zachary, sporting a new beard, emerged from the crowd and came to lean at the bar next to him, he found it near impossible to play it cool – instead, he pulled Zachary into a big hug, exclaiming how good it was to see him. Luckily, Zachary wasn't repulsed by his enthusiasm – quite the opposite. He gushed about how he'd been looking for James since he arrived.

As soon as they started talking, they couldn't stop. James asked Zachary all about his job, listening in amazement and expressing his envy, before glumly informing Zachary that, despite graduating a year ago from his media course, he was yet to land a job in journalism. While he continued to apply, he was working at a stationery shop, and he'd interviewed last week for a local paper in Brighton and was yet to hear back.

'So you never know,' James had said loudly over the music. 'Maybe I'll get lucky and this time next year I'll be an actual reporter!'

'Nothing to do with luck,' Zachary replied, matter-of-factly. 'Someone with your passion and dedication – it will happen, I know it. In the meantime, you know what you should do? Start a blog or a website.'

'A blog.' James snorted. 'Why?'

'Why not?' Zachary shrugged. 'A Eurovision blog.'

'What would I say?'

'There is so much to say! You could write about the contest, about the performers, about what people can expect from each country. You can write about the history. It can be a big celebration of all things Eurovision. You could do videos of you talking about it, maybe speaking to fellow fans, people who make the effort to come wherever they are in the world, just like you and your friends.'

James blinked at him. 'Maybe. That could be quite a fun idea.'

'You'd be brilliant at something like that.'

'Really?'

'Really. I'd like to see it.'

James grinned at him, his eyes twinkling. 'So, if I created this blog, I could guarantee at least one subscriber.'

'Your number one fan, right here,' Zachary replied, gesturing to himself.

Butterflies had danced around James's stomach.

They barely left each other's side all night after that. They eventually made their way back to the table where Millie, Noah and Ingrid were and spent some time with them, before heading to the dance floor where they had their first kiss. When James sought Millie out later to tell her that Zachary had suggested going back to his, he had barely been able to contain his excitement.

Now here he is this morning, happy to confirm that he hasn't dreamt up the whole evening. As Zachary opens his eyes and says 'good morning' in an affectionate, dozy voice, James knows that, on his return, he'll be able to inform Millie's grandpa with some certainty that he, too, met the love of his life at Eurovision.

Too excited to fall back asleep, James waits for Zachary to wake up properly and eagerly agrees to his suggestion of breakfast together before James has to go back to the hostel to pack up to go home. They get ready and then hold hands strolling down the pavement together, looking for a nice place to eat. They find an outdoor table for two and take their seats, chatting about last night, laughing about their hangovers and kissing across the table, like an established couple. James couldn't be happier.

'I don't want to leave,' James confesses dreamily.

'I know, me neither,' Zachary says, taking a sip of his coffee. 'But at least we had one perfect night, right? And hopefully we'll see each other next year.'

Everything comes crashing down so suddenly and spectacularly that James physically recoils. He can't speak. And Zachary, casually adjusting his sunglasses, doesn't even seem to notice.

'Just one perfect night,' James eventually manages to get out, his throat tightening as he forces out the words. 'That's ... that's all this was?'

Zachary turns to him in surprise. 'James, you know this could never work. You live in England and I live in Switzerland. It's not like we can ... date.'

'But ... I ... I just—' James feels like his face is on fire as his brain scrambles to find the right words. 'I guess I hoped ...'

He trails off. He's not sure *what* he had hoped. Zachary was making sense. What did James expect? Did he think that Zachary would declare his love for him and, after one night together, they would commit to a long-distance relationship?

Without thinking about any kind of logistics, James had hoped things would magically work out. Just like they had for Julie and Tom. He'd lost himself in the fantasy.

He suddenly feels an overwhelming urge to cry, which would make this excruciating moment even worse. He already must look so immature and naïve to Zachary right now. He *has* to find a way of pulling himself together.

'Sorry, of course, you're right,' he says, plastering on a smile and lifting his mug of coffee. 'So, Austria next year, huh? That will be fun! I've never been! Have you?'

Zachary leaps at the change of conversation, but the damage is done. The rest of their meal is overshadowed, the conversation stilted, and James feels both eager to leave and desperate to stay.

After they've paid the bill, Zachary offers to walk James back to the hostel, but James insists he doesn't. He wants to walk back alone.

'Well, then,' Zachary says, taking off his sunglasses, 'I guess we say goodbye.'

James nods. 'Yes, guess so.'

'I hope you have a safe journey home.'

'You too.'

Zachary hesitates. 'Last night was …'

He trails off.

'Like you said earlier,' James interjects with a sad smile, 'it was one perfect night.'

'Yes,' Zachary says. 'It was.'

After standing a few more moments in silence, James can't take it any more and leans towards him for a peck on the cheek, not wanting to overdo it, but as he moves away, Zachary grabs his hands and pulls him back towards him, giving him a long, lingering kiss that makes James's head feel light and his shattered heart ache.

CHAPTER SEVEN

Vienna, Austria

2015

Saturday 23 May

Millie watches as Noah talks into the ear of the club's DJ, an attractive redhead in a tiny green strapless dress and thigh-high spangly boots, while she's been left guarding the booth they've managed to secure as James and Ingrid get the drinks. There's something different about Noah this year. He certainly *looks* different. He's grown his hair long – too long in Millie's opinion – so that he continually sweeps it back from his face, tucking it behind his ears. He's lost weight, too, and his style has evolved from his relaxed traveller look of a t-shirt, faded jeans and an absurd amount of grubby, fraying wristbands, to tight, skinny black trousers turned up at the ankles, expensive patterned silk shirts and black loafers with no socks – at least, that's what he's wearing tonight. He's obviously making a lot more money now than he was before.

When she admitted her surprise at his choice of shirt earlier, he said that it was a gift from an ex-girlfriend. It's Dolce & Gabbana, apparently. Millie wondered if the ex he referred to was Clara, the model he was dating this time last year, but according to today's anecdotes, there have been a few women in his life recently, so it could be anyone.

His attitude is different, too. He was always confident, but this year he seems overly zealous about everything, radiating intense fervour and energy, frantic almost – like he's trying too hard. The easy-going side to him has taken a backseat.

Millie knows she should be happy that he seems so enamoured by his life, and she's pleased that he's doing so well.

But she can't shake the feeling that he's not entirely himself.

'Here we go,' James says, appearing at her side and setting down a couple of bottles of beer as Ingrid follows suit.

'Thanks so much,' Millie says, making room for both of them to slide into the booth next to her.

'Yeah, thanks again James. I'm so sorry, I can't believe I left my purse in Berlin,' Ingrid says hurriedly. 'So stupid of me. I promise I'll transfer you all some money when I get back.'

'Ingrid, stop apologising! It's really no problem,' James assures her, as she lowers her eyes to the table, her hair falling in front of her face.

Millie's brow furrows in concern as she watches Ingrid anxiously fidget with the label on her bottle. She's not sure if she's reading too much into everything, but she feels like Ingrid has been acting strangely all day – she's seemed distracted, and has brushed off a lot of questions with short, vague answers, wearing a smile that doesn't quite ring true.

She wants to get Ingrid on her own at some point tonight to ask her if everything is really OK. Millie knows that the music industry is notoriously fast-paced and she hopes that Ingrid is coping with all the pressures that come hand in hand with success.

'Hey, where's Noah?' James asks.

Millie nods across the dance floor to the DJ. 'He said he wanted to introduce himself.'

'Ah,' James says, a knowing smile spreading across his face. 'He wanted to let her know that a fellow artist was in the building. Poor woman is probably getting an earful about how he's a big-shot DJ in Europe.'

Millie giggles. 'No doubt about it.'

'At least we're not having to listen to him talk about his amazing DJ life,' James points out, taking a swig of his drink. 'I didn't think he'd shut up about it today when we were doing all that sightseeing – my memories of the Schönbrunn Palace will forever be intertwined with his story about that girl climbing up on stage when he was DJing in Barcelona and twerking on him. I'm all for him doing well in his career, but I'm not sure I needed to hear so many stories about how many famous DJs in Ibiza complimented his "natural flair". Two or three would have been enough.'

'I hadn't even heard of the people he was talking about,' Millie admits, looking at Noah again as the DJ throws her head back to laugh at something he's saying.

'Me neither,' James says. 'Some of their names sounded made up, if you ask me.'

'I had no idea Noah was even that into music.'

'Or the "cool Europe party scene" as he put it earlier,' James teases. 'No, I didn't think so, either, but I guess he's found his calling. He seems to be having a great time, anyway. Doesn't look like he'll be heading back to Australia any time soon, does it?'

91

Millie shakes her head. 'I thought photography would be his calling. Not DJ decks.'

'I don't think photography offers the kind of opportunities that DJing does to give you … that *rush* he's after, shall we say,' James comments pointedly, raising his eyebrows. 'He's basically been partying for an entire year and getting paid for it.'

It's none of her business and she doesn't know why she cares so much, but Millie is strangely bothered by Noah giving up on photography. When they arrived yesterday and met up with him to begin the Eurovision weekend festivities, she noticed he didn't have his camera on him, an accessory that she realised she'd rarely seen him without before now. During their catch-up when she got round to asking him about his photography ambitions, he wrinkled his nose and brushed it aside with a dismissive wave of his hand.

'I've told you before, that was only ever a hobby,' he said. 'Nothing serious. I don't do it any more.'

She gawped at him. 'At all? Not even for fun?'

'Nope, don't have time. I did chat to a professional photographer about it once and showed him some of my stuff – he thought it was good and we had a chat about getting into it. But, you know, it sounded a bit rubbish. You don't get paid much; I'd have had to do a course in it, probably, and then maybe get an apprenticeship. It sounded like a lot of hard work for not much gain,' he concluded with a shrug.

'The gain would surely be doing what you love,' Millie argued, thrown by his casual attitude.

'I'm doing what I love now,' he retorted, leaning back in his chair and putting his hands behind his head. 'And trust me, the gain is a *lot* better.'

She dropped it, because there didn't seem to be any point in telling Noah her opinion. It's his life, his choices. She's disappointed that he would give up on photography so easily, especially when he was so good at it, but then again, it makes sense that he would choose to do something that's clearly paying him nicely and that he enjoys. He gets to travel a lot with this line of work, too, and she's caught on to the fact that he doesn't like staying in one place too long. He always seems to be on the move. With him still refusing to be on social media, none of them knows where Noah is throughout the year until he randomly messages the group with a photo of him in whichever city he's landed in.

She wonders what his family think of his current lifestyle. She knows that they were never exactly supportive of him leaning towards anything in the arts – she remembers him saying his dad would never back him taking up photography seriously, so it seems unlikely he's thrilled about Noah becoming a DJ.

'Do you know what the best thing is about Sweden winning today?' James says, prompting Millie to tear her eyes away from Noah. 'That next year, we get to go there again and I can prove to you all that I am now able to hold my schnapps.'

Millie laughs. 'I'm pleased Sweden won. I loved the graphics of the performance. The singer was literally interacting with the background. So cool.'

'That's another great thing about Eurovision. It's not just the performer, it's the team creating the *performance*,' James asserts passionately. 'It must be so fun to be a part of it – you can really go wild with creativity when it comes to the design and set.'

'Don't forget the costume, too,' Millie adds. 'I liked the UK's '20s flapper vibe.'

'Who doesn't like a nod to Gatsby?' He grins, glancing over at the DJ booth. 'Anyone else think it was sweet how excited Noah got at Australia doing so well in the contest? He's never really got into it before like we have – I mean, I know he likes it because he comes every year, but let's be honest, that's the pact keeping him in line. He hasn't been crazy about the actual show before. But tonight, he was screaming at the screen, up on his feet cheering whenever a country awarded Australia a decent number of points.'

'It was lovely,' Millie laughs. 'About time they let Australia take part.'

'And great that they did so well. Much better than the UK.' He hesitates, turning to Ingrid with a grimace. 'Sorry about the German result tonight, Ingrid. I've said it once and I'll say it again: she did not deserve last place. I thought the song was good!'

Ingrid shrugs. 'It happens.'

'It won't happen when *you're* representing Germany,' James says brightly. 'Speaking of your singing prowess, when are we going to hear your music? I feel like Noah was prattling on so much today that none of us got a word in edgeways! You need to tell us more about your life. Which record label was lucky enough to sign you and when can we download your stuff? I want to brag about you to everyone!'

'Oh, um, soon hopefully. These things take time.' She frowns, reaching for her bottle and taking a large glug, before shoving it back down on the table. 'I'll be back in a minute.'

'Are you all right?' Millie asks, noticing her troubled expression.

'Great, perfect,' Ingrid replies, shuffling out the booth. 'I have to go to the toilet.'

She turns on her heel and starts pushing her way through the crowd of people throwing themselves around the dance floor. Millie watches her go before turning to James.

'Do you think something is going on with her?'

'Maybe,' he says thoughtfully. 'She's being very quiet.'

'She's usually so excited, but this year she seems less … vibrant.'

'Maybe it's because Germany came last. Or she might just be tired,' James points out. 'Come on, let's be honest here. She's the only one of us who really has her shit together.'

'True. She's probably exhausted from writing and recording all the time, and going to fancy business meetings and celebrity parties.'

'Oh how I wish that my life was half so glamorous as hers,' James sighs. 'But alas, I'm stuck writing about a rogue seagull that managed to get into a seaside restaurant and cause havoc by stealing a lemon sole off someone's plate and proceeding to fly about with it, shitting everywhere. What a rollercoaster of a tale.'

'Hey, I like your articles,' Millie says. 'At least you're writing for a living, right?'

'Yeah, and I do know how lucky I am to do that, don't get me wrong,' he insists. 'But working for a local Brighton paper is hardly the journalism I envisioned doing. The news stories are barely news. You know someone emailed me a picture of their cat wearing a homemade Sherlock Holmes costume and asked if it was worthy to print in the paper.

A cat wearing a *deer stalker hat and cape*. And you know what the most depressing thing about that is? My editor genuinely considered it for the front page!'

Millie tries to hold back a laugh. 'It does sound cute.'

'Don't worry, it made page two,' he admits, rolling his eyes. 'We got several letters about it.'

'In favour or against?'

'Oh, it was all fan mail. The owner got in touch to happily let us know that they have set up an Instagram for the cat now on the back of the picture's success.'

'OK, so it's not quite the pace of journalism you're after, but you are putting smiles on readers' faces,' Millie points out, unable to suppress her giggles any longer. 'That is important. Sometimes people need to see a cat in a Sherlock Holmes outfit. That will have made their day. The seagull story sounds thrilling, too.'

'I can't keep doing this forever,' James groans, burying his face in his hands.

'You won't! It's only been a year. Remember, you're getting the experience you need to apply for much better jobs. Keep the end goal in mind.'

'Yes, yes, I know you're right. But that doesn't stop me from wanting to die a death every day that I head into the office and my editor asks me to cover another hot-dog-related incident at the pier.'

'There's been more than one hot-dog incident?'

'Believe it or not, yes.'

'Hey, it will all work out for you, I know it,' Millie says encouragingly. 'One day, you'll be a big-time music journalist – maybe Noah could put you in touch with some cool DJs to interview! Or you could ask Ingrid for an exclusive when she releases her single.'

He snorts. 'An exclusive for what? My tiny newspaper in Brighton? I don't think so.'

'I was talking about your *blog*,' she clarifies. 'Don't even pretend like it's not going well.'

'It is going surprisingly well,' he admits, brightening. 'Who knew people would be so interested in anything I had to say about Eurovision?'

'Um, *I* did?' she says, raising her hand. 'I still don't understand why you're keeping your identity anonymous, though. Don't you want people knowing it's you who founded it and is writing all that amazing content? I think it would help spur on your career! Surely editors would be impressed with it doing so well.'

James hesitates. 'I don't know. Not everyone admires Eurovision like we do; people can look down on it, especially in the music industry. The last thing I need is a big music magazine seeing that on my CV and not taking me seriously.'

'They'd see you write passionately about an event that's popular all over the world,' Millie counters, unable to mask the hint of frustration in her tone. She hates the idea of James feeling embarrassed by Eurovision.

'I'm not so sure. I like the idea of a bit of mystery behind the blog's creator,' he justifies to Millie, the same reason he's been giving her since he launched it last year. 'Subscribers might think that it's someone genuinely involved with Eurovision or even a former artist who took part in it. They think I'm in the know, behind the scenes or something. If they found out I was some random fan from Brighton they might be disappointed and I could lose them.'

Millie doesn't look convinced. 'I still think they'd love it no matter what. Your articles are so interesting and fun.

You need to expand it into a proper Eurovision-dedicated website. Not just blog posts. If you removed your anonymity, you could start uploading videos of yourself. Don't you think video content would make it even more accessible?'

'Maybe. I guess we'll see how it goes and if it really takes off, I can rethink,' he muses.

'It seems like it's already taken off to me,' she says proudly. 'You have so many comments on your pieces now! Including all those supportive notes from a certain someone …'

James shoots her a warning look. '*Millie*—'

'I'm just saying that the username "NumberOneEuro-Fan" could be a nod to the fact that Zachary told you that he was your number one fan when he suggested you start the blog in the first place,' she says carefully.

'We've talked about this. There's no evidence that "NumberOneEuroFan" is Zachary,' James says matter-of-factly. 'They could be absolutely anyone.'

'Whoever they are, they commented on the very first post you ever wrote, saying how happy they were that you "decided to launch the blog".' Millie raises her eyebrows. 'That sounds like they know you *personally*. And they've commented on almost every post you've written since! A very loyal fan. I've been keeping an eye on them and don't pretend like you haven't, too.'

A sheepish smile creeps across his face. 'Fine, I won't pretend that I don't scroll through all the comments on my blog posts to check if "NumberOneEuroFan" has left a message.' He sighs. 'I'm constantly looking for clues that it might be him. But it's probably not – I'm probably reading too much into things. How would Zachary even know it's my blog?'

'He would know,' Millie says confidently. 'You did launch it right after he suggested you do so, and you have a unique style to your writing. Whenever I'm reading something you've written, I can hear your voice in my head.'

'That's because you know it's me.'

'And so would Zachary, I bet.'

James rolls his eyes. 'OK, stop. I can't keep obsessing over him and you know it. He has a boyfriend now, remember?'

Millie purses her lips. 'You don't know that for sure.'

'There are couple photos of them together all over Zachary's Instagram.' James looks pained, his eyebrows knitted together. '*Nikolas* is a gorgeous Swiss blonde who, it would seem, is very good at skiing and loves to cook. It makes sense that Zachary would be with someone like that. It also helps that they live in the same city.'

Observing his downcast expression, Millie feels the urge to hug him. It seems a great injustice that James and Zachary can't be together because of distance.

'Maybe you could message him,' she suggests gently. 'He'll be somewhere here in Vienna and ... you could still be friends?'

'He doesn't want to hear from me,' James says dismissively. 'Although, it would be nice to stay in contact so that we can one day get tickets to the Grand Final again. As fun as it is spending all this money to fly to these different countries every year to sit in a bar and watch it on a TV screen, it would be a little bit more entertaining to be in the audience.'

'Yes, well, it's difficult and expensive to get tickets, even to the rehearsals,' Millie reminds him. 'Remember, we're here to soak up the atmosphere.'

'Maybe with your flashy new job, you'll be able to snag us some tickets,' James suggests and Millie promptly snorts.

'*Flashy?*' she baulks. 'I'm a nanny to two kids! You know I have a tiny salary.'

'A nanny to two kids of a wealthy family,' he points out. 'They might give you a *very* nice bonus at Christmas.'

Millie smiles into her drink. The parents who hired her, Judith and Michael, may have money, but the majority of her job involves her desperately trying to get two-year-old Isaac to poop in his potty, playing hide-and-seek for the twenty billionth time with four-year-old Elena, and praying that she's found all the little bits of playdough that have toppled onto the floor from the table – a few weeks ago, Judith stepped in some while she was wearing a pair of Jimmy Choos, about to leave for an evening event, and needless to say her anger over the incident was not directed at her children, but rather the person in charge of them. Millie won't be letting that happen again any time soon. Judith is terrifying.

Michael is nice, though. He's so different to his wife – warm, funny, welcoming – and Millie wonders how they ended up together. Opposites attract, she supposes.

Owner of a recruitment firm, Judith works long hours and Michael, an estate agent, can occasionally end up needing to work evenings, which is why they thought it worth hiring someone to help with the kids. Millie drops off and collects the kids from nursery and school, feeds them and keeps them busy until bath and bedtime. She's also on hand to look after them if Judith and Michael have something on after work and she's happy to work weekends if they need and they've given her enough notice. She's been working for them a few months now and the kids adore her. Both parents can see how valuable she is and, although it would be nice if Judith was a little less frosty, Millie really likes the job. She's become quickly attached to Isaac and Elena.

'How was dinner with your mum last week?' James suddenly asks. 'You never told me how it went.'

Millie snorts. 'That's because there's nothing to tell.'

'She knows about your new job, right? I thought Aggie would be pleased that your days of wearing a cupcake hat were behind you,' James says with a teasing smile.

'Oh yes, she was sure to ask if I was still "babysitting",' Millie reveals through gritted teeth. 'When I told her that I was really enjoying being a nanny, she remarked it didn't seem like it had a "decent career trajectory".'

James winces. 'She is wound so tightly. Do you think she ever relaxes and has fun? Or ever goes on a date?'

'HA!' Millie shakes her head. 'And allow anything frivolous to distract her from her *career trajectory*? Don't be so ridiculous, James.'

'She makes me feel so lazy, your mum,' James chuckles, taking a sip of his drink. 'You have to admire her success and work ethic, though. She is unbelievably intimidating. Why do you think she never gives herself a break?'

Millie shrugs, looking down at the table. 'Grandpa says it's for me – that ever since she had me, she felt desperate to secure my future. But I don't believe him. She's just wired that way.'

James tilts his head at her. 'I don't know. Aggie has always said that if you wanted to go to university or take a course in something, she would fund it for you. And your grandpa isn't the type to lie. He always—'

'Hey, you two! How's it going?' Noah interrupts, plonking himself down in the booth and flicking back his hair. He's sweaty and slurring his words. 'Sorry I was so long. I went over to say hi and see what her deal was, but we ended up chatting about our work for ages. We have some mutual friends in the business.'

'Really?' James says, unimpressed. 'That's nice.'

'Yeah, she knows this guy, Dice, an Austrian DJ who I met in Ibiza! Random, right? Dice is awesome. He was there for this set I did and he said to me, "I know you're new to this game, Noah, but you have to see it through."'

'How inspiring,' James says drily. 'Anyway, Ingrid has been a long time. I think I'll go check on her.'

'Is this for me?' Noah asks, gesturing to the full beer bottle.

'Yeah, that's yours,' James confirms before squeezing out of the booth and giving Millie a good-luck look. 'I'll see you in a bit.'

'See you,' Millie says. She turns back to Noah when he's left. 'You all right?'

'I'm great!' he cries, holding up his bottle before shuffling along the seat of the booth to be closer to her. 'I may have done a couple of shots with the DJ while we were chatting.'

'Sounds fun.'

'Get this, she said that if I want to stay in Vienna for a bit, she can get me on the circuit here, speak to some people and get me some slots. I could DJ at this club, like tomorrow or something. Look how busy it is! This is a great crowd. Isn't that nice of her? She thinks I'd go down really well here.'

'Very nice.' Millie glances over at the redhead, who catches Noah's eye and gives him a winning smile. 'So good of her to appreciate how talented you are despite never having heard you DJ.'

Noah raises his eyebrows at her as she innocently takes a sip of her drink.

'There's some of that famous British sarcasm,' he comments with a smile. 'I'm telling you, it was a strictly professional conversation.'

'I'm sure.'

He gazes out at the crowd, bopping his shoulders to the beat.

'How great was Eurovision tonight?' he says, continuing to dance next to her. 'Australia smashed it.'

'They did. You should be very proud.'

'What did *you* think about our act, Guy Sebastian?' he asks loudly, the drink obscuring his ability to control the volume of his voice.

'I told you earlier!'

'I know, but tell me again.'

'Why?' She laughs. 'Have you already forgotten?'

'Your opinion is the one that means most,' he says simply. 'To me, anyway.'

Thrown by the sweetness of the comment, Millie swallows the lump in her throat and tries to ignore how close he is next to her, his arm brushing against hers any time he sways too close.

'I thought it was a really catchy song and a great performance. He has a lovely voice, he deserved to do well. I liked the build-up to the chorus, too. It was one of those uplifting songs that you can't help but dance to, you know? It was a lot of fun; it had ... pizzaz.'

Noah bursts out laughing.

'What?' she asks, blushing. 'OK, so "pizzaz" is a stupid word, but you know what I mean.'

'Don't apologise,' he says, waving his hand. 'I LOVE that you use the word "pizzaz". This is why I love talking to you about Eurovision. It's like something inside of you ... lights up. As though it's in your bones.'

'It *is* in my bones,' she insists. 'My grandparents met because of it, remember?'

'Oh right, yeah, the great love affair that began with ABBA,' he recalls, nodding. 'It's a good story.'

'And they love to tell it,' Millie informs him. 'My grandma does, anyway.'

'What's she like, your grandma? Do you take after her?'

'I wish!' she cries, shaking her head. 'She's fun and loud and eccentric. She doesn't care what anybody thinks of her and everybody loves her. I'm more like my grandpa – not that he's not wonderful, too. He's the best. But he's more … reserved.'

'I like that about you,' Noah blurts out. 'You see everything.'

Millie stares at him, not sure what to say.

'I'd like to meet your grandparents,' he continues, oblivious to her reaction. 'They sound great.'

'They are. I'm lucky to have them. They've always supported me. Even though sometimes I feel a bit lost. They won't give up on me, or make me feel bad about my choices like my mum does.'

Noah stops bobbing about, his brow furrowed as he lets her words sink in.

'You sometimes feel lost?' he questions.

'Of course! I think everyone does.'

'But, you're so …' he squints at her, searching for the right word.

'*Yes?*' she prompts.

'I don't know,' he shrugs. 'To me, you don't seem lost, that's all. And especially this year when you're' – he gestures at her – 'taller.'

She throws her head back as she laughs. '*Taller?* Noah, how many shots did you do?'

'There's something about you that's made you taller,' he insists, jabbing his finger in her direction. 'Maybe you hunched lots before.'

She nods, smiling to herself. 'Maybe.'

He may be drunk, but Millie wonders if he's onto something. Her job has given her a new sense of purpose. She's proud of what she does and she's excited about what's to come. She's even started thinking about moving out of her grandparents' house and finding somewhere where she has her own space.

Noah's right. Lately, she *feels* taller.

'What are you thinking?' Noah asks.

'Nothing,' she says, smiling up at him. 'I'm just pleased to be here.'

'Me too. Do you think we'll always do this? Meet up every Eurovision?'

She shrugs. 'I hope so. We did make a pact.'

'We have to stick to it,' he says, shifting near to her and closing the gap between them. 'As long as you keep coming to Eurovision, then I'll keep coming. That's a promise. I mean it.'

'All right,' she grins. 'I take promises seriously, Noah. Make sure you don't break it.'

'I would never.' He stares at her. 'Millie?'

'Yes?' she says, feeling weak under his intense gaze.

'Sometimes … sometimes I wonder if you and I were destined to meet,' he says. 'Maybe we were meant to be.'

Her heart thudding against her chest, she notices his eyes flicker to her lips. He reaches out and brushes her hair away from her face with his fingertips, leaving his hand lingering at her cheek. She swallows as he leans in towards her, his eyes closing.

She puts a palm on his chest, stopping him.

Her heart aches as he recoils, bewildered by her reaction. *She wants him so badly.*

'Not like this,' she whispers.

She's not sure if she hears her. He tilts his head, his eyebrows furrowed, his eyes bloodshot from the alcohol. She feels sick, wondering if she's being an idiot, terrified she's ruined it forever.

She knows that in this moment, he's not himself and not thinking straight. He's so drunk that she could be anybody and she won't let herself be just anybody to Noah. She doesn't want to be another fling, someone he can brush aside and forget about. She knows she deserves more than that. But that doesn't make it any easier to stop him. She's dreamt of kissing Noah ever since they met. Maybe she should have just gone with it, even if he is drunk. Maybe it wouldn't mess things up between them. Maybe it would be the start of something.

The music changes.

His face lights up.

'Oh my god, I love this song! Come on!' he cries, grabbing his beer, scrambling out of the booth and bounding onto the dance floor before Millie can say anything.

She helplessly watches as he barges through the crowd on his own until he reaches a spot in front of the DJ, where he throws his hands up in the air and applauds her. The DJ sees him and gives him a wink. He begins to dance with whoever is around him.

So quickly abandoned, Millie can at least rest assured that she did the right thing by stopping him from kissing her tonight. She takes a sip of her drink and slides out of the booth, ready to go back to her room. She doesn't know where James and Ingrid have got to, but she's not willing to sit and wait on her own any longer.

With a sinking heart, she knows that Noah won't notice her leaving.

CHAPTER EIGHT

Sunday 24 May 2015

Noah wakes up with a raging headache.

With a muffled groan into his pillow, he opens his eyes and reaches down for his backpack that's strewn on the floor with the rest of his things, hauling it over towards the bed and unzipping the front pocket where he knows there's a packet of paracetamol. But after triumphantly grabbing it, he lifts it towards him only to find the box empty.

He buries his face back in the pillow, scrunching up his eyes. He needs to sleep this hangover off, but there's no chance he'll be able to get back to sleep with his head thumping so badly. He remembers there's a pharmacy just across the way from his hotel; he can nip out, buy some painkillers and return to the sanctuary of his bed in just a few minutes. He's meant to go for brunch with the Eurovision group, but he'll probably skip that. They've had their annual catch-up and, as lovely as a farewell brunch would be, sleep has to come first. Plus, he doesn't have to check out today because last night he extended his stay here for a week. He can stay in bed all day. Perfect.

He just has to build up the willpower to crawl out from under the duvet to get that much-needed paracetamol.

Realising that he actually has no idea what the time is, he raises his head to look around for his phone, but can't see it anywhere. It's not on charge and it's not on the bedside table. His trousers are crumpled in a heap on the floor, so he musters the energy to swipe them up and is relieved to find his phone and wallet still in the pockets. There has been more than one occasion recently when he's lost one or both of those items. His phone tells him it's early – not even 8am – and he also has a message waiting for him from an unknown number. He smiles as he reads it – it's from that hot DJ he met last night. He remembers now that she said she'd message him.

She was gorgeous AND talented. They got on really well, chatting away about their work and, though his memories of last night are hazy at best, he thinks she said something about him DJing at that club? Yes, that's it, because he remembers telling Millie and she thought it was funny because the DJ hadn't heard him play but offered him the job anyway …

Oh god. *Millie.*

Noah lifts his hands to cover his face and lets out another groan. An unwelcome memory from yesterday flits across his mind and he wishes he could delete it immediately.

He hit on her.

They were sitting alone in that booth at the back of the dance floor and he can't remember what she said, but it was something nice and he had this overwhelming urge to kiss her, which is so STUPID. Why did he do that? Thankfully she stopped him. He's not embarrassed about the rejection. But he's mortified that he tried anything with her, because it's not fair.

He sees the way she looks at him.

Noah may act like an idiot a lot of the time, but he isn't one. He can tell that Millie is into him. She's always had a crush on him, he knows that. And it's not as if he wouldn't jump at a night with her – there's been chemistry between them ever since they first met. But he knows that wouldn't be enough for her, and he can't risk putting their friendship in jeopardy and ruining the dynamics of the Eurovision group. As strange as it is to admit, this tradition they have of following the song contest wherever it leads them next has become one of the few constants in Noah's life. He'd hate to throw that away.

Last night was a close one. It could have been a disaster. Thank god Millie had enough common sense to think through the consequences, and didn't let him cross the line. *Argh*. He rubs his eyes. He can't remember what he said to her, but he hopes it wasn't anything that might lead her on. He'll definitely have to skip the brunch later today. It's much easier to pretend nothing happened than face her.

Recalling the awkwardness of the incident has made his headache a hundred times worse, so he pushes himself up and swings his legs out of bed, pulling on the outfit he was wearing last night, purely because it's the closest thing in reach. His shirt stinks of booze and sweat, and he grimaces as he buttons it up, shoving on his shoes and remembering the room key before he stumbles out the door to head to the lift. At least he doesn't have to worry about bumping into any of the others in the corridors of his hotel. They did tell him where they're staying, but he wasn't really listening so he can't remember. The most important thing is they're not staying *here*, in this grand hotel right in the centre of town.

He lied to them about where he'd booked. As well as he's doing with his DJing, they'd still find it hard to believe that he could afford such luxury accommodation, so it was easier to skirt around the truth and give them a vague description of where he was staying without providing an actual name of a hotel.

Noah has got very good at lying. He's been lying to his family all year – they're under the impression that he's working for a multinational company in Amsterdam. If his dad found out that he was DJing, he'd cut him off instantly, and while Noah has been earning something through his newfound career, he couldn't maintain his current lifestyle without his credit cards. So, the corporate job is a lie that suits all of them very nicely.

He got into DJing in Dublin last July – one evening, having infiltrated a group of lads out on a stag night, Noah found himself lost in an alcohol-influenced deep conversation with a guy called Aiden about how he had no idea what he was going to do with his life.

'I've been there. But I was lucky to have someone who got me into mixing. There's nothing like the feeling of being up there behind the decks, putting on the right song and watching the crowd go wild in response, throwing their arms up in the air,' Aiden admitted, taking a drag on a cigarette. 'You can't beat it.'

'Yeah? Maybe I should try it,' Noah said, half-jokingly.

'Tell you what, come with me tonight when I play later and see what you think. If you want, I can teach you how to do it, show you the software, whatever.'

Noah looked at him in surprise as he exhaled a plume of smoke.

'You'd do that?' he asked.

Aiden shrugged. 'Sure. I think you'd like it.' He turned to give Noah a grin. 'There are some great parties.'

Witnessing Aiden behind the decks that night, Noah had an epiphany. On arrival at the club in the centre of Dublin, they'd been treated like VIPs. They were given a bottle of Champagne and told to shout when they wanted another. Noah stood by the side of the stage as Aiden played, watching everyone packed onto the dance floor moving to the music, having the time of their lives, cheering adoringly for Aiden when the next song came on. No one in there was thinking about their worries or troubles. They were living in the moment; a moment of great music and pure ecstasy. Noah wanted to be a part of it; he wanted to create those moments.

He took Aiden up on his offer, learnt the ropes and was quickly introduced to others in the industry, which is how he ended up meeting a couple of London DJs who had flown over to Ireland for special appearances. Hitting it off with them, he joined them as they headed for Ibiza. It stemmed from there and now Noah was having the most incredible time, playing in different cities all over Europe thanks to his new network of contacts.

Noah pushes through the revolving door of his hotel out into the fresh air and nods good morning to the doorman before shoving his hands in his pockets and setting off in the direction of the pharmacy. He crosses the road and then takes a right, remembering that it was on the road across from the big car park there.

Strolling past the rows of parked cars, he does a double-take when he sees someone lying across their back seat fast asleep. At first he thinks it's quite funny – maybe they had a big night celebrating Eurovision and ended up sleeping in their car, unable to find their hotel in a drunken stupor. But when he looks closer, he sees that they're tucked into a sleeping bag. He comes to a sudden stop when he's near enough to make out the face of the person: Ingrid.

What is she doing?

She's meant to be staying in some swanky hotel a few minutes away, put up by her record label. He's sure that's what she told everyone. Or he, at least, *assumed* that's what was happening. When he said it out loud, she didn't disagree.

Stepping closer to the car, he bends down to peer through the window. There are duffel bags piled up in the front passenger seat. A washbag is perched on top of them. He can make out that underneath the sleeping bag Ingrid is wearing a cosy jumper and has a beanie shoved on her head – not the outfit she was wearing last night. It doesn't look as though she ended up crashing here because she couldn't make her way back to the hotel.

It kind of looks … it looks as though she'd *planned* on sleeping in her car. Why else would she have a sleeping bag handy?

Baffled, Noah straightens. He rubs his temples with his forefingers, trying to remember if she said anything yesterday about her hotel booking being cancelled at the last minute or something along those lines that might explain why she'd end up staying in a sleeping bag in her car. But nothing is ringing a bell and, anyway, if she'd been at a loose end because her hotel had cancelled, wouldn't she just book somewhere else or ask to stay with them? None of this makes sense.

Now that he thinks about it, Ingrid was acting strangely yesterday – she was much quieter than usual. Usually she arrives for the Eurovision weekend bouncing off the walls and full of ideas for what they can do, but she showed up looking tired and downcast.

He can't remember if he asked her if something was up – he doesn't think he did.

Noah isn't sure what to do next. He doesn't want to wake her. She might be … embarrassed about him finding her like this. He quickly walks away, heading for the pharmacy as he'd originally planned. It's none of his business where Ingrid sleeps, right?

But something feels wrong. He can't forget about it or pretend.

There is one person he trusts to know what to do.

Exiting the pharmacy, he throws two paracetamols into his mouth and swallows them down with some glugs of water. Screwing the lid back on the bottle, he gets his phone out, scrolls for her number and presses the call button.

Millie answers on the third ring.

* * *

'You were right about me being a dreamer,' Ingrid says, clutching the warm mug of coffee in her hands, her eyes fixed on the table. 'But dreams don't work out.'

Across the table, Noah and James share a look. Millie, sitting next to her, reaches out and places a comforting hand on Ingrid's shoulder. Her eyes glistening with tears, Ingrid smiles gratefully, but looks down at the table, embarrassed.

After Noah had spoken to Millie, she'd suggested that they meet for brunch as planned and gently approach the subject with Ingrid, making sure that they were only bringing it up to make sure she was OK, not to be nosy or judgemental.

Ingrid was shocked that Noah had seen her sleeping in her car and floundered with her answer at first, attempting to come up with a story that would explain it, but it was obvious she was lying and eventually she cracked. Looking deflated and exhausted, she started crying and told them the truth: not one record company had been interested in signing her.

'None of them even asked to meet me after listening to my songs,' she says, her voice shaking as tears flow down her cheeks. 'I put everything into that EP. I dropped out of music college; I lost the waitressing job I had because I kept missing shifts whenever Emil needed me to work on the music. It was all for nothing.'

'Surely that can't be the end,' Millie says in a soothing tone. 'Maybe there is someone else you can send the record to?'

Ingrid shakes her head. 'Emil said he'd sent it to everyone he knew in the industry. He promised me it would be snapped up by a label; he was so confident. But it kept getting rejected until there was no one else left. Then he stopped returning my calls.'

James frowns in confusion. 'Who, Emil? Do you mean, in a personal or professional capacity?'

'Both,' she states, fiddling with a napkin. 'No calls, no replies to my messages or emails. I contacted him every day. When he wouldn't get back to me on his mobile, I tried his office. His receptionist kept telling me he was in a meeting and he'd call me back, which was obviously bullshit. I'd run through my savings and I couldn't pay the rent – I needed somewhere to stay and was hoping, since we were meant to be ... you know ... *together*, that I could stay with him. But he wouldn't fucking talk to me.'

She pauses to blow her nose. Millie feels sick just listening to her story. She can't imagine what Ingrid has been through.

'I stayed on my friend's sofa for a bit, but I didn't want to outstay my welcome, so I made up a story about how I'd found a place of my own, but instead I started sleeping in my car,' Ingrid continues in a softer, defeated tone. 'One day, when I still hadn't heard from him, I ended up driving to Emil's home and waiting outside. So desperate and humiliating. But I had to know what was going on. He owed me an explanation.'

'Did you speak to him?' James asks gently.

She nods, dabbing at her eyes with the fresh napkin that Millie passes her. 'I confronted him and he told me it was over. All of it. Our relationship and his representation. He told me that no record company was interested in me, he'd done all he could, and unfortunately, I was no longer the right fit for his talent agency.'

'*What?*' Noah looks appalled. 'Can he do that? Just … cut you out like that? As your agent, isn't he meant to find you work, even when things get tough?'

'Emil does what he wants,' Ingrid states plainly. 'He was so formal and cold. It was like I didn't know him at all. You should have seen his face when I pointed out that I was supposed to be his girlfriend. He looked' – she wrinkles her nose – 'disgusted. He said that our personal relationship had never been serious and he'd never made out that it was.' She pauses, holding up her finger. 'He *did* say, however, that if I ever wrote any new music in the future, I'd be welcome to send it to the agency for their consideration.'

'Oh my god.' Millie shakes her head. 'What an *arsehole*.'

'He's a businessman,' Ingrid shrugs.

'He used you,' James says angrily. 'He treated you so badly and you were supposed to be his client, someone he looks after and guides through a very pressured and difficult

116

industry. No matter which way you look at it, Millie is bang on: he's an arsehole.'

'I shouldn't have taken all those risks,' Ingrid surmises. 'I should have been more sensible. My dream is over before it even began. I gave up everything for nothing.'

Millie shakes her head. 'Your dream isn't over.'

'I've been doing some busking to get a bit of money,' Ingrid reveals, chewing her thumbnail. 'I thought it would be helpful, because at least I'd be doing some singing every day, but it's made everything worse. Every day, I pick a spot and stand there singing. People walk on by. They don't notice me. I'm invisible. The record labels were right: I don't have what it takes. I so easily fade into the background.'

'That's not true,' Millie says firmly, James and Noah looking equally horrified by Ingrid's statement. 'You are brilliant and you will make it. You've had a little setback, that's all. But you'll come back from this.'

Ingrid shakes her head, fiddling with her tissue. 'It doesn't feel like it. It feels like all hope is lost. I was so close to having everything I always wanted. Emil promised me my dreams and I was stupid enough to believe that they might come true. My college tutors were right – I took such a big risk with no safety net.'

'You know, I admire you for that,' Noah says suddenly with a determined look in his eye. 'Taking that risk.'

Ingrid looks up at him in surprise. 'What do you mean?'

'I mean, you took a risk to get what you want and you weren't taking no for an answer,' he begins. 'You weren't willing to accept an alternative. You knew what you loved, you knew what you wanted, and you were going to achieve that no matter what. No compromises. OK, that was a big risk, but it doesn't mean that it wasn't an admirable one.

Take it from someone who has never taken a risk or had the courage to go after what they really wanted in the face of a bunch of challenges. If you ask me, what you did was really brave. I'm proud of you.'

As Noah comes to his conclusion, the three of them stare at him in awe. He said it with such sincerity and feeling, Millie realises they were just treated to a glimpse of the true Noah, the one with worries, insecurities and vulnerabilities like everyone else. They so rarely get to see that side of him.

'Thanks Noah,' Ingrid says, offering him a smile through her tears. 'That means a lot.'

James nudges Noah's arm. 'You're right.' He turns to look back at Ingrid. 'You have nothing to be ashamed or regretful about. It didn't work out this time, but next time it might. You can't give up. You're only twenty-three! Just because one dickhead took advantage of you and screwed things up doesn't mean you should throw away your potential and your talent.'

'Why do you think you love Eurovision so much? Because it's full of dreamers!' Millie adds, beaming at her. 'Every dreamer gets knocked back once in a while, but you get up again. And we're here to help you.'

'Oh my god, Conchita Wurst!' James gasps.

'WHERE?' Millie cries, looking round the café wildly.

'No, no, I'm not saying she's here,' he explains hurriedly, as Millie's shoulders slump in disappointment and Noah chuckles at her overreaction. 'But think of her Eurovision song, "Rise Like a Phoenix". You are the phoenix, Ingrid. You're going to rise out of these ashes and you're going to fly!' James places a hand on his heart. 'That song has so many levels.'

'What if I can't fly? What if signing with Emil's agency was my chance and now it's over?' Ingrid says, wincing at the idea. 'If I can't be a singer, I don't know what I'll do. I've never considered doing anything else.'

'You don't only get one chance,' Millie assures her. 'Like James says, you have to channel Conchita and believe in yourself again. You need time to rebuild your confidence, that's all. Deep in your heart, do you truly believe that your Eurovision dream is over?'

Ingrid sighs heavily. She looks to James to Noah and back to Millie. All of them are staring back at her, wide-eyed and hopeful.

'I suppose I don't *entirely* believe that the dream is over,' she admits.

'Exactly,' Millie says, while Noah claps his hands together. 'We're not giving up on you and, most importantly, *you're* not giving up on you.'

'You're a magnificent phoenix,' James whispers.

Ingrid smiles at him. 'I'm not sure how being a phoenix is going to help me pay the bills back in Berlin, though. The restaurant I was waitressing at while I was recording won't take me back and I haven't managed to get a job anywhere else. I'll have to get in touch with my parents and see if they'll take me in.' She groans. 'Time to swallow my pride and face them – they always said that it would be impossible to make it as a singer. I was so desperate to prove them wrong.'

'Hang on. I have a couple of friends based in Berlin and one of them owns a bar,' Noah says, his face lighting up. 'I can call her! I met her in Munich when I was DJing there. I'm sure she can get you a job at her place. If not, then she'll probably know someone else who can help. Let me call around and ask if one of my mates there can put you up or if they know anyone with a spare room for you to rent or whatever – I can cover paying for it until you're back on your feet.'

'No, Noah,' Ingrid gasps. 'I can't accept that!'

'Sure, you can,' he shrugs, focused on his phone screen as he scrolls through. 'Here she is – Lisa. She's the one who owns the bar. I'll just be a second.'

He pushes his chair back and gets to his feet, wandering out the café to make the call. James turns to the other two and exhales, raising his eyebrows.

'His DJing must be going *really* well,' he comments.

'I can't let him do this,' Ingrid says with a frown.

'Why not?' Millie grabs her hand. 'He's helping out a friend. If he knows someone who can get you a job, take it! And if he's able to put you up so that you're not sleeping in your car, then you can't turn that down. Like he said, it's until you're back on your feet.'

'This is so embarrassing,' she sighs, rubbing her forehead.

'No, it's not,' James assures her. 'Let him help you. If you want embarrassing, then I have an entire album on my phone dedicated to photos of Millie wearing a giant cupcake hat.'

Millie scowls at him. 'You WHAT?'

'They're there for whenever I need cheering up.'

'You told me I looked good in that hat,' she mutters, narrowing her eyes at him. 'And you never mentioned that you were taking any photos, let alone enough to fill an ALBUM.'

'This isn't about you, Millie,' James says loftily, taking a sip of his coffee.

Noah saunters back into the café and gives Ingrid a thumbs-up. 'She has a spot for you on the bar staff if you want it.'

'Wow. *Thank you*, Noah,' Ingrid says, clasping a hand over her mouth. 'I honestly don't know how I'll ever thank you enough for this.'

'It's no problem,' he says, leaning down to give her a hug. 'Plus, she told me to come to Berlin myself, which I've been meaning to do for a while, so I guess I'll see you there in a couple of weeks! I've heard it's got the best DJ scene in Europe.'

'You don't want to come back with me now?' Ingrid offers, as he pulls away. 'I can give you a lift.' She hesitates, adding quietly. 'You've seen the state of my car, though, so it might not be very comfortable.'

'I'm going to stick around here in Vienna for a bit,' he says with a grin. 'That DJ from last night has been in touch. I'm actually going to go meet her now.'

'Cool! Exciting!' Millie says, a little too enthusiastically. 'We should go, too. We need to get to the airport.'

Noah, Millie and James split the bill and then the four of them head outside to say their goodbyes. Ingrid thanks them from the bottom of her heart for their support and understanding, but mostly for not letting her give up on herself yet.

'That Eurovision stage is within your reach,' James says, resting his hands on her shoulders. 'I *know* that you'll end up there somehow.'

When Noah and Millie go to hug each other, it's brief and awkward, neither of them quite comfortable with holding the other one tightly after last night. Both wonder whether they should say something, but in the end, neither of them say anything.

'You OK?' James checks, nudging her while they wait with their bags for a taxi.

'Yeah,' she says, smiling up at him. 'Of course.'

He looks unconvinced, glancing at Noah as he walks away and then back at her. 'If you're sure.'

She rolls her eyes. 'I'm fine, James.'

Her phone starts ringing and she's glad for the distraction, but confused when she sees the name flashing up on her screen: Aggie. Her mum rarely calls her and she knows she's flying back from Vienna today. Millie doesn't want to speak to her, but she's too curious not to pick up. Her mum would only bother calling her for a specific reason.

'Hello?' she answers.

'Millie, hi,' her mum says, and her voice is edged with panic.

'What's wrong?' Millie asks urgently.

'It's Grandpa ... he ... it's not good,' Aggie responds, her breath shaking. 'How soon can you get home?'

CHAPTER NINE

Brighton, UK

2016

Thursday 12 May

'Elena, did you hear me?' Millie asks, putting her hands on her hips. 'I said it's time to put the iPad down and head upstairs to brush your teeth.'

Yet again, Elena stubbornly ignores her, not even bothering to acknowledge Millie's instructions, while Isaac sits on the sofa running his fire engine back and forth over the cushion, lost in his own world. Millie frowns. Elena is normally so sweet and well-behaved, but the last couple of days she's been in a foul mood, acting up, breaking rules and refusing to listen to anything Millie says. It's surely just a phase, but Millie feels like a lot of Elena's anger at the moment is directed at her personally. Millie puts that down to her simply being the one who's around Elena most of the time, but still. She can't shake the feeling that something is off between her and the little girl.

'All right, you've had your warning,' Millie says, marching over to her. 'You have three seconds to put the iPad down. Three – two – one.'

When Elena doesn't move, Millie reaches down and grabs the iPad, attempting to tear it from Elena's fingers. Elena yells, 'NO!' and when Millie pries it from her grip and puts it high on the bookshelf where it can't be reached, Elena starts howling on cue.

'Why are you crying?' Millie asks, bewildered at her reaction. 'You know it's bedtime. Come on, upstairs to brush your teeth.'

Isaac dutifully slides off the sofa and waddles to the stairs, while Elena dramatically face-plants the sofa and wails into the cushions.

'Elena. Elena! What is *wrong*?'

'I want Daddy!' she shrieks at Millie, her face scrunched up and red.

'He's on his way home. By the time you brush your teeth, maybe he'll be here. Come on.'

Millie bends down to pick up Elena from under the shoulders, but Elena swats her hands away, refusing to move.

The sound of the front door opening at that moment could not have been more welcome and as soon as Elena hears her dad stepping into the hallway, her expression brightens and she shuffles off the sofa, running out of the sitting room.

'Daddy!' she cries, rushing into his legs and wrapping her arms around them, while Isaac totters along behind her.

Michael laughs at such an enthusiastic greeting, lifting and kissing each of his kids, getting accidentally knocked in the head by Isaac's fire truck in the process. He asks them about their day and Elena tells him how she drew him a picture at school and runs to get it from her bag in the kitchen.

'We were just about to go brush our teeth and get ready for bed,' Millie informs him, appearing in the doorway of the sitting room having straightened all the cushions on the sofa and made sure the room was as tidy as it was left this morning.

'I was hoping I'd be back for story time,' Michael grins, before beaming at Elena as she comes rushing back to him with her drawing. She holds it up for him and he studies it.

'I haven't even been allowed to see it,' Millie says, folding her arms and leaning on the doorframe. 'So I hope you feel honoured.'

Michael hesitates. 'Wow! This is … great! Is this me?'

Elena nods vigorously. 'It's you, me, Isaac and Mummy.'

'Very good,' Michael says nodding. 'Thank you. Now, shall we go upstairs and get ready for bed so we can have story time? Let's go!'

'I get to pick the story!' Elena cries happily, heading to the stairs with Isaac in tow.

'I'll be down in a bit,' Michael tells Millie, following his children.

Before climbing the steps, he balances the drawing on the end of the banister and then pretends to be a monster chasing them up, prompting a chorus of excitable squeals.

Millie waits until they've reached the landing before she leans over to look at the picture of the four members of Elena's family, standing on the grass outside a house with the sun shining down on them. Knowing it will only fall to the floor if she leaves it resting on the banister, Millie takes it into the kitchen with her, leaving it on the island.

Taking the opportunity of having a bit of free time, she tidies up the remnants of the kids' tea and loads the dishwasher. When lights are turned off upstairs and everything seems calm, she hears Michael's footsteps coming down the stairs and makes herself busy by wiping down the surfaces.

'All OK?' she asks, washing her hands in the sink and drying them on the nearest tea towel hanging on the AGA.

'All fine,' he confirms, heading straight to the fridge and getting out a bottle of open white wine. 'Isaac went out like a light and Elena will crash soon. She seems exhausted.'

'She's had a busy day.'

'Mmm,' he says, getting out a glass before reaching for another. 'You want one? You're officially off duty.'

She smiles. 'All right. Thanks.'

Pleased at her answer, he places the two glasses next to each other on the side and begins pouring.

'Work was awful today,' he informs her, sliding her glass onto the kitchen island. 'A string of house showings and no one bit. I'm not going to reach my monthly target at this rate.'

'I'm sure you will.'

He takes a sip of wine and his shoulders relax instantly. 'What about you? Were the two horrors OK today?'

'They were great.' She pauses, deep in thought, wondering whether to voice her concerns or if it would be premature.

Michael notices her hesitation. 'What happened?'

'Nothing,' she assures him. 'Nothing in particular. It's just … Elena's acting funny around me.'

He frowns. 'In what way?'

'I don't know, I may be reading into things, but she seems to be … angry. The last few days, she's been shutting me out, not wanting to play or do anything I say.'

'She's probably being a diva to get your full attention,' Michael says, rolling his eyes. 'Gets that from her mother. I wouldn't worry about it. It will pass and you'll be back to being best friends in no time.'

Millie nods. 'I hope so.'

Elena and Isaac mean so much to Millie. She knows that it's natural for children to go through difficult phases, but

Elena's behaviour towards her still hurts. She loves that little girl so much.

'Anyway, I should probably head home,' Millie notes, glancing at her watch.

Michael puts his glass of wine down and comes towards her. Sliding an arm round her waist, he pulls her close to him and dips his head, kissing her gently on her ear. She closes her eyes, her breath shuddering as his lips make their way down her neck.

'Are you sure you have to leave so soon?' he whispers.

A smile creeps across her face.

'I suppose I could stay a little longer,' she says softly.

Grinning, he leaves a trail of kisses up her throat before finding her lips, and she kisses him back, melting into him as her arms reach up to wrap around his neck.

Millie never set out to fall in love with him. It happened gradually and her growing feelings for him took her by surprise. She'd always thought he was kind and funny – not to mention handsome – but it wasn't until after he separated from Judith a few months ago that Millie realised there might be something between them. She started noticing that he'd make excuses to be near to her, suggesting flimsy reasons for her to stay later in the evenings than needed, asking her to join him for a drink before she went home, his eyes lingering on her a little too long during their conversations.

They slept together for the first time one Saturday evening, after he'd asked her if she'd help out with the kids for the weekend. Judith had moved out and he wanted to keep them distracted from his marital problems with a fun day out at an adventure farm park. Judith and Michael had agreed it made sense for Isaac and Elena to stay in the family house with their dad until they'd worked out a long-term plan, due to Judith's longer work hours. Michael thought Millie being at the farm to help would be a good idea for both him and the kids, and they ended up having a wonderful day all together. Judith picked them up at four from the house after having to be at the office that day, and when she'd left, Michael thought he and Millie had earned a drink – he added that he wouldn't mind the company.

When they'd started kissing on the sofa a few drinks in, it just seemed *natural*. The sex was incredible and got better as they became more relaxed and familiar with each other. She loved that he was quite a bit older than her – he didn't play games or try to impress. He made her feel sexy, despite her daily wardrobe consisting of t-shirts and loose high-waisted jeans, practical clothes that she wouldn't mind getting dirty when playing with the kids. He mentioned that she'd suit a shorter haircut, and he was right – she had it cut and loved the way it framed her face. 'I think I should cancel my trip to Sweden,' she says to him now, as he entwines his fingers through hers and picks up his wine with his other hand before leading her through to the sitting room.

'Why would you do that? I thought you were into the Euro-vision thing,' he says, pulling her down on the sofa with him.

'Yeah, but I could stay here instead,' she offers with a leading smile.

'You know I'd love that,' he grins, before letting out a dramatic sigh. 'But it would be pointless, since I have that party on Saturday and I'm taking the kids. Ugh.' Closing his eyes, he pinches the top of his nose with his forefinger and thumb. 'I *really* don't want to have to spend time with Judith this weekend.'

Millie blinks at him. 'Judith is going to be there?'

'Of course,' he says, opening his eyes and dropping his hand to his lap. 'It's her parents' anniversary. It would be a bit weird if I went without her.'

'It's … it's their anniversary party? I didn't know what the party was for. I didn't realise it was *her* family.'

Michael nods, taking a large gulp of wine. 'Total nightmare. We have to put on a show for them all. Pretend that everything is fine. Such a bore.'

'They think you're still together,' Millie says slowly, letting this information sink in.

She feels absurdly and unreasonably jealous. She knows it makes sense to keep things between them a secret from the outside world, but it's unsettling to think of him and Judith behaving like a couple.

'They're very traditional and she doesn't want to upset them,' he says, rolling his eyes. 'It's not important, it's all very—'

'But she'll have to tell them eventually, right? Why is she putting it off? Won't it just be more of a shock when you start divorce proceedings?'

'I'm not going to pretend to understand what's going on in Judith's head, so I'm going along with what she wants for now because it's easier,' he insists, before leaning forwards and sliding his hands up Millie's thighs. 'You know, I can think of a lot more interesting things to do than talk about this.'

That's all it takes. As he presses against her and kisses her, she closes her eyes and the rest of the world fades away. She feels safe and comforted. Everything is OK.

All that matters is him.

* * *

'Millie, is that you?'

She jumps at Julie's voice coming from the sitting room as she quietly steps through the front door later that night.

'Grandma, what are you doing up?' she asks, putting her bag down in the hallway and going through to find her sitting on the sofa.

'You're back late,' Julie remarks.

'Michael got stuck at work, so I offered to babysit last minute.'

'You do so much for him. He's always keeping you late these days. I hope he's paying you overtime.'

Millie's eyes flicker to the framed photograph resting in Julie's hands on her lap. Her heart sinks. It's the photo of her wedding day that is usually up on the mantelpiece. Millie wonders how long Julie has been sitting here on her own staring at the picture.

'You OK, Grandma?' she asks gently, coming to sit next to her.

Julie gives a small nod. They both know she's not.

'I love that photo,' Millie comments, gesturing to it. 'Everyone always sees it and says I look like you. Such a compliment.'

'You're sweet,' Julie says, gripping the frame tightly.

'Do you want me to make you a cup of tea before bed?' Millie offers.

'No, thank you.'

Millie watches in silence as Julie slowly pushes herself up off the sofa, before padding over to the mantelpiece in her slippers and carefully returning the photograph to its spot. She can't bear how tired and frail Julie looks at the moment. Even just a few paces across the living room seems to be a chore for her.

'Mum will be arriving tomorrow morning,' Millie says brightly, attempting to distract herself from dwelling on how vulnerable Julie looks. 'She's got lots of fun things planned for this weekend. Nice walks and I think she mentioned she'd booked lunch at that restaurant you love; you know, the one with the pink door?'

Julie sighs, leaning on the mantelpiece for support. 'That's very thoughtful, but I think I'll have a quiet weekend here at home.'

Every weekend is a quiet weekend at home for Julie now.

'Well, see how you feel,' Millie says. 'It will be good to get out and about.'

Millie's forced chirpy tone is grating even to her, but it's the only way she can get through these conversations with Julie – as though sounding positive will somehow magically make them both feel that way. But since Tom died of his heart attack last year, it feels as though any cheer returning to this house is a long way off. Julie doesn't want it, as though finding any joy in life without him would be some kind of betrayal.

Aggie and Millie have done all they can to bring Julie out of the isolation she's retreated into since losing him, but she's fiercely resisted all their attempts. When her grandpa died, Millie felt suffocated with grief, but watching her grandma become a shell of her former self has almost been worse.

'Maybe I won't go to Sweden tomorrow,' Millie ponders out loud, looking down at her lap.

'No, you should go,' Julie replies wearily.

'Grandma, I know this weekend is going to be difficult for you and—'

'I'll be fine.' Julie rubs her forehead, turning away from the photo on the mantelpiece. 'You might as well go and enjoy the …'

She trails off, her face crumpling, before she waves her hand dismissively. Julie can't bring herself to talk about Eurovision. She can barely fathom it's still happening without Tom here with her. Millie should have backed out of the trip, but she'd lose so much money to cancel at this stage.

At least Aggie will be here for the weekend to look after her. The past year, Millie has had to depend on Aggie a lot more than she would have liked – she has to admit, Millie doesn't know what she would have done without her mum when Grandpa died. She wasn't exactly an emotional crutch, but Aggie was the one who sorted all the paperwork and she insisted on staying a few weeks with them in Brighton to sort the funeral and make sure everything was in order with the house. She didn't want Julie or Millie to have to worry about any admin. Julie has been such a mess that Millie and Aggie found themselves forced to find a way of working together to look after her and occasionally, in very low moments, Millie has been surprised to find that it's been Aggie who has helped her through.

There was one incident last year where Julie didn't get out of bed all day and Millie couldn't bear to see her refusing to leave the darkness of her room. Through sobs, she confessed to her mum that she was worried Julie was giving up altogether.

'I can tell you with great certainty that she is going to be OK,' Aggie had told her firmly. 'She's stronger than anyone you know. She was just very much in love with Dad and she's going to have to navigate the world without him now. That will take some getting used to, and no one will rush her through it, but she'll get there. I know it.'

Millie had felt a wave of gratitude for her mum, then. When Aggie said something in that manner, you believed her. She must have used that trick to get to where she was in business, because after weeks of feeling like she was drowning, Millie had suddenly felt reassured.

'Is James coming here tomorrow so you can go to the airport together?' Julie asks, making her way back across the room to the door.

'No.'

'That's a shame,' she comments. 'I haven't seen him in a long time. He hasn't been over to visit for a while.'

Millie doesn't say anything, pressing her lips together.

'Well, I'm off to bed,' Julie announces. 'I'll see you before your flight tomorrow?'

'Of course.'

'Night, Millie.'

'Night, Grandma.'

Once she hears Julie's bedroom door close upstairs, Millie leans forward, resting her elbows on her knees and burying her face in her hands. She doesn't know if Julie's comment about James was a simple observation or pointed remark, but either way it stung.

Millie and James have grown apart – or rather, Millie has purposely grown away from him. It's been essential that she keep her relationship with Michael a secret. He doesn't want Judith finding out yet, because it's complicated with her as it is, and the children can't know as that would be too confusing for them.

And even though Millie knows she's not doing anything wrong because they didn't start seeing each other until after Michael and Judith separated, she doesn't want James knowing. He was so upset about his dad's affair, she knows that he'd disapprove of her involvement with someone who's technically still married. She doesn't need or want his judgement. Her relationship with Michael has been what's kept her going during a horrible year; she doesn't want anything to taint it.

Such a big secret has created a rift, though. She kept having to cancel on James so she could spend time with Michael and she ran out of good excuses. She felt guilty lying to him, so it was easier to avoid chatting to him. He knows something is going on and he's tried to get it out of her, but she's stayed strong. Protecting what she has with Michael has come at the cost of her friendship with James. Once everything is out in the open, though, it will be OK. One day, James will understand why it had to be like this.

She does *not* want to go on this trip to Sweden. In fact, she's dreading it. She really should have cancelled so she could spend more time with Michael and look after Julie.

She should have cancelled so she wouldn't have to face James.

CHAPTER TEN

Stockholm, Sweden

Saturday 14 May 2016

'Whoa! Sorry!' Noah cackles with laughter after knocking into James while he was dancing a little too vigorously. 'Did I spill your drink?'

'It's fine,' James mutters, looking down at the damp patch on his shirt.

'What's going on with you two?' Noah blurts out, pointing at James and Millie, who immediately tenses. 'You're standing there like statues! This is meant to be a *party*! We're literally at an event called "Party House" or whatever.'

'It's called "Eurovision The Party",' Ingrid corrects, laughing at him.

In Noah's defence, he didn't properly read the messages that Ingrid sent about this thing when she organised their tickets a few months ago. He had no idea it was an official side event to the Eurovision Grand Final, hosted in the Tele2 Arena in Stockholm. There's a huge screen behind the stage showing the contest and backstage interviews with the artists; it's felt like a huge celebration in there all night, but James and Millie are acting like they don't want to be here.

'Right, "Eurovision The Party". That's the one,' Noah nods, bopping from side to side. 'Party is in the *title*. You two' – he gestures to Millie and James – 'are bringing down the vibe. Come on, have fun!'

Neither of them answer. Millie looks down at the floor and James takes a sip of what's left of his drink to avoid his gaze. Noah shrugs and turns away.

He's having way too much fun to let them ruin his night. At least Ingrid is having a good time, dancing along to the music next to him. She's in such a better place this year and he's glad he was able to help get her back on her feet. She worked at his mate's bar for a while and then started working temp jobs for a personal assistant recruitment company – everything she owed Noah for covering her rent the first couple of months has been paid back in instalments and she's now completely out of his debt. She told him earlier that she lives in a shared house on the outskirts of Berlin and she's genuinely enjoying the temp work. She's much happier, he can tell.

He's proud of her.

He has no idea what's going on with James and Millie, though. Maybe they're mad at him for missing out on their sightseeing excursions today, which, to be fair, would be understandable. Noah appreciates that part of the tradition of the four meeting up at Eurovision every year is to see the city to which they've travelled together, largely because they never have tickets to the *actual* Final, so they have to make the trip worth their while. He did originally plan to meet them this morning as they'd arranged, but he ended up losing track of time after a big night with some new friends, and the thought of trekking round the ABBA Museum this morning suddenly didn't seem so tempting.

He probably shouldn't have drunk so much before meeting them tonight at this weird Eurovision party thing, either. That wasn't his fault. He blames that on the influence of the new people he's met out here – he'd been put in touch with them by his friends in Amsterdam. He's been staying in The Netherlands a while now and has got a great group there, a lot of them in the nightlife industry – DJs, club owners and promoters. They're a lot of fun. When he said he was off to Sweden for the weekend, one of them insisted he meet up with someone she knew out here and *voilà*. They'd clicked straight away.

Noah looks over at Millie and, seeing that she still looks miserable, he takes another large swig of his drink. She's distracted. He can't tell what's bothering her. He hopes it's nothing to do with what happened last year.

Hitting on her was a drunken mistake – they both know that. With anyone else, he'd have forgotten about it. He wouldn't have cared.

'This is a great song!' he calls out to Millie above the music.

She gives a nod.

'It's so uplifting and it's got a great beat,' he continues with a lot more enthusiasm than he feels. 'You just have to dance to a song like this, right?'

She replies, but he doesn't catch it.

'Sorry? What did you say?' he says quickly, leaning closer to her.

'I was just agreeing that it's great,' she explains.

'Oh, right, yeah! It's great.'

She returns her attention to the stage. Trying to think of another conversation starter, he continues dancing alone, occasionally stealing glances at her.

Noah has spent a long time honing his ability to simply not care what people think.

But he hates the idea of *her* thinking badly of him.

He's about to ask her who she thinks will win this year, when his phone rings again: Charlotte. That's the fifth phone call from her today. She's always hassling him to speak to her and catch up, but not like this. He decides to answer.

'Hello?' he shouts into the phone, pressing his finger into his other ear so he can hear her above the music.

'Noah, finally!' she replies. 'I've been trying to get through to you all day!'

'Sorry, it's the Eurovision weekend. You know I meet up with those friends every year. We're in Stockholm at the moment!'

'I know,' she says. 'That's why I'm calling. I'm here too.'

'What?'

'I'm in Stockholm. Where are you? I'm going to come find you.'

Noah freezes in shock as the song comes to an end and the audience goes wild.

* * *

'I'm not going to lie, I always thought your Eurovision tradition was kind of weird,' Charlotte confesses, leaning back in her chair. 'But now that I'm here in the midst of the celebrations, I'm starting to see where you're coming from. There's a really positive energy around this contest, isn't there. Everyone seems …'

She searches for the word.

'Happy?' Millie suggests with a smile. 'Excited? Drunk?'

Charlotte laughs. 'I was thinking more along the lines of "hopeful".'

Noah shifts in his seat. They've met Charlotte after 'Eurovision The Party', joining her at an upmarket bar in the centre of town. He'd tried to persuade the other three not to come with him, but they were all keen to meet his sister and since they hadn't spent the day with him, they didn't want to say goodbye yet anyway.

It's strange to see Charlotte after so long apart. She looks the same: glamorous and immaculate as ever in slim-fitted black trousers and a tailored cream blazer, accessorised with gold dangle earrings and bright red lipstick. He thought that he noticed her look a bit shocked at his appearance when he first walked into the bar, but that's understandable – his hair is much longer now and he's wearing a green silk short-sleeved Gucci shirt. Safe to say his style has evolved since they last met.

When the other three introduced themselves to her, it struck Noah that she might scupper his well-guarded secret of the Pearce fortune, but there's been no giveaways so far. James and Ingrid have taken themselves off to the bar and seem to be having a laugh over there, and Millie and Charlotte are getting on well.

Noah has gone a bit quiet, though – seeing Charlotte is making him confront his family troubles, something he never likes to dwell on for long. He feels guilty that he hasn't seen his mum in so long and about the lies he's been spinning …

Oh god.

He's been so worried about Charlotte revealing their background to Millie that he hadn't considered Millie saying something that would blow open the lies he's told Charlotte about his job. He's now more tense than before.

'Yeah, you're right,' Millie says in response to Charlotte's observations about the song contest. 'The first time we met,

I bored Noah with a long speech about why it's so unique. At Eurovision you can be whoever you want to be, no judgement, only good vibes. So, I suppose "hopeful" is a nice way of putting it – it's how the world should be all the time.'

'Particularly apt considering what's happening in the UK at the moment.' Charlotte grimaces. 'What do you think the outcome will be?'

'Remain, of course! There's no way we'll leave the EU,' Millie states firmly. 'There's "remain" posters up in almost every window I pass.'

'That could just be the feeling where you live, though. Britain is a big country,' Charlotte reasons. 'And the Leave campaign seems to be … louder.'

'I guess we'll find out in a few weeks.' Millie sighs. 'Let's not talk about it now, though. It's too depressing. What did you think of Ukraine's winning song today?'

'I missed it,' Charlotte admits. 'They were playing the contest on the TV here, but I was going through emails and not really concentrating.'

'It was so moving. Some very powerful lyrics.'

'A ballad, I assume?'

Millie nods. 'It's called "1944" and was about Stalin's deportation of Crimean Tartars that year. A heavy subject for a song, but somehow it worked.'

'Wow. That can't have been an easy one to write.'

'Yeah, the lyrics really grabbed you. About how everyone dies in the end, and we need to live and love – you know, it was powerful stuff.'

Noah notices Charlotte looking distinctly pained, affected by Millie's words. He watches curiously as she collects herself.

'Wise words,' she comments, taking a sip of her drink.

'It genuinely sent a shiver down my spine. You should watch her performance back if you get the chance; she really put everything into it,' Millie recommends.

'I will,' Charlotte nods. 'I have to admit, I thought Eurovision was all upbeat pop songs.'

'You never know which one is going to hit the mark. And Australia was so close to winning! You know you came second, right?'

'I did see that,' Charlotte says, relaxing a little again. 'I'm impressed!'

'Dami Im – she is incredible. What a voice. And that song, "Sound of Silence"! I can't get the chorus out of my head. Imagine if you had won!' Millie's eyes widen at the thought. 'We'd all be heading to Australia next year. That would have been so cool! Noah, you could have been our tour guide.'

'He would have been a useless one,' Charlotte remarks. 'He hasn't been back in so long, I'm not sure he'd remember anything about his home country.'

There's an awkward silence. Sitting between them with his arms folded across his chest, Noah doesn't say anything, his expression stony, his jaw set.

'So, how come you're in Sweden?' Millie asks Charlotte, clearly deciding it best to change the subject.

'I've been in Europe for a few days for meetings and decided to seize upon the opportunity of surprising my brother, so I thought I'd drop by,' Charlotte explains, lifting her chin. 'I knew he would be here for Eurovision.'

'That's so nice. A great surprise! What do you do that's brought you to Europe?'

'We're thinking of expanding the property business over here,' Charlotte explains.

Noah clears his throat pointedly.

'Wow, you're in property?' Millie looks at her, impressed. 'That's so cool.'

'Yes,' Charlotte says, glancing at Noah in confusion. 'It's the family—'

'It's an amazing career,' Noah says loudly over her. 'Charlotte's always been the high-flyer. Hey, James and Ingrid are really taking their time with that other round. Maybe we should go help them.'

'I think they're fine,' Millie observes, glancing over her shoulder at them. 'They're just having a chat, I think. They'll bring them over in a minute.'

'Great,' Noah says with a fixed smile. It's time to take control of this conversation before everything is pulled apart. 'Charlotte, Millie is a nanny for two children. She's brilliant at it.'

Charlotte notes Millie blushing furiously at Noah's compliment.

'I'm not brilliant,' she contests, nudging Noah's arm. 'But I do love my job. I'm lucky to work with a great family, they're really …' – she hesitates – 'they're, um … well, I love it.'

'That's wonderful, what a lovely job,' Charlotte smiles.

'Not very glamorous, though, unlike Noah's line of work,' Millie says, beaming at him. 'You must be so proud of him. He's doing so well.'

'He doesn't speak about it much,' Charlotte comments.

'Really? That's weird! You don't shut up about your DJing skills around us,' Millie teases him, giggling. 'But he's obviously amazing at it, otherwise he wouldn't be jetting all over the place, playing at huge events all over Europe. I'm yet to make it to one, though. Hoping to get a VIP invite soon, right Noah?'

He forces a laugh, unable to meet Charlotte's eye.

'I wish he'd get back into photography though, as well,' Millie continues boldly. 'He was so good at it.' She turns to him in admiration. 'You have such a talent.'

Noah reaches for his drink and takes a swig.

'Maybe you can persuade him to pick up his camera again,' Millie says brightly to Charlotte. 'He might listen to his sister.'

'Oh, it's doubtful,' she mutters. Glancing from Millie to Noah and back to Millie again, Charlotte clears her throat. 'So, are you in a relationship, Millie?'

'Me?' A shade of pink rises up Millie's neck as she answers. 'Oh … um …'

'Sorry, it was a personal question.'

'No, no, it's fine. It's … actually, I am sort of seeing someone.'

Noah looks up at her, his eyebrows knitted together. 'Really?'

'Yeah, he's great,' she gushes, tucking her hair behind her ears. 'Really great.'

'Is it serious?' Noah asks.

She nods. 'I think so, yeah. We'll have to see I guess.'

'Cool,' Noah responds, surprised by this information. 'I'm happy for you.'

The table falls into silence. Noah's jaw twitches.

After a few moments, Millie hops up from her seat.

'I'm just going to the loo. Back in a minute.'

As Millie leaves, Noah inhales deeply, still refusing to meet Charlotte's eye. She waits a moment before speaking.

'Millie seems nice.'

Noah gives a sharp nod. 'She's great.'

'She clearly has a thing for you.'

He frowns. 'She just said she has a boyfriend.'

'Yeah, but she likes you, Noah, anyone can see that. Or she *did* like you at one point and there's still some feelings there. You've dated her in the past or something?'

'No. I'm not interested.'

Charlotte snorts. 'That's a lie. She may be easier to read, but I'm your sister. I can see the way you look at her, too. Why didn't you go for it when you had the chance?'

'Like I said, I'm not interested,' he repeats. 'I don't want to be tied down.'

Charlotte sighs, noticeably irritated by his response.

'What?' he snaps.

'That's just you all over, isn't it,' she states with a surly expression. 'Running away from anything serious. From anything real.'

'I haven't run away.'

'Could have fooled me.'

They glare at each other.

'You know what, I don't have to put up with this,' Noah grumbles, standing up. 'Enjoy your night.'

'I thought you just said you don't run away,' Charlotte says. 'Proving my point right now, don't you think?'

Noah storms out of the bar, throwing open the door and stepping into the cold, night air. Taking a moment to work out his bearings, he starts walking in the direction of his hotel. He feels too tired and drunk to listen to a lecture from his sister. They can catch up tomorrow. He might have more patience for her then.

'Noah!' Charlotte calls out after him, emerging from the bar. 'Noah, wait!'

'I don't want to talk to you,' he replies, knowing as he says it how petty it sounds.

'You have to,' she insists, rushing to catch up with him.

And something in her tone of voice makes him stop. She doesn't sound annoyed any more, but desperate. He turns to face her.

'I'm sorry for lying about my job, but I couldn't be bothered with yours and Dad's disappointment,' he says, shoving his hands in his pockets. 'I would probably have told you eventually, but I needed—'

'I've known for a while that you've been lying about what you do for a living, Noah,' she admits wearily.

'You … you have?'

'Yes. When you told us about it, I rang the Head Office in Amsterdam of the big corporation you mentioned and they'd never heard of you.'

He looks at her, disgusted. 'You *checked up* on me? What the fuck, Charlotte?'

'I was right, wasn't I? I wasn't doing it to rumble you. I was looking out for you. That's all I've ever done. Look out for you. You're my brother.' She sighs, her eyes falling to the pavement. 'I haven't told Mum and Dad. They are completely under the impression you work there. I don't know why they're so willing to just take your word for it, but lucky for you, they have.'

'You didn't tell them,' he states with some surprise.

'No, I didn't tell them,' she emphasises, insulted at the insinuation. 'And I don't plan on telling them. But I do think that you need to start growing up, Noah.'

He rolls his eyes. 'Here we go.'

'Why are you pissing away your life?' she asks, taking a step towards him. 'You've been *DJing* this whole time? You've never been into music.'

'I am now.'

145

'You like partying.'

He narrows his eyes at her. 'You wouldn't understand.'

'You're running away from your future. You can't avoid real life forever, and you can't keep shutting out your family as though we don't matter.'

'I'm not coming home, Charlotte,' he practically yells.

'You have to!'

Suddenly, she bursts into tears. She covers her face with her hands, sobs spilling out of her as though she's been holding them back for a long time and can't keep them pent up for one moment longer.

Noah stares at her in shock, not sure what to do. She's usually so strong and controlled; he hasn't seen her cry like this before. His anger towards her quickly fades to sympathy, and he moves towards her.

'Charlotte,' he begins gently, but she raises her head from her hands to speak before he can ask her what's wrong.

'Dad is sick, Noah,' she reveals, sniffing. 'Mum needs you. I need you. Please come home. It's time.'

Her face crumples as she starts to cry again, tears streaming freely down her cheeks. Noah steps forward and wraps his arms around her. She presses her forehead into his shoulder and holds him, her hands gripping him tightly.

They stand like that for a while, the muffled sound of the bass from the bar reverberating down the street and a group of Eurovision revellers stumbling past them, gleefully singing at the top of their lungs.

CHAPTER ELEVEN

'Did you see where Noah and Charlotte went?' Millie asks James and Ingrid, approaching them at the bar.

She'd returned to find the table empty and had waited there, assuming they'd be back any second, but she's been sitting on her own for a while now.

'I thought I saw them go outside,' Ingrid mentions, nodding to the door. 'But they should have come back in by now.'

'Maybe they've popped out for some fresh air,' James suggests with a shrug.

'Noah looked angry,' Ingrid notes. 'Both of them did, actually.'

'We should check on them,' Millie determines, heading towards the exit.

When she gets outside, she can't see them anywhere. She looks up and down the road, but there's no sign of them. Getting out her phone, she calls Noah, but it rings out. She hangs up, biting her lip.

'Do you think he went back to his hotel?' Ingrid asks, as she and James emerge from the bar behind Millie. 'He was very drunk.'

'I'd be impressed if he took himself home. He's usually the last one standing out of us four,' James says. 'Maybe Charlotte wanted to go and he insisted on walking her home.'

147

'He would have let us know,' Millie reasons. 'If Ingrid saw him storming out the bar and Charlotte looking upset too, then it doesn't sound good. I'll try calling him again.'

'Or we could just leave it,' James offers, raising his eyebrows at her. 'He's a grown-up. He can do what he wants. If he doesn't want to hang out with us tonight—'

'Of course he wanted to hang out with us,' Millie counters defensively.

'He was trying to shake us off before we came to meet his sister,' James reminds her. 'It was obvious he didn't want us here.'

'He's private when it comes to his family. You know he hasn't been back to Australia in years. We don't know what's gone on between them; maybe he wasn't sure how it would be with Charlotte and he didn't want to involve us in any family drama,' Millie says sharply.

James holds up his hands. 'All right, all right. You don't need to jump down my throat. I'm talking about Noah, not you.'

'I'm not jumping down your throat, I just don't think we should assume he was trying to ditch us. That doesn't seem fair and wouldn't be like him.'

'He literally ditched us all day today,' James says, his expression clouding over.

'Why would he even bother coming to Sweden if he didn't want to see us?'

'Why do you care so much about Noah's intentions?' James cries.

'He's my friend.'

'He's mine too! There is no point to this conversation, I was only making an observation. Seriously, Millie, it's like you're trying to start an argument with me over nothing.'

Millie looks away. Agitated, James shakes his head.

'Maybe you two need to talk,' Ingrid suggests softly, looking from one to the other. 'I don't know if something is going on between—'

'There's nothing we need to talk about,' Millie interrupts bluntly, lifting her phone to her ear as she tries Noah again.

'That does seem to be the case these days,' James mutters under his breath.

Millie turns away from them and huffs irritably as she gets Noah's voicemail. When her phone vibrates in her hand with a call coming through, she lifts it hopefully thinking it's Noah ringing back, but it's from a withheld number. Strange. That's the second call this evening she's received from a withheld number. She's tempted not to answer in case it's a cold call, but then she considers it's late and might be Michael phoning from his in-laws' house. She's too curious not to pick up.

'Hello?'

'Millie. Hi.'

She recognises the woman's voice straight away.

'Judith!' Millie exclaims, her voice a few pitches higher than usual. 'Is everything OK? Are the kids all right?'

'They're fine,' Judith snaps.

She knows.

It's late at night, there's nothing wrong with the children – why else would Judith be calling? Millie's blood runs cold.

'I know everything,' Judith says, confirming Millie's suspicions. 'I know about you and Michael and your *disgusting* affair. Elena told me today.'

'E-Elena?' Millie whispers, horrified.

'She saw Daddy and the nanny kissing this week. You can imagine how confusing that is for a five-year-old. She asked me today if you were going to live in the house now instead of Mummy. She was scared that Mummy might not be part of the family any more. She was very upset.'

Millie places a hand over her mouth, feeling like she might throw up. Poor Elena. Suddenly her strange behaviour over the last few days makes sense. *Oh my god*. How did she see them together? They have been a lot more reckless recently. Elena must have crept down the stairs one evening this week and seen them.

'*How dare you?*' Judith spits down the phone with such venom that Millie's heart thuds against her chest so hard and fearfully, she can hear it ringing in her ears. 'How dare you try to destroy my family?'

'Judith, please, I would never—'

'I hire you and bring you into my home and you try to break my family apart! What kind of *monster* are you?'

'I wasn't trying to destroy your family. I swear nothing happened when you and Michael were together!'

'That's what he said when he was grovelling this evening, but you don't honestly expect me to believe that, do you?'

'I promise, Judith. I would never have—'

'What a cliché, the husband and the nanny,' Judith says. 'I mean, it's *embarrassing*! You should be ashamed.'

'Judith, please—'

'Did you honestly think he was going to leave me for you? Are you under the impression that we're going to get divorced and you'll be able to swoop in and become part of the family? Is that the delusion you've created for yourself?'

'You and Michael should talk,' Millie says quietly, her voice trembling.

'Oh we've talked,' Judith growls. 'We've been talking all night. I wasn't going to let him stroll out of here, after my

150

daughter reveals his affair at my parents' anniversary celebration. He told me everything. The entire truth. He's very apologetic and, quite rightly, mortified about the entanglement. He's told me what you are to him.'

Millie grips the phone in her hand so tightly her knuckles go white.

'Nothing,' Judith states bitterly. 'You are nothing to him.'

Millie tries to remain calm, reminding herself that Michael has been put into a horrible position; he's been cornered and confronted, and she doesn't blame him if he's had to lie to Judith until she's calmer and in a better place to process the news. She also doesn't know if Judith is telling the truth. For all Millie knows, this phone call is Judith's way of getting back at her, an attempt to hurt her as much as possible by making up a conversation between her and Michael that hasn't been had.

'We're going to fight for our family,' Judith continues. 'You may have done your very best to destroy everything, but you're not going to win.'

'I wasn't trying to win anything,' Millie insists. 'I promise you Judith – Michael and I … it began after you were separated and we didn't plan on any of it.'

'Well it's over now, I won't let you do any more damage,' she seethes. 'When I hired you, I thought you were a decent, kind person, someone I could trust. But now I see you for what you really are: a homewrecker. You're pathetic. You won't ever see Michael again. And you will never – *never* – be allowed anywhere near my children. You come to my home, I'll call the police. Stay away from me. Stay away from my husband. Stay away from my family.'

Judith abruptly hangs up.

Millie stands in shock, unable to move a muscle. Eventually, she lowers her phone from her ear. She realises she's crying; her cheeks are wet. She needs to go back to her hotel now. She has to get out of here.

She spins around to find James right behind her.

She'd forgotten they were even there. He and Ingrid overheard all her side of the conversation. He's looking at her in dismay, his eyes flashing with anger behind his glasses.

'Millie,' he begins. 'What the—'

'Spare me the lecture,' she snaps, marching past him. 'I don't need your judgement. I'm going home.'

'Why wouldn't you tell me something like that?' he asks, following her as Ingrid brings up the rear. 'I'm supposed to be your best friend. You've been having an affair with Michael?'

'We aren't having an affair,' Millie cries, turning to face him. 'We're in love. We fell in love. And it was after Judith moved out, so I didn't do anything wrong. So please don't start yelling at me, accusing me of ruining a family.'

James recoils, stung. 'In case you haven't noticed, Millie, I'm not the one yelling. I wasn't going to go all judgemental on you; it sounds like you're doing a very good job of doing that for yourself.'

'What's that supposed to mean?'

'You feel guilty about the affair and so you're acting defensively towards me before I've even had a chance to speak!'

'I know what you're thinking. Just because of what happened to your parents, you think that—'

'Whoa, whoa.' James lifts his hands, staring at her in bewilderment. 'Don't bring what happened to my parents into this. This is about you, Millie, and your actions and their consequences. Nothing else. And yes, OK, I happen to think affairs are not a good thing. I also know that you don't think they are, either. So I don't really understand why you've done what you've done.'

'I don't need to explain myself to you,' Millie huffs.

'I wasn't asking you to!' he replies, his voice rising with anger. 'But at least now I know why you've pushed me away. You've been keeping this huge secret from me and our friendship has suffered as a result. I thought I'd done something wrong!'

'You don't understand. You wouldn't get it.'

'Get *what*?'

'Everything has been shit for me!' she cries in exasperation. 'Ever since Grandpa died, I've felt aimless and alone! I *need* Michael. You wouldn't understand because everything falls into place for you, but I was lost!'

James glares at her. 'You think everything falls into place for me? That's what you think. Bloody hell, Millie, I knew you'd become self-indulgent, but I didn't know you were this bad.'

'*Excuse me?*'

'You have spent your life waiting around for something to come along and happen to you, complaining about your lack of a future or whining about being stuck in a rut. Well, guess what, Millie, if you want things to change, sometimes you have to have the guts to do something about it.' He looks at her in disappointment. 'If you'd been a little less self-pitying and self-involved, then you might have noticed that things *don't* actually come easy to me. They don't come easy for anyone. Things haven't felt all rosy, recently, but I don't wallow in my problems and act out like a teenager.' He gestures to Millie pointedly, prompting her to drop her eyes to the ground. 'You've obviously been so intent on protecting yourself from my "judgement", or whatever excuse you've made up in your head, that you haven't stopped to consider that *I* might need you, too.'

James throws his head back and exhales.

'Sometimes I wish I didn't know what I wanted to do with my life,' he continues in a softer, wearier tone. 'I spend every day sat at my desk, writing shit articles that no one cares about for a pitiful amount of money, attempting to convince myself that one day, it will all be worth it, because it *has* to be. It has to be worth it. I can't compromise on what I want, and what I want is to write about music. So, I'm stuck, chasing a dream that probably won't come true. How pathetic.' He pauses, running a hand through his hair, looking her right in the eye. 'I feel like a failure, Millie. I get really down about it. And I wish my best friend had been there so I could talk about it to someone.'

Millie lets his words sink in. She hates that he considers himself a failure and that he's been unable to lean on her when he's needed to, but he has to understand that she hasn't had the strength to be that person for him this year. Even now, his anger towards her is too much for her to handle when she's just been shouted at down the phone by her boyfriend's soon-to-be ex-wife.

She doesn't know what to say. She's too upset about everything to speak.

'OK, that's it, I'm done,' James says finally, tired of waiting for her to respond. 'I'm going back to the bar, because I need a drink. Ingrid, fancy joining me?'

'Sure,' Ingrid nods, before looking at Millie hopefully.

But Millie doesn't move. James turns on his heel and marches back into the bar, Ingrid following behind him, and doesn't look back.

* * *

Millie exits the hotel lift at her floor, her room key swinging from her finger, to find Noah slumped against a door down the corridor. She starts on seeing him. He doesn't notice her at first. His eyes are glazed over and his shoulders slumped forwards. He looks smaller somehow.

'Noah?'

He glances up and offers her a sad smile.

'Hey,' he says quietly, giving a wave, not attempting to stand up.

'Are you looking for your room?' she asks, approaching him. 'I think you're on a different floor.'

'No. I was waiting for you,' he says. 'Is that OK?'

She blinks at him. 'Yeah, it's OK.'

'I wanted to talk to someone. No. Wait. That's not correct. I didn't want to talk to just anyone.' He frowns, pointing his finger at her. 'I wanted to talk to *you*.'

'All right, you can talk to me,' she says, looming over him. 'But let's go to my room.'

He squints up at her. 'Is this not the door to your room?'

'Afraid not.'

'Ah.' He winces. 'I really hope this room is empty, otherwise these people may have been woken up when I knocked earlier.'

'Why didn't you call me?' she asks, offering her hand to help pull him to his feet.

'My phone is in my room. I thought you might be back by now, so I just came up here without it,' he explains, tripping over his feet as he follows her to the correct door.

As she turns the key, she glances up at him in concern. 'Have you had more to drink since you got back?'

'Two words for you,' he says with a lopsided grin. 'Mini bar.'

'OK, let's get you inside.'

She ushers him in and watches as he stumbles towards her bed. He climbs onto it and makes himself comfortable, propping up the pillows behind him and slumping back into them.

'How was the rest of your night?' he asks, pushing his hair back from his face.

'Terrible,' she answers honestly, sitting down on the edge of the bed.

She thinks back on the phone call with Judith, the hatred and disgust in her voice, and how much of a mess she's landed herself in. Even if Michael manages to calm Judith down, there's still no way Millie can stay in her job. She feels an ache in her heart at not seeing Elena and Isaac's little faces every day. And then there's James. He looked so disappointed, so let down by her. Some of the things he said were brutal. But also, they might be a little true.

'My night was also not good,' Noah reveals.

She turns to look at him. 'Did you have a fight with Charlotte?'

'Sort of. Then we talked for a long time. She went back to her hotel and I came here to drown my sorrows.'

'Do you want to talk about them?' Millie asks gently. 'Your sorrows, I mean.'

He nods. 'Yep. That's exactly why I came looking for you. And it had to be you, Millie, I didn't want to talk to anyone else. Isn't that strange?'

She shrugs. 'Not really. I feel like I can talk to you about stuff, too. We're friends.'

'Hmm.' He takes a deep breath and rests his head back, his eyes on the ceiling. 'Charlotte came here to Sweden to deliver a message. My dad is sick. He's got cancer.'

'Oh, Noah!' Millie whispers.

She stands up and moves around the bed to climb up next to him, reaching for his hand and clasping it in hers. He starts to cry. She lets go of his hand and wraps her arms around him, pulling him towards her so he can rest his head against her shoulder.

'I'm sorry,' he croaks eventually, wiping his face with the back of his hand.

She passes him a tissue from the box next to the bed. 'Don't say sorry.'

'I'm a mess.'

'You're not a mess. You're sad. It's OK to be sad.'

He wipes his eyes, scrunching up the wet tissue in his fist.

'Do you remember in Oslo you said to me that Eurovision was an escape from the world and its problems?' he asks.

'Sounds like something I'd say,' she admits.

'That's what you said, I haven't forgotten.' He sighs, despondent. 'Well, it hasn't delivered on that promise, Millie. This year, there's been no escape. Instead, my problems have come collapsing in on me all at once.'

He sounds so vulnerable and lost. Millie feels an overwhelming wave of sympathy for him. She wishes she could click her fingers and make his pain disappear.

She pulls away so Noah is forced to lift his head to look at her.

'It's going to be OK,' she tells him, as though saying it confidently might make it be true. 'And you always have me for the times that it doesn't feel that way.'

He nods, his eyes glistening with tears as they meet hers.

'I know,' he says.

They don't say anything else. Noah goes back to resting his head on her shoulder and Millie holds him. And for that moment, it feels as if there's no one else they need.

Neither of them would remember exactly when, but at some point, they shift down the pillows until they're lying flat. Millie reaches for the switch on the wall to turn off the lights. They fall asleep, her on her back, him on his side facing her, his nose nestled in her hair, his arm around her waist.

They remain like that all night.

CHAPTER TWELVE

London, UK

2017

Friday 12 May

Wheeling his suitcase behind him, James stops as he reaches the security gates and turns to his boyfriend with a warm smile.

'You didn't have to take me to the airport. Now you have to go all the way back to the office.'

'I wanted to come,' Mark insists. 'I wasn't about to let you get the train on your own. It really isn't any trouble. And I can make some business calls from the car on the way back.'

'Even though I'm only going for two nights, I'm going to miss you, you know,' James admits shyly. 'I'm readily admitting to being completely pathetic.'

'It's not pathetic,' Mark assures him. 'I'll miss you, too.'

James reaches out to grab his hands and pull him closer for a kiss. With a quick glance around, Mark allows him a swift peck on the lips.

If it was someone else, James would have found Mark's distaste for public displays of affection frustrating and maybe even a little bit hurtful, but there's something endearing and sweet about Mark's reserved nature. James teases him about it all the time, purposely throwing his arms around Mark in queues and busy shops, revelling in Mark's embarrassed sighs and eye rolls. But James knows Mark secretly enjoys it, because he'll always do this small knowing smile afterwards, as though James's outlandish behaviour amuses him really, but he doesn't want anyone but James to know.

James and Mark met in December at a small but prominent live music venue in Brighton. James was there for work, reviewing a local indie band, Wandering Bow, who had seemingly sprung out of nowhere and become a YouTube favourite for their incredibly catchy latest single, 'Explain Yourself', but James had noticed them a while earlier and first mentioned to his boss, Errol, back in September that they were a band to watch.

At the time, Errol had been dubious, but he allowed James to write a short column on how Wandering Bow were the next big thing. When a couple of months later they were all anyone could talk about, Errol told James he was a 'talent-spotting genius' – James was instantly rewarded with more column inches and gig reviews. The press spot for Wandering Bow's sold-out December gig was given to James without any argument from anyone else on the team.

James loves his new job. It pays a fraction more than his former paper job, so he's earning hardly anything, but he's finally where he wanted to be: a journalist for popular online music magazine, *Jagged*. His role title is Junior Reporter, working largely with the Features Editor, Amy, and helping her with a lot of the boring admin that comes hand in hand with being a journalist, like transcribing her interviews with bands, as well as writing the odd piece here and there. But his passion and drive has quickly impressed both her and Errol, the magazine's editor. He started with small articles and gig reviews until he graduated to full-blown interviews and profile features.

James can't remember a more thrilling career moment than when he was handed a press lanyard on his arrival at Wandering Bow's gig. It was such a big moment for him. He hung it round his neck proudly, feeling like he'd finally achieved what he'd been working towards all this time, and then he kept it afterwards – it's safely tucked away in his desk drawer at home.

Before the band came onto the stage, he spoke to the publicist for a little while and then found a spot at the back, standing alone with his flip notepad and pen. He wanted to soak in the atmosphere so he could capture it correctly in his review, scanning the room and observing the people there who made up the audience: lots of teenagers wearing all-black outfits and lace-up boots, their eyes lined heavily with dark make-up.

As James took them in, Millie's ex-boyfriend, Louis, popped up in his head and he chuckled to himself – this is exactly the sort of gig he and his friends would have come to, not because they listened to or cared about the music, but because it made sense with the image they were trying to project.

The venue was fairly intimate and got crowded quickly, so James stuck to the back corner where he had a good view of the stage but was set apart from the space that was filling with fans ready to dance.

He noticed Mark during the first song. It was difficult not to notice him.

James had glanced to his left and there he was, standing on his own, too. He looked unbelievably uncomfortable and out of place. For a start, he was wearing a suit. And not just that, but he had made absolutely zero effort to make his get-up a little more casual. He hadn't loosened his tie or taken off his jacket – he was determined to look smart, despite his surroundings. He had short dark hair and bold eyebrows that were deeply furrowed, as though he was trying to work out how he'd ended up in this place. Everything about him screamed a serious personality: his sober expression, his meticulously groomed appearance, his confident posture that made him seem taller than he was. He was even holding what looked like a tumbler of whisky and ice.

This man had come to a gig and ordered a *Scotch*? His drink choice made him a captivating curiosity. James *had* to know his story.

He didn't approach him for the next few songs, wanting to make sure that he wasn't waiting on anyone, but the man remained standing by himself. James made notes on the band's energetic performance and their lively, engaging rapport with the audience, and then, finishing off his drink for a last-minute boost of confidence, he wandered over.

'What do you think of the band?' James asked over the music.

Surprised at being addressed, the man leant closer to him.

'Sorry?' he replied.

'What do you think of the band?' James repeated louder, nodding towards the stage.

'Oh! Um.' He noticed the lanyard around James's neck and the notepad and pen in his hands. 'Are you a reporter?'

James hadn't meant for his opening line to come across as though he was asking a question for his work, but he realised that it was a nice cover as to why he approached in the first place. It was a clever in, even if it was accidental.

'Yeah, I'm reviewing the gig and gathering quotes from the audience for the piece. I'm James,' he said, holding out his hand.

His companion politely shook it. 'Mark. I'm afraid you picked the wrong audience member for a quote, James. I shouldn't really be here.'

'What do you mean?'

'My little brother and his girlfriend are the big fans. They're in there somewhere,' Mark explained, gesturing to the crowd jumping up and down to the beat pulsating through the room. 'Their friend was meant to come but dropped out at the last minute and my brother insisted I took the spare ticket so it didn't go to waste. But this isn't really my thing.' Mark suddenly looked panicked. 'Don't … don't put that in your article.'

James laughed. 'This is all off the record, don't worry.'

'Oh good,' Mark replied, visibly relaxing. 'I'm sure the band are great if you like this kind of music. Sorry for not being able to help. I would offer to go get my brother for a quote, but that would involve tackling that crowd and I have no idea where they are.'

'No need to go through the stress of that,' James assured him, hesitating, before adding, 'Besides, you wouldn't want anyone spilling a drink on your suit.'

Mark raised an eyebrow at him, picking up on his teasing tone. 'No, as a matter of fact, I wouldn't. I'm not exactly dressed for the occasion, am I.'

'The moment I saw you I figured you weren't a diehard fan of Wandering Bow.'

'The suit was the giveaway.'

'The tie, in particular. And your drink.'

Mark held up his glass. 'What's wrong with a whisky?'

'Nothing. A strange choice for a rowdy music gig, that's all. It's the type of drink reserved for quiet libraries in the highlands of Scotland.'

The corners of Mark's mouth twitched into a smile. 'I think you'll find that whisky brands and their publicists would strongly disagree with you. It's a versatile beverage.'

'For a sophisticated palate.'

'Now that I won't argue with,' Mark said.

James smiled up at him. The song came to an end and the room was filled with cheers and applause. The two of them stood side by side without saying anything while the lead singer of the band introduced the next song.

A few seconds into the first verse, Mark leant towards James again.

'You've got quite an exciting job, then,' he commented. 'It must be glamorous being a music journalist.'

'I love it,' James admitted. 'But not so glamorous. I spend a lot of my time in venues where the bottoms of your shoes stick to the floor.'

Mark nodded, glancing at his feet. 'That is a downside.'

'What do you do?'

'I'm a solicitor.'

'Wow. I should have guessed from the whisky.'

'If I'd have known I'd be judged so much for the whisky, I would have ordered something else. Or at least got a mixer.' Mark grimaced at the thought.

'I'm only jealous because I can't pull off having a whisky,' James laughed, touching his arm. 'I would look like an idiot, whereas you' – James leant back and gestured to Mark – 'you look like the sort of refined, worldly type.'

'Simply because I'm wearing a suit?'

'It's *how* you wear it,' James clarified.

Looking him in the eye, Mark swallowed. James noticed his throat bob and realised – *hoped* – that Mark was … nervous?

'And how do you think I wear it, James?' Mark asked, holding his eye contact.

'I think … I think you wear it very well,' James said, his stomach flipping as he lost himself in Mark's intense, dark eyes.

James can't really remember the second half of the band's performance, his memories of that night consumed by the handsome and charming Mark and their easy-flowing conversation, which spanned several songs and culminated in Mark's straight-to-the-point question as to whether James would like to go for a drink with him that week.

James loves Mark's no-nonsense attitude. In their first few weeks of dating, James would spend ages carefully composing messages, agonising over how every phrase would be read or could be misunderstood, checking over and over that they were suitable before pressing send – and, unless he was in a meeting, Mark would reply straight away. The first time Mark messaged James to arrange their date, James replied and added a 'X' at the end of his text. Mark's message back did not have any kisses, sending James into a spiral of mortification. It was only as he got to know Mark that he came to learn that he didn't ever put kisses at the end of his messages.

One of James's favourite exchanges between the two of them was when they were a good few weeks into their relationship and were deep into the honeymoon phase of seeing each other almost every night. He'd just wished Mark goodbye on the doorstep, the morning after an amazing evening spent at a posh restaurant that Mark picked, and an amazing night at his gorgeous, and meticulously neat, apartment. Unable to stop grinning as he walked away, James got out his phone and messaged Mark five kisses: *Xxxxx*

His phone vibrated with an instant reply: *I know*.

It was perfect. It reflected them as a couple. James, extroverted, impulsive, sensitive; Mark, grounded, collected, unflappable. It shouldn't really make sense, but somehow it does. Both so different, both undeniably crazy about the other.

James's mum likes Mark a lot, too. He is the first boyfriend James has brought home to meet her. He is fiercely protective of his mum – the divorce had escalated that emotion – and he has always been wary of introducing her to anyone in case she might disapprove, which would put James in an impossible position. He realised that, before Mark, there was never anyone who he really felt good enough to meet her.

'He's *lovely*,' she said when James visited her alone the weekend following the introduction. 'He knows his own mind and he's very respectful. Nice manners, too, which is a rarity.'

'You like him, then,' James checked eagerly.

'Yes, I do, very much!' She hesitated. 'Does he make you laugh?'

'Course he does!' James said, arching back in his chair, surprised at the question. 'Don't be fooled by that stern exterior. He's got the kind of comic timing that someone like me can only dream of.'

'You've always been very funny,' his mum countered defensively, before reaching over to pat his hand. 'I'm so pleased you've found someone who makes you happy. That's all I care about. It's wonderful to have that spark with someone. You have that, don't you?'

'Definitely.'

She sighed. 'One day, I hope to find it again!'

'You will, Mum.'

She'd gone on to fill James in on the coffee date she'd set up the following day with a man named Jeremy, who she met online. James listened, smiling and nodding, as she listed Jeremy's matching interests and hobbies.

But he'd been distracted, trying to shake someone out of his head, someone who had sprung to mind when she brought up the sought-after spark: Zachary.

James thinks about him a lot less than he used to. He doesn't stalk him on social media or pine over the idea of him and what could have been. But it is impossible to forget about his existence altogether, because James still wonders if it's him cropping up in the comments of his Eurovision website: NumberOneEuroFan continues to follow his work closely.

The blog has expanded to become a fully-fledged enterprise that takes up more and more of James's free time. To James's surprise, it has grown to become one of the leading sources for Eurovision fans all over the world. He remains anonymous as its creator, something which is becoming a little more of an issue – he knows that video content would help boost subscribers even more and aid his associated social media channels. But he's not ready to reveal himself. When James told Mark, his reaction proved that not everyone understands the appeal of Eurovision and James doesn't want to risk losing the respect he's earned from his colleagues.

He didn't tell Mark about it until they were a couple of months into the relationship. At first, Mark had thought James was joking. His eyebrows knitted together, his forehead creased and he stared at James as though trying to work out what the point of this joke could possibly be.

'What do you mean you run a Eurovision website?' he asked, tying his apron round his waist as he got ready to cook dinner.

Another thing that James adores about Mark: whenever he cooks, he puts on his apron. Even if it's for a meal that takes a few minutes. Like everything else in Mark's life, he approaches cooking fully prepared. James has never worn an apron in his life. Apart from his mum, he's not sure he knows anyone who *owns* an apron. But Mark wouldn't contemplate making even a salad without his apron on.

'I mean exactly that,' James chuckled, resting his chin in the palm of his hand as he leant his elbow on the kitchen table. 'I founded this Eurovision blog and it's now become a really popular website. I write articles about the song contest, its history, the people involved in it, and there are news updates and a subscriber newsletter. I've managed to build up a pretty big fan base – big enough to get noticed. This year the EBU have invited me to the Grand Final in Ukraine. I get a VIP pass and everything.'

Mark had put his hands on his hips before responding, and James could see from his quizzical expression that he was still trying to work out what was going on.

'The EBU?' he asked.

'The European Broadcasting Union. They run Eurovision.'

Mark blinked at him. 'You've been invited to the Final of Eurovision?'

'Yeah. Would you like to see the site?' James reached for his laptop, loaded it and then turned his screen to face Mark. 'There you go.'

Mark pulled the laptop towards him. He scrolled down the homepage. James waited in silence, scrutinising the way Mark's eyes narrowed as he focused on the screen, the way his mouth formed a straight line as he read through the headlines of the various posts.

'This is all … you?' he said eventually.

James nodded. 'I love Eurovision. Always have.'

'Really,' Mark replied, turning back to the laptop. 'I didn't know that.'

'I didn't mention it.' James paused, still studying Mark's face. 'What do you think?'

'Of the website? It's very … colourful.' He clicked on the author's bio page where there was a picture of a man's silhouette and a couple of paragraphs next to it describing the passion of the person behind the website who shall, for now, remain anonymous. 'Why the secrecy?'

'Oh, when I set it up it was just a fun side project.' James shrugged. 'I wasn't sure how colleagues would feel about it so thought it best to keep it under wraps.'

'I can understand that. Probably best not to shout it from the rooftops.'

'Right.' James smiled weakly. 'So, I take it you're not a fan?'

Mark pulled away from the table, getting back to prepping their dinner. 'Honestly, I don't really have any feelings on it. I mean, I know what it is, and I guess I may have watched bits of it in the past. I once went to a Eurovision party, actually.'

'Yeah?'

'We were all given countries to come as. I got France.'

'Nice! What was your costume like?'

Mark snorted, running the tomatoes under cold water. 'I think I was wearing a white shirt and blue jeans, and then bought a red cap last minute from a cheap stall somewhere.'

'You went all out, then,' James murmured, sliding the laptop back towards him and closing the website.

'You know I'm not good at that kind of thing,' Mark said, giving him a look. 'You've probably been to a lot of Eurovision parties, since it's your … uh … passion.'

'I used to go to the same one every year – the grandparents of a friend hosted one. It was a lot of fun.' He brushes it aside with a wave of his hand. 'Anyway, I wanted to tell you about the website, because, you know, it's a big part of my life and it's doing well now, so …'

James trailed off. Mark looked up from cutting the tomatoes.

'I'm glad you told me. I think it's … really interesting.'

James raised his eyebrows. 'You do?'

'Yeah,' Mark insisted. 'The most amazing thing about it is that you've done something so successful on the side of your day job. I'm not exactly surprised; everything you do is brilliant.' James smiled modestly. 'You know I'm in awe of your creative, artistic side. This Eurovision thing is just another fascinating layer to you. I'll have to learn more about it, if it's one of your passions.'

James felt a surge of love towards him. He knew that Mark didn't get it – he may never fully understand it – but the fact that he was trying was all James needed to know about him. He knew then that he was in this for the long haul, so long as Mark was, too.

As the Eurovision weekend crept up on them, Mark found James's excitement entertaining, but he'd been unable to drum up any enthusiasm himself. He wasn't one to pretend – he was a straight-talking guy, and if he didn't like something, he didn't like it – but he was fully supportive of how hard James had been working on his blog posts in the lead-up and now here he was to wave James off at the airport, having insisted on driving him.

Mark may not be a fan of Eurovision, but he's here for James anyway. And that means so much more.

'Are your friends meeting you in Ukraine?' Mark asks, checking his watch.

'Yes,' James confirms, fidgeting with the bottom of his shirt.

Proud to announce that his blog had provided him with a VIP pass to the Grand Final, James had messaged the Eurovision group earlier this year to reveal that he had also managed to snaffle three more tickets so that Ingrid, Noah and Millie could join him. It would be the first time in a while that they actually had the opportunity to watch the show live, rather than on a TV screen in a bar somewhere, and James was thrilled to be the one to make it happen. No matter what had gone down last year, he wanted to stay loyal to the Eurovision pact.

Which wasn't easy, considering he hadn't seen Millie in a long time.

They've had sporadic contact ever since they returned from Sweden. It was silent between them for a long time. James had felt guilty about his outburst, but not enough to be the first to reach out and apologise. Millie had treated him poorly and distanced herself from him, so, in his opinion, it was up to her to get in contact and start repairing their friendship. He was hurt that didn't happen straight away. She clearly didn't value their relationship in the same way he did. He was still angry at her for having an affair with a married man; a stupid decision he didn't think she was capable of.

He missed her, though. He really missed her.

On numerous occasions he started composing messages to her, but got flustered thinking about what to say. That would lead to irritation and resentment that *she* wasn't the one getting flustered over messaging him. His stubbornness always won and he left it.

She took her time but she'd eventually got in touch. In true contemporary style, the first he heard from her was when she liked one of his Instagram posts. She began to leave brief messages on others – 'gorgeous! Hope you're well x' – and when he posted about his new job, she went so far as to send him a congratulatory box of brownies.

He loves brownies.

When James had explained the pact to Mark, he'd given him a brief overview of his argument with Millie that had caused the deterioration of their friendship. Mark patiently listened as James reeled off the saga and, when he finished, Mark swirled his glass of wine and shrugged.

'She's probably embarrassed,' he remarked.

'About *what*?'

'About the affair. You say that before this happened, you two were best friends? She knows you well, then, and she knows what you would think. She probably couldn't stand the idea of letting you down. She should have told you, rather than avoiding you altogether, but she was obviously scared.'

James had been floored by Mark's simple explanation. He'd been so angry at her decisions, he hadn't really delved into why she'd made them in the first place.

His fingers drum nervously against his suitcase as he thinks about the weekend ahead. He has no idea if Millie's still with Michael, although he does know she doesn't work for him any more. He hopes that Julie is doing better than she was. He's never known so little about his best friend's life and, as much as he can try to pretend otherwise, he hopes they can find a way back to each other.

That was part of the reason he wanted to offer the three of them these tickets. To show her that he was still willing to try.

'You'd better head on through,' Mark says, nodding to the security gates.

'Thanks again for accompanying me to the airport.'

'Of course, although I do have to rush off for a call. Message when you get there and have a great time. I'm looking forward to hearing all about it.'

'You'll watch it on TV?' James prompts with a hopeful smile.

Mark looks torn. 'I'll have it on in the background while I cook.'

'Good enough. Love you.'

'You too.'

He leans forward and kisses Mark on the lips – a proper kiss this time – before Mark can protest. When he pulls away, Mark reveals that secret smile of his, his eyes dropping to the floor, shaking his head.

'If you want, I'll shout my love from the rooftops,' James offers, basking in his adorable discomfort.

'Not necessary,' Mark affirms, getting his phone out of his pocket. 'Safe flight. Don't forget to let me know you're there safe and sound.'

James promises he won't and then waits to watch Mark walk away. His phone pressed to his ear, Mark turns to look back over his shoulder and wave at James, before gesturing that he should head through security. James rolls his eyes. He's got plenty of time before his flight, but he loves that Mark is determined for him to get going so there's no risk of his being late. Mark is always on time or early for everything.

James grabs the handle of his wheelie case and is about to turn when someone passing Mark, heading towards security, catches his eye. Tall, blonde, strikingly handsome, he's in a smart, beautifully tailored and expensive-looking suit. He looks so well-groomed and sophisticated, it takes James a moment to get his head around the fact that it really is him.

'Noah!' James calls out, his voice echoing around the terminal.

Noah glances up at the sound of his name, spotting James straight ahead of him. James waves him over, excited that they're probably on the same flight.

'I had no idea you were flying to Ukraine from London,' James says when Noah reaches him, pulling him into a hug. 'What are you doing in the UK?'

'I've been meaning to message you,' Noah responds, his cheeks flushing. 'I live here now.'

CHAPTER THIRTEEN

Kyiv, Ukraine

Saturday 13 May 2017

'I'll try a Ukrainian beer, please,' Noah says, leaning on the bar.

The barman raises his eyebrows in pleasant surprise. 'Which one?'

'Whichever one you'd recommend,' he says, as the barman nods and gets pouring. Noah notices a group of British Eurovision fans drinking from bottles of a famous American brand at a table nearby and shares a conspiratorial smile with the barman, rolling his eyes.

'I'm impressed,' Millie comments, sliding onto the stool next to him. 'First you have a giant plate of varenyky for lunch and now a local beer. You're really throwing yourself into sampling the local delicacies. It's that adventurous spirit of yours.'

'You know me,' he replies, clasping his hands together.

She nods slowly. 'I do.'

He glances over his shoulder. 'Have James and Ingrid left?'

'Yeah, I think James had some work to do and Ingrid wanted to sneak in a nap before the Final – I think she's been working really hard this week.'

'I thought you wanted to go back to your hotel, too, and get ready for tonight.'

'I did,' she admits. 'But then I changed my mind. I thought I might as well join you for one more drink.'

'Can I buy you a local Ukrainian beer?' Noah offers when his pint is slid across to him.

Millie looks unsure. 'I don't know. Will I like it?'

'She'll have the same,' he instructs the barman. 'No idea if you'll like it, but if not, I'll drink it for you and order you something else. It's good to try something new. Broaden your horizons, Millie, you won't regret it.'

'Says a true pro,' she remarks. 'You are the king of changing scenery.'

'Yeah.' He hesitates, bowing his head. 'I'm sorry, by the way. I should have told you I was living in England.'

'That's OK,' she shrugs. 'You only just moved there, right?'

'Right,' he lies.

Noah has been living in London for two months now, plenty of time to send Millie and James a message to let them know and arrange to meet up. At first, he gave himself the excuse that he'd need a few weeks to settle in, and then after a few weeks, he thought he might as well wait a few more and mention it when he met them in Ukraine.

The truth is, he's been nervous to see Millie. She saw him at his most vulnerable last year in Sweden and he wanted to be in a really good place when he saw her again, hoping that her memory of him crying into her arms would be wiped away and replaced by the image of a guy who has it all together.

Noah pays for their beers and they clink their glasses before taking a sip.

'That's good,' Noah declares, receiving a warm smile from the barman before he turns to check Millie's expression. 'What do you think?'

She puts her glass down. 'That I should step out of my comfort zone more often.'

He breaks into a grin.

'You didn't fancy staying put in Australia, then?' she notes, swivelling on her stool to face him properly.

'It was only ever going to be temporary. As soon as Dad was better, I started planning on coming back to Europe.'

She nods, gently saying, 'I'm really glad he's OK, Noah.'

'Thanks. Me too.' Noah picks at the coaster sitting underneath his beer as condensation from his glass dampens it. 'It will take time for him to fully recover, but the cancer is gone.'

'It must be a relief to see him getting back to himself.' She pauses. 'I know you found it hard seeing him so ...'

'Yeah, it's always a shock when someone seems to become a shell of their former self. But don't worry, he's back to throwing his weight around the place.'

After so many years apart, his reunion with his father was distinctly lacking. Even in the throes of exhausting chemotherapy, Noah's father was a master of manipulating the conversation away from himself and his illness, determined to prove that his condition had not obscured his disappointment in Noah's flippant attitude to his life and career.

'You want to look back and know you had meaning, that what you did *meant* something,' his dad had told him grouchily. 'That's what I want you to understand, Noah. You've had your jaunt around Europe. Time to get serious.'

Thank goodness Charlotte never told her parents the truth about Noah's DJ lifestyle – he was already on the receiving end of enough snide comments from his father, and that was when his dad was under the impression he had a steady job.

On learning that the chemo was working and he was on his journey to a full recovery, his father demanded that he be allowed to get back to work and begrudgingly accepted a compromise of working from home, so he could be closely monitored by his wife, while Charlotte and others on the board continued to keep things ticking over nicely in his absence. Noah, meanwhile, was itching to leave Melbourne. He was glad he returned for a while – it was important he'd been with them at a trying time for his family – but it was obvious he didn't belong there.

'I owe you a thanks,' Noah says to Millie hurriedly.

'Why?'

He gives her a pointed look. 'You *know* why. All those phone calls when I must have kept you up late into the night so I could ramble on about my problems—'

'Noah,' she interrupts, holding up her hand, 'your dad was really sick. You don't have to thank me for letting you talk about it.'

He shrugs. 'It meant a lot, that's all.'

'I liked our chats,' she says with a sincere smile.

He looks her right in the eye to say softly, 'Seriously, Millie. Thank you.'

She holds his gaze for a moment and then looks away, her cheeks flushing, as she replies, 'What are friends for?'

Going back to Australia was daunting and overwhelming, and Noah hadn't wanted to face it alone, so when he first arrived, he found himself messaging Millie more than usual. She'd done the same, checking in on him much more regularly, asking about his dad, reminding him she was always there if he needed a chat. And last summer – or winter, in his case – he did need chats. Lots of them. So he'd call her and she'd always pick up. If he's honest with himself, Millie was a major player in getting him through a dizzying and painful period in his life.

He really should have messaged her when he moved to the UK.

What a coward.

'So tell me what your plan is for London,' Millie says brightly, seeming eager to move the conversation on. 'I overheard you telling James earlier something about real estate when we were walking through Maidan Square.'

'That's right, I got a place on a real estate training and development programme.' He straightens up.

'You weren't tempted to return to the glamorous world of international DJing?'

He chuckles, shaking his head. 'I came to the realisation that maybe it wasn't for me after all. I felt exhausted just thinking about it, to be honest. The real estate course is interesting with a guaranteed job attached to it – it will be good to stay in one place for a while with a steady salary. I'm excited to get stuck in.'

Noah wonders if Millie can tell he's trying to convince himself of that, too.

It had been Charlotte's idea to pitch a real estate training programme in Europe to his dad – that way, Noah would likely gain his support, personally and financially, to leave Australia. A steady day job didn't mean he had to give up his DJ passion either, Charlotte had pointed out. He would have evenings and weekends to pursue any artistic endeavours without his dad needing to know. When Noah said

179

that he wasn't sure any more if DJing *was* his passion, Charlotte gave him a look and muttered, 'No shit.'

But her idea was a good one. Noah suggested a few course options he'd researched to his parents and London was declared to be the most attractive option – his dad was hoping to expand his property business out there some day and having a man on the ground already might be helpful to him, even if it was Noah.

'I have to admit, I never had you pinned for a guy who would be excited to get stuck into a steady job,' Millie comments, echoing his words and watching him curiously.

'It will be a change, but I'm genuinely looking forward to it.'

'Then, I'm happy for you,' Millie says, nudging his arm with her elbow. 'It sounds like a great plan and, best of all, we'll be living in the same country, so that's an extra perk.'

'Exactly.' He pauses. 'You'll have to come visit me in London. You'd be welcome any time. And I could come see you in Brighton, maybe. If you'd like.'

She smiles warmly at him. 'I'd like that a lot, Noah.'

'Good. Great.' He holds up his glass and tilts it towards her and, with a wry smile, declares, 'To steady jobs?'

'To broadening horizons,' she corrects, raising her glass and clinking it against his.

* * *

As the arena audience of the Eurovision Grand Final gives a roar of cheers and applause later that night, Ingrid claps slowly, her brow furrowed as she stares up at the stage, her mind racing with ideas.

'And now to round off my review of that wonderful performance from Germany with a quote from a lifelong German fan of Eurovision,' James cries above the noise, nudging Ingrid as he taps furiously into his phone, providing live updates on his blog. 'Ingrid, what were your thoughts?'

'I thought Levina was great,' she replies. 'The song is uplifting and she has a beautiful voice. But ...'

She hesitates. James glances up from his typing, intrigued.

'Go on,' he prompts.

'But I think they could have done so much more with the staging,' she relays regretfully. 'The song would have more of an impact if they'd been a little more creative with how it was performed. Altogether, the production felt flat. This stage in Ukraine is absolutely incredible, it has been designed to almost integrate the audience. Look how close the people can get to the performer this year, but we didn't make use of that at all. We could have done more with costume, props, set, chorus performers – all the elements that make a show a *show*. The song was good, but it could have really been brought alive with more of an exciting production.'

James does his best to keep up with her, but has to ask her to repeat some of her thoughts so he can quote her accurately. When he's finished typing it up, he posts it to his blog and looks at her, impressed.

'Thank you, Ingrid, that was great,' he enthuses. 'No general quotes from you this year, that's for sure.'

She shrugs, smiling up at him. 'I have to speak the truth. Your fans may disagree.'

'Now that you've pointed it out, *I* agree with you if that helps,' he reasons. 'And even if they do disagree, it's always fun to have some lively debate. Music is subjective. But your point about all the elements that come together to make a performance a production is very interesting – it's easy to forget there's so much more to it than someone walking onto a stage and singing.'

Ingrid nods. Until recently, she never thought about that herself.

Her girlfriend, Andrea, says it was a stroke of luck that brought Ingrid into the remit of Carl Beck, but Ingrid believes it was more than that. She thinks it was fate.

When her temp agency rang her and asked if she'd be interested in a four-week PA job that had come up at the Theater des Westens, Ingrid said yes before hearing any of the details. It didn't matter to her what exactly she'd be doing there; being involved in a theatre in some capacity was all she needed to know to accept the job.

It turned out that one of the PAs working for Stage Entertainment, the production company that develops shows at the Theater des Westens, had quit without warning because he suddenly got offered a place at drama school. The production team were desperate for someone to step in straight away. With a new show opening next month, they didn't have time to advertise for the role and they needed someone reliable, enthusiastic and available immediately. Enter Ingrid stage right.

She loved it from the start. The chaos of the theatre, the hustling activity everywhere you went – it was all magical to her. On her first day, she arrived and was immediately bustled into an office to meet Madeline, a fierce producer who began listing what she needed Ingrid to do before she'd even taken off her coat. That didn't faze Ingrid one bit, though. Having worked as a temp PA for a while by then, she'd become very good at being prepared for anything and swiftly learning the ropes. While Madeline barked orders, Ingrid grabbed her notebook and pen from her bag and jotted them down, even if she didn't quite understand them yet.

Madeline took to Ingrid, which, Ingrid was told, was a rarity. She respected that Ingrid got the job done without fuss, took the initiative to action certain things before Madeline had asked, and knew when to stay out of her way. Ingrid managed Madeline's diary, took her messages, accompanied her to meetings and acted as her gatekeeper when creatives dropped by without having made an appointment.

One of those creatives was Carl Beck, the stage manager at Theater des Westens. Ingrid had seen him marching about the place before, usually trailed by one or more people who'd either be badgering him with questions or noting down his requests as he reeled them off. In his sixties, he had a thick mop of greying hair, a permanently stern expression and a pair of reading glasses that hung around his neck on string and were constantly being propped up on the end of his nose to aid him in studying whatever piece of paper had been thrust in front of his face and then dropped again as he strode off with purpose. He was *always* going somewhere with purpose, Ingrid observed.

She got to know Carl well through his meetings with Madeline, some of which were scheduled, others that came about by his lurking outside her office until she was off the phone and he could poke his head around the door with Ingrid's permission to ask a quick question – Ingrid had cottoned on quickly to which creatives Madeline would make time for and which ones she wouldn't. She'd make time for Carl.

On one occasion that he visited, Madeline was out at a meeting, but Ingrid informed him that if he had time to hang around for five minutes, he might catch her on her way back before she had to go to another meeting.

'I never have time to "hang around", Ingrid,' he informed her, pacing impatiently in front of her desk. 'But I do need to know the answer to this budget question quickly, so I suppose "hanging around" will have to do.'

'Stage managers have to deal with budgets?' Ingrid asked curiously as she typed an appointment into Madeline's schedule.

'Stage managers deal with everything,' he replied. 'We control it all. We may not be at the forefront of anyone's mind, but we're the ones who put it all together. Performers, directors, producers, set design, costumes, lighting, sound, props – we coordinate everything. If someone has a question, they come to me and I provide a solution to the problem. I am the chief of organisation without any of the credit.'

Ingrid smiled, standing up to place a file on Madeline's desk.

'I know how that feels,' she said over her shoulder.

Carl watched her curiously as she returned to her desk. 'Yes, I imagine you do. You've got to grips with this place very quickly. And you've achieved something no PA of Madeline's has been able to do so far. Either they're organised but she dislikes them, or she likes them, but they're useless at the work. But you, Ingrid, can claim to be an excellent assistant *and* to have won her favour. How did you do it?'

Ingrid laughed. 'I don't know. I guess part of my job is to read the people I'm working with and make sure their life runs smoothly. Remove the stumbling blocks before they get to them.'

'You get a rush from finding the solutions to the problems,' he remarked.

'Yes.'

He rubbed his chin thoughtfully for a moment. 'Ingrid, did you once tell me that you studied music?'

'I never graduated,' she admitted, reaching for print-outs and stapling them together.

'But you are interested in all this' – he gestured at his surroundings – 'showbusiness.'

'Yes!' she exclaimed, filing the papers away neatly and returning to her keyboard to bring up some notes on the screen that Madeline wanted her to neaten and finish. 'It's the world I've always wanted to be a part of. It's all I dream about.'

'You know what's interesting, Ingrid,' he said, moving to lean on her desk. 'The entire time we've been talking, you've also been working.'

She looked up from her screen, her cheeks flushing with embarrassment. 'Sorry, I've been rude.'

He shook his finger at her. 'No, no. I'm not pointing out a fault. It's a talent. You're a multi-tasker. You're smart, determined, organised, perceptive and you're head over heels in love with the performing arts.' A smile spread across his face. 'Ingrid, have you ever thought about stage management?'

She stared at him.

'Because if you're interested,' he continued, 'I have a space on my team that I'd like to fill. And I think you would be the perfect candidate.'

Before she could answer, the door swung open and Madeline glided in, greeting Carl and informing him she could give him two minutes and not a second longer. Carl tapped Ingrid's desk, said, 'think about it', and followed Madeline into her office.

Ingrid hasn't been able to stop thinking about it, and watching the Eurovision Grand Final only seems to be cementing the idea in her head.

She hasn't spent the evening losing herself in the music, but, instead, has been examining all the different components of the production, fascinated by how every different aspect has come together to tell a story. She's been looking out for the tiniest details of each set, scrutinising the choreographed steps of the artist and their dancers, questioning every lighting decision, musing over the costumes and noticing prop placement.

Somewhere behind that curtain, she knows that there's one person responsible for coordinating all those little components that bring each nation's production together: the stage manager.

The audience erupts as the act for the host country takes to the stage. Ingrid is aware that James has to concentrate on live blogging, so she quickly takes the opportunity to speak before the band representing Ukraine begins.

'James, can I ask you a question?'

'Go for it,' he responds, his eyes fixed on the stage.

'Do you think dreams can change?'

He looks at her quizzically. 'What do you mean?'

'You always wanted to be a writer from when you were little, but what if you realised you might be better at something else? Do you think it would feel like you were giving up?'

James takes a moment to consider her question before turning to face her properly. 'I think that taking the steps towards doing something that makes you happy, even when it's not what you thought you'd do, is always a brave move. Dreams can change, because people can change. Sometimes your dreams evolve as you do.' He raises his eyebrows at her. 'Does that help?'

She smiles. 'Yes. Thank you.'

The lights go down and they are dramatically plunged into pitch black as a spotlight shines on the lead singer of O. Torvald. The audience cheers wildly and his voice fills the room.

CHAPTER FOURTEEN

'Why don't you go talk to him?' Noah suggests quietly in Millie's ear.

She realises she's been openly staring at James as he frantically blogs into his phone.

'Go on,' Noah encourages. 'Make the first move.'

'He's busy working,' she hisses back, running a hand through her hair and turning her attention to O. Torvald up on the stage. 'He doesn't want to be disturbed.'

Noah gives her a look. 'Chicken.'

She narrows her eyes at him. 'I'm not being a chicken. I just don't want to distract him when he's busy!'

'Sure, you tell yourself that,' Noah says with a mischievous smile.

Millie sighs, lifting her eyes to the ceiling. 'How would I start the conversation? What would I even say?'

Noah shrugs. 'I'm not exactly the best person to ask for this kind of advice, but I reckon being honest is the way to go here. Tell him how you feel.'

She bites her lip.

'Millie, he's your best friend,' Noah reminds her gently.

'Not any more,' she mutters.

'Yes, always,' Noah emphasises. 'You've had a hiccup, but a friendship like you two have – it doesn't just fizzle out. You have to make it better.'

'I don't know how, though,' she insists anxiously.

'Talking to him is a good place to start. All that stuff you told me earlier in the bar about how much you miss him? Tell *him* that. Go on. I'm not going to let you avoid him all night. You said you were determined to get this sorted before we leave Ukraine.'

'You know, I'm starting to really regret opening up to you about this, Noah,' she remarks grumpily.

'To be honest, it's odd for me to be the voice of reason or take the moral high ground in any situation, so I'm going to go ahead and really relish this moment.' Noah grins. 'Millie, you can do this. You owe it to him to make the first move.'

Millie takes a deep breath. Noah is right. She has so much to say to James and had promised herself that this weekend, she'd do everything in her power to put things right with him, but now she's here, her nerves are getting the better of her.

She glances over at him as he focuses on his blogging. It's amazing how fast he types into his phone, pinging out his live updates for his ever-growing fan base. Millie is so proud of him and how much he's achieved with his Eurovision site. She desperately wants to tell him that. So much has changed between them, she wonders if he'd even want to hear it.

But, as she said to Noah over a glass of delicious Ukrainian beer earlier, she's determined to talk to James about what's happened, no matter what. She's not going to hide her head in the sand any longer.

For a long time now, Millie has been afraid.

She's come to realise that, in a flummoxing contradiction, she's been scared of life happening to her while being terrified nothing would happen at all. James was right to stand in the street in Stockholm last year and yell at her for refusing to change her life. He was right about lots of things. She just didn't want to hear it then. If only she'd listened, she could have been more prepared for the heartache that was coming her way.

She's been too embarrassed to call him or ask him to meet. She loathes her behaviour a year ago. And more than that, she's so ashamed of how she treated James. It took her a while to build up the courage, but she started to show that she wanted to make amends by commenting on his social media, just to remind him that she existed. It was pathetic, but she was too scared to reach out properly in case he told her to fuck off. He would have every right to.

When he messaged the group about Ukraine, she finally saw the opportunity to speak to him face to face without pressurising him into spending time with her. She secretly hoped that the ambiance of Eurovision might help matters – everyone would be on a high; he would be in his happy place and potentially more willing to forgive.

As O. Torvald's song comes to a finish, Millie exhales.

'I can do this,' she tells herself out loud, mustering the courage.

'Yes, you can,' Noah affirms as he joins in the applause.

With a sharp nod, Millie steps around Ingrid, who happily moves to stand next to Noah, and sidles nervously up to James.

She opens with a nervous, 'Hey.'

James finishes his sentence and clicks 'publish'.

'Hey,' he replies, looking up from his phone.

'Sorry, I know you're busy, but I wanted to … uh …'

'Talk?' he suggests.

She swallows the lump in her throat. 'Yes. Talk.'

Nodding, James waits patiently for her to speak. Her mind is scrambling as she tries to work out where she can possibly start. She decides that Noah is right. The only way forward is to be honest. No beating around the bush. All she has to do is tell him the truth.

'I'm so sorry, James,' she blurts out finally. 'I'm so, so sorry. I've missed you so much and I was a terrible friend. I *am* a terrible friend. Oh god, I was so stupid. You were right. All those things you said to me last year, I needed to hear them. I didn't want to hear them, but I needed to. I know it may not have seemed like it at the time, but I heard what you had to say. I needed to make a change and I've done that. I … I'm going to be a primary school teacher. I'm doing this degree in Brighton. And everything with Michael – it's over. A long time ago. A really long time ago. That was so fucked up. I'm embarrassed. What a loser. Oh god, I'm prattling on, probably not making any sense.'

She covers her face with her hands, shaking her head at how terribly this is going, but when she lowers her hands again, she sees the corners of James's mouth have twisted into an encouraging smile. She sighs, deflating.

'I'm really sorry that I let you down,' she continues. 'The affair with Michael – you must think I'm the biggest idiot on the planet.'

James looks down at the floor.

'No, I don't,' he says, his brow furrowing. 'I never thought that.'

'Well, you would have been right if you had. I was blind. He was never serious about me. The moment his wife found out …'

She trails off. She knows she doesn't need to finish the story. James can guess the rest. Anyone could guess how that one ended. In fact, most people would have probably foreseen it long before the whole sorry saga played out.

Millie hadn't, though. She was the classic fool.

As soon as she landed back in the UK from Sweden after Eurovision last year, she phoned Michael, but he didn't pick up. She realised he might still be at Judith's parents' house and it would be inappropriate for him to answer, so she left it, even though she was desperate to hear his soothing voice. He didn't answer any of her calls that Sunday night. He didn't answer the following morning, either.

By Tuesday, his phone went straight to voicemail and she began to panic. It crossed her mind that Judith might have murdered him and maybe she should contact the police. Returning to rational thought, Millie decided she'd go to his house that afternoon around the time the kids would return from school to see if he had done the pick-up in Millie's absence – it was much more likely that Judith had smashed his phone in a rage and that's why he wasn't contacting her.

Throwing on her hoodie, she called out to Julie that she was heading out for a bit and would be back later, and then walked the route she knew so well to Michael's. Pulling up her hood as she got nearer, she kept a good distance from the house and pretended to be on her phone. After a few minutes, his car pulled up and she ducked behind one of the trees lining the pavement, watching carefully. He stepped out the driver's seat and went to help the kids out the back. Judith climbed out from the front seat.

Millie gasped.

They were laughing about something, being playful with the children as they got out from the car and ran to the house. Michael opened the front door and Elena and Isaac sprinted in. Judith followed and, as she did so, Michael put his hand on the small of her back. He closed the door shut behind them.

Millie couldn't breathe. She leant against the tree, feeling as though her legs might give way beneath her. Clutching at her chest, she pushed her hood down, suddenly feeling much too hot, and then her fingers fumbled in her pocket for her phone. She tried calling Michael again. It went to voicemail.

She doesn't remember getting home. Her feet managed to get her there, but her mind was in a blur, her heart aching so badly she felt dazed by the pain. She asked Julie if she could borrow her phone and then dialled Michael's number.

It rang.

He'd blocked her.

'Hello?' he said, picking up.

Millie gripped the phone desperately at the sound of his voice.

'Michael. Michael, it's me.'

Silence the other end.

'What's going on? I've just seen you with Judith? You have to talk to me, Michael. I need to know what's happening. You have to—'

'I'm afraid you've got the wrong number,' he said curtly.

He hung up.

She remained in shock the next few days, barely able to function. Michael finally contacted her a week later. He apologised and said he'd had to wait until an appropriate time. He explained that he and Judith had talked it all through and they'd decided to give it another go. Judith was going to step back from her work a bit more, so they could spend some quality time together. They were going to work at their relationship. He had to give it a try, he said, for the children's sake. He was sorry and he wanted to reassure Millie that he'd give her an excellent reference so she could find a new job.

He'd give her an excellent reference.

Later, Millie would come to see him and their relationship for what it was: two broken people who were looking for someone else to come along and make them whole again. But that never works. James was proven right: Millie had been under the illusion that Michael could sweep in and make her happy.

'I'm sorry it didn't work out,' James says, studying her expression as she thinks back on her naivety. 'I never wanted you to get hurt, and I promise I wasn't judging you. I … I only wanted you to talk to me about it. You shut me out.'

'I know,' she admits, pained. 'You told me that it was my own guilt that was stopping me from talking to you and you were right about that, too. But honestly, the break-up with Michael was the best thing that could have happened.'

'Yeah?'

'Yeah.' She offers him a hopeful smile. 'It kind of shook Grandma out of her misery.'

James tilts his head in confusion. 'How?'

'I think seeing me so upset and confused gave her a bit of a fright,' Millie tells him. 'When Michael went back to Judith, I was out of a job and spent a lot of time wallowing around the house, heartbroken. Grandma said that seeing me like that made her realise she'd been so caught up in her grief that she'd neglected the loved ones she still had around. I guess she could see that I really needed her. It didn't happen overnight or anything, but she's so much better now. She's got her spark back.'

'That's wonderful,' James says earnestly, looking relieved.

'Yeah, she's got this new lease of life. She's really got into her gardening. The garden looks incredible now, full of colourful flowers. And she swims.'

'She *swims*?'

'She got a swim membership at the local leisure centre and she goes three times a week. She's made some friends there and she's talking about signing up to these other classes they offer.' Millie hesitates. 'She still can't bring herself to watch Eurovision, though.'

'I'm sure that will come with time,' James says gently. 'Don't worry, she'll find her way back to it.'

'I hope so.' Millie pauses, biting her lip. 'She'd love to see you soon. She keeps asking after you. She's missed you popping in.'

'That's sweet of her.' He runs a hand through his hair. 'I've missed chatting to her about everything. She was always a very good guide when it comes to life's problems. Actually, that's not entirely correct' – he chuckles – 'Julie's advice tended to be a little outrageous.'

'I was going to say. Her advice would get us in *more* trouble. Grandpa was the one to go to for gentle wisdom.'

'Very true.' James nods. 'He always knew the right thing to say. He could tell you how to handle any kind of situation, good or bad.'

Millie gives a small smile. 'Mum always says that was the great irony after his death – the only person who would have known how to cope with the change in Grandma was him, and he was the only person we couldn't ask.'

'How are things with your mum?' James asks tentatively.

'Actually, things are … better,' Millie admits. 'We've been talking a lot more recently and she's been making a lot more of an effort.' Millie rubs the back of her neck. 'She even apologised.'

James looks confused. 'You're kidding.'

'I'm not,' she asserts, still finding the truth surprising herself. 'She gave me a serious, full-on apology at Christmas.'

'Of course she did it at Christmas,' he grins. 'The season of goodwill and forgiveness. It would have been disappointing if she'd picked a different time of year to finally realise the error of her ways. Twinkle lights have the power to thaw even the hardest of hearts.'

Millie laughs. 'Exactly. She sat me down and said she'd been thinking about how she should have done more to be there for me. Apparently, losing Grandpa had made her realise that she'd like to rejig her priorities and she may have been a little too focused on work.'

James snorts. 'A *little* too focused.'

'I know.' Millie smiles. 'Anyway, she told me she was always there if ever I needed a chat about anything. And to be fair to her, she's been true to her word. I called her about career advice and, thanks to her guidance, we worked out that I should consider teaching.'

It's strange for Millie to look back now and realise that, although the Sweden weekend last year was truly a disaster, it was a key turning point to get her life back on track. She was released from a toxic relationship; Julie began to emerge from her all-consuming grief; and thanks to Judith firing her, she was forced to get a new job, ending up as a waitress in an upmarket restaurant in the centre of town.

That job was fine to tide her over, but come January, Millie made it her New Year's resolution to find herself the same kind of fulfilment she'd experienced when she was working with Elena and Isaac, even if that meant reaching out to Michael to ask for that excellent reference he'd promised her so she could get another job as a nanny.

After some helpful conversations with Aggie, she decided it was worth applying for the Primary Education with QTS degree at the University of Brighton. When she got the email saying she'd secured a place to start this coming September, she felt a whole new kind of excitement: primary teaching seemed so perfect for her, she wondered why she hadn't considered it before. But then, as Aggie pointed out, this step has come at the right time in her life – maybe she wouldn't have been ready for it before or wouldn't have been so convinced it was the right path.

'Life works in mysterious ways,' Aggie had said, when she came over to toast Millie's course acceptance with her and Julie.

'Doesn't it,' Julie agreed, immensely enjoying the posh Champagne Aggie had brought with her. 'I'm only just learning to trust in that myself.'

Millie knew that evening they were celebrating her achievement, but she'd also had a moment acknowledging how proud she was of the other two women in that room. There had been many obstacles and hiccups along the way, and the three of them were so different, but it felt like they were finally beginning to understand each other and were willing to help each other face the challenges still to come as a family.

Grandpa would have been proud, too.

But Millie's family wasn't quite complete yet. Not without James.

'I'm pleased you're in a good place with your mum. And teaching sounds like a really good idea,' he says. 'Did you say earlier that you were doing a degree in Brighton?'

'Yep, following in your footsteps.'

'You'll love it,' he says, raising his voice over the final chorus, before glancing up at the Eurovision stage as Belgium's performance comes to an end.

'Sorry, you need to get back to work, don't you, and I'm just standing here telling you all this stuff about my life,' Millie says hurriedly.

'No, it's fine,' James insists, turning back to her. 'This,' – he gestures to the space in between them – 'this is more important.'

She feels an overwhelming surge of love for him. After everything that's happened, the distance that formed between them all because of her, he's still reassuring her that she means something to him. His words give her all the courage she needs to finish telling him the truth about how she feels.

'James,' Millie says firmly after taking a deep breath, as though making an important speech at a podium. 'You tried to make me see sense, and instead I pushed you away because I wanted to be blind to it. But I want you to know that no matter what, I'll always be here for you. I know it may not have seemed that way, but it's true. And I've missed you so much and I hope … I really hope we can be friends again.'

He sighs, his forehead creased as he looks deep in thought. For a moment, she's terrified that there's no hope.

But then, he breaks into a smile and holds out his arms.

Filled with a surge of relief, she collapses into him, breathing in his comforting smell, a tear running down her cheek as she feels his arms tighten around her.

'I've missed you, too,' he says simply.

He doesn't say anything more. He doesn't need to. They stand holding each other while 'Beautiful Mess' plays in the background, and Millie feels the weight that's been pressed on her heart all year finally lift.

Watching them, Ingrid nudges Noah.

'You see?' she says to him proudly. 'Eurovision brings people together.'

CHAPTER FIFTEEN

Lisbon, Portugal

2018

Thursday 10 May

'Let me get this straight,' James says slowly, looking at Millie across their table in the Time Out food market, 'you're going to tell Noah how you feel about him *tonight*?'

'That's correct. It's time. I'm taking the jump,' she states.

James and Mark share a look.

'Oh god, I feel nervous enough as it is without you two making me doubt my decision,' Millie huffs, reaching for the plate of cured meats and selecting some slices with her fork. 'I need to know I have your full support or else I'll bottle it.'

'You definitely have mine,' James assures her. 'It's about time you and Noah got together. It's been eight years of longing looks. I'm all for it.'

'Thank you,' Millie says, relieved. 'Mark? Your thoughts, please?'

'I don't really know the guy or your relationship with him, so I'm not sure I'm the best person to ask,' he begins cautiously, prompting James to roll his eyes, 'but what I'd say is to trust your gut. If you think this is the time to tell Noah how you feel, then why not?'

Millie is happy with that answer. It *is* the time to tell him.

Since he moved to England, Noah has been in a lot more regular contact with Millie and they've met up for drinks several times in Brighton and London. Every time they see each other, it's so easy and fun and flirty, and Millie has come to accept that her feelings for him have grown to the point where she's not interested in dating anyone else.

At last, it feels like her life is on track. One year down in her degree, she's enjoying it and on the hunt for a flat to rent with one of her new friends, Tina, somewhere close to her grandma. Not that Julie is encouraging her to stay close; if anything, Julie is excited for Millie to 'spread her wings' and experience living with someone her own age rather than being holed up with her grandmother. Aggie agrees that it's important for Millie's independence to move out from home and has even offered to help with the flat search if she needs.

Millie thanked her, but she can handle it just fine.

There's just one piece of the puzzle missing: Noah. James and Mark's contentment in their relationship has inspired her to make her move, and something Julie said before she left struck a nerve, too.

'Are you sure you won't be watching Eurovision this year?' Millie asked as she gave her grandma a goodbye kiss on the cheek. 'You might see us on TV. Now that James is a big name there, we have incredible seats.'

Julie shook her head. 'I'm still not ready. But you have a wonderful time in Portugal.' She glanced at the framed photo of her and Tom that sat in the middle of the mantelpiece. 'Life is short, darling. Make the most of it and go after what you want. Time slips away faster than you think.'

Millie knows that what she wants is to be with Noah. And she has a good enough inkling that he feels the same way, but is too scared to admit it to himself. They have amazing chemistry and they've ignored it all these years because they've been protecting their friendship. But Julie is right. Life is short. Millie has to take that leap of faith and if it all goes wrong, then at least she can say she tried.

Noah seems in a good place, too. He's doing well in his real estate job in London and he's got into running, so he looks and feels healthier, and – praise the lord – he rid his wardrobe of silk shirts. Whenever she sees him, he's dressed in a suit or a smart shirt with chinos. Millie has observed that he does seem quieter and more introverted now. A little more tense. She puts that down to him getting to grips with his new life in London. In her opinion, he didn't really suit the steady office role he'd landed for himself – she can see his eyes glazing over when she asks about his work. But she can understand why he's sticking with a secure job.

If he and Millie really make a go at being together, she could help him work out if there's something else he'd rather be doing that would make him happier. She knows they would be good together. Right now, their friendship is almost torture for her.

She has to take the risk.

'I'm excited for you, Millie,' James declares. 'Here's to finding love at Eurovision!'

As she giggles and they both take a sip of their drinks, James's phone buzzes. He puts his glass down and digs into his pocket to find it, while Millie asks Mark if he's enjoyed his time so far in Portugal. James has been invited to both rounds of Semi-Finals, as well as the Grand Final this weekend, due to the huge popularity of his website. He took the week off work and managed to convince Mark to join him, promising they could make the most of Lisbon in between the Eurovision events. Millie joined them today and Noah and Ingrid are arriving tomorrow.

On seeing the message is from Zachary, James inhales sharply.

He hasn't heard from him for a long time. Still, just the sight of his name has an effect on James, causing his heart to beat faster and his mouth to go dry.

'What is it?' Mark asks, noticing his reaction.

'Nothing, no one,' James assures him, fumbling with his phone as he attempts to slide it back into his pocket. 'One of my Eurovision contacts.'

'Oh.' Mark looks unimpressed. 'Do they need to bother you during the day? You're going to be there all evening and most of the afternoon, too, probably. I don't really understand why there needs to be so many rounds to this thing – why don't they just do it all in one go on one big night?'

'There have to be Semi-Finals before a final round,' James laughs, nudging him with his elbow. 'Come on, you can't seriously say you didn't enjoy Tuesday night.'

'It was fine. But I'm going to have to sit through the same songs again on Saturday,' he groans, covering his face with his hands. 'It seems very … long.'

James's eyes flicker to Millie, who is keeping her mouth firmly shut.

'Yes, but Saturday night is a completely different atmosphere,' James says as brightly as he can muster. 'It's electric, trust me. And Noah and Ingrid will be there, too, so we'll have a really fun group. You'll love it.'

'I doubt it,' Mark huffs. 'It seems like a waste to be here in Lisbon and be spending our nights in an arena at the same concert.'

'I said you didn't have to come to the Semi-Final tonight,' James responds, growing irritated. 'You can do whatever you want.'

Mark sighs, his expression softening as he reaches for James's hand and squeezes it. 'No, I want to be there. It's important to you. Sorry for being a downer. I'm sure it will all be really fun to experience.'

'The spirit of Eurovision is infectious,' Millie insists, jumping in with an encouraging smile. 'It will get to you, Mark, you wait and see. It's going to be a wonderful week-end ahead, I just know it.'

* * *

Friday 11 May

'I'm sorry, I'm being rude,' Ingrid says, putting her phone face down on the table. 'I had to answer that, but now I'm done. I think.'

'No worries,' Noah says, sitting back with his beer. 'I've been enjoying the view.'

Ingrid glances out the window at the beautiful lights of Lisbon, the city stretching out before them. They've come to a rooftop bar that Mark has chosen, one of the many 'must-see' places listed in his Lisbon guidebook that he's scribbled a star next to. Normally, Noah prefers to stumble upon places while wandering the streets of a new city, rather than aim for the tourist traps, but it was clear that Mark did not agree with that way of doing things. And now he's here, Noah has to give it to him – it really is spectacular.

'I figured you might be messaging the new love of your life,' Noah tells Ingrid, tearing his eyes away from the view to offer her a mischievous smile. 'Who is it this time? I hope they're good enough for you. I don't think Andrea was anything close.'

'She definitely wasn't,' Ingrid confirms, grimacing at the memories. 'At least we weren't together too long before she went off with that hot drummer. I think they're still in a relationship, too, which is something. It would have been worse if she'd cheated on me with someone who wasn't even worth it.'

'Generous of you to find that silver lining,' Noah mutters.

'There is someone new on the scene, though – a very charming saxophonist. But we're taking it slowly.'

Noah raises his eyebrows. 'Yeah?'

She shrugs. 'Sort of. I'm quite impatient about these things.'

Noah laughs, shaking his head. 'You know, Ingrid, I really admire that about you.'

'My lack of self-control?'

'Your dedication to falling in love, actually,' he corrects, taking her by surprise. 'I know that sounds strange, but even when you have your heart broken, you're not willing to give up on it. It's … amazing.'

'It's the dreamer in me,' she acknowledges with a knowing smile. 'But I have to admit that you didn't catch me in the middle of messaging the saxophonist. I had to answer a work email. It's a very busy time at the moment. We're opening a new production in a few weeks and everything that could go wrong is going wrong.'

'You'll sort it out, I know,' Noah says firmly. 'If anyone can handle it, you can.'

'Yes, I hope so.' She exhales. 'It's scary. This is the first production I'm the lead stage manager on. Carl has left it in my hands; he's trusting me to get it right. If it all goes wrong—'

'It won't go wrong,' Noah assures her, reaching over to squeeze her arm. 'You're THE Ingrid Vogel, remember?'

She laughs as she recalls the night they met in 2010, burying her head in her hands.

'Oh my god, I can't believe I tried to get in past security by saying that! That poor guy having to put up with people like me shouting my name in his face as though it meant something.'

'It does mean something! Look at you, you're the stage manager of one of the leading theatres in Berlin,' Noah reminds her. 'I'm sure they'd usher you in now without a second's thought.'

'Because stage managers are *so* famous.' She shakes her head, still chuckling at the memory. 'It's funny. I really did want to be famous and now, I don't want that at all. Much better to be in the real world. I was right to let go of my dream to be a singer. I was a shit songwriter, too. You know what doesn't rhyme? "Appear" and "Forever". But I sang them funny so that it might work. It did not.'

Noah laughs along with her, but he feels a little forlorn at Ingrid's lost dream. He knows she's happy now, but there is something melancholy about accepting a childhood dream isn't going to happen. All those hopes and big ideas fade to nothing.

Maybe the reason it hits him hard is because he's accepted the same fate: entering the real world and shutting the door on unrealistic ambitions. He hates working in real estate, but here he is, doing well in it in London and making his family proud.

'There you are!' Millie cries, plonking herself down on the chair in between them. 'I went to the loo and then I tried looking for James, but I can't find him anywhere!'

'He left with Mark about half an hour ago,' Noah reminds her, laughing. 'They didn't want a late night. You said goodbye to them, remember?'

'Oh yeah!' She slaps her forehead. 'Whoops!'

'Uh oh, how many shots have you had?' Ingrid giggles, reaching over to stroke Millie's hair, tucking it behind her ears.

'Only one or two,' she replies innocently, before pretending to whisper to Ingrid behind her hand. '*Or four.*'

'I'm going to go hunt down some water,' Ingrid decides, picking up her phone as it starts ringing. 'And I have to take this. It's a producer. I'll be back with water in a bit.'

Millie gives her a thumbs-up and then gazes out at the view in amazement.

'There are *so many* lights,' she observes.

'It's a big city,' Noah replies, amused. He's happy she's having a good time.

'It's so beautiful here in Lisbon,' she declares, going to gesture at the view but hitting her hand hard against the glass. 'Ow.'

'You OK?' Noah checks, raising his eyebrows.

'Of course. Of course, I'm OK.' She turns to smile at him. 'Are you OK, Noah?'

'I'm good thanks, Millie,' he laughs, sipping his beer. 'Glad to be here with you.'

'I'm glad to be here with *you*,' she echoes, reaching forwards and pressing her finger into his chest. 'You know why?'

'Why?'

'You're my favourite.'

He smiles at her. 'You're my favourite, too.'

She suddenly frowns. 'Where did Ingrid go?'

'She's gone to take a call and get some water.'

'Uh oh.' Millie winces. 'Is that because she thinks I'm too drunk?'

'No, I think all of us could use some,' he assures her.

'I had to have a lot of drinks today.'

'Sure, it is Eurovision weekend. Good to blow off steam.'

She shakes her head dramatically, her hair swishing across her face. 'No, for a different reason. I needed it for courage.'

He gives her a strange look. 'Why would you need to drink for courage?'

She squints at him suspiciously, attempting to focus on his face.

'I … I don't think I should tell you, yet. I need to check with James. I'll go find him.'

Millie stands up too quickly and stumbles. Noah leaps to his feet and grabs her arms, steadying her before she falls. Regaining her balance by gripping him tightly, she tilts her head up to see Noah's face close to hers.

'Are you all right?' he asks.

Before she can lose her nerve, she reaches up to hold his head in her hands and pulls his face towards her, kissing him right on the lips. As he starts to kiss her back, she leans into him, his hands sliding down to her waist, his fingers gripping her as though he won't let her go. She's waited for this for so long and it's perfect.

Until suddenly, it shatters. 'I can't do this,' he whispers, breaking away from her. His brow is creased, and in that moment, she's not sure if he's telling her or himself. '*I can't do this.*'

* * *

Saturday 12 May

Millie wakes up the next morning in a pool of sweat in her hotel bed, consumed by a painfully heady mix of anxiety, shame and nausea.

She kissed Noah and he recoiled from her. Oh god, there is no chance she can get out of bed today and face him! She'll have to stay right here ... forever. She groans into her pillow, muttering 'Why? *Why?*' over and over, begging time to go back so she can save herself from this agonising state of humiliation.

The only positive thing she can cling on to is that, for a moment, she's pretty sure he kissed her back. She was very drunk, yes, but she's sure of it. He definitely kissed her back. But then, he whipped his head away and held her at arm's length, repeating, 'I can't do this.'

He must have been physically repulsed by her. This is Noah, for goodness' sake. He's got with almost every girl in Europe. But not Millie. He turned her down. Flat.

She will have to make this bed her new home, because she is never leaving it. Never.

Curling up into a ball, she manages to fall asleep again and wakes up to a loud knocking on her door.

She sits bolt upright and whimpers, planting her palm across her forehead as it throbs mercilessly at her moving too fast. At least she feels better after that extra doze than she did earlier. The sickness has ebbed, she just needs to get rid of this headache.

Whoever is at her door knocks again. She stares at it in horror.

It wouldn't be Noah, would it?

No. No, it can't be. He's in a different hotel. She remembers Ingrid taking her home. Pushing herself up from the mattress and letting the sheets fall off her, she checks she's wearing pyjamas – which she is in a manner of speaking: a t-shirt and pants – and gingerly creeps up to the door to look through the peephole. She breathes a sigh of relief and opens it, allowing Ingrid to stroll in holding two cups of coffee.

'How are you feeling?' Ingrid asks, grimacing as Millie plods back to bed and falls face down onto her pillows. 'I thought as much.'

'It's not a good day.'

'Here, this is for you if you can stomach it,' Ingrid says, putting one of the coffees down on the bedside table while she perches on the edge of the bed. 'You want some paracetamol? I have some in my bag.'

'Yes, please,' Millie whines, forcing herself up into a sitting position. 'I think I'm going to need some food soon. Plain toast or something.'

'That can be arranged. We're all meeting for brunch soon, anyway.'

'We are? What time is it?' Millie asks, gratefully taking the tablets and washing them down with gulps of water from the bottle Ingrid offers her.

'Nearly half eleven. We're meeting at twelve, that's why I thought I'd come and get you and check how you were getting on.'

'When I woke up earlier I thought I was going to die. I feel slightly more human after a lie-in,' Millie answers honestly. 'I don't think I should go to brunch.'

'You'll feel better once you've showered. James and Mark are at a museum, so we'll meet them after at the—'

'Wait. What?' Millie looks at her in confusion. 'James has gone to a museum? He hates museums. On school trips, the two of us would literally run through them and then spend the entire time in the gift shop.'

'I think it was Mark's idea.'

Millie nods. 'Makes sense. They're so grown up.'

'We're going to meet them at the brunch restaurant, and I said we'd meet Noah downstairs at reception. He has to walk past here from his hotel anyway,' Ingrid explains, holding out the coffee for Millie.

Taking a sip, Millie sets down the cup again.

'Ingrid, I can't go to brunch,' she announces.

'The smell of the coffee might not be helping, but you do need some food, so—'

'No.' Millie holds up her hand. 'I'm not saying I'm too hungover to go to brunch. I'm saying I can't go to brunch because Noah will be there.'

Ingrid gives her a strange look. 'Why not?'

At least this confirms that Noah didn't tell Ingrid what Millie did. He spared her the embarrassment and kept it to himself, which is something. But Millie can't handle this on her own; she needs all the support she can get. Since James has abandoned her to look at a load of old artefacts, Ingrid is her confidante of choice.

'I did something stupid last night,' she begins, scrunching up her face and closing her eyes. 'I kissed Noah.'

Ingrid gasps, her face lighting up. 'You did? FINALLY!'

'No, no, it's not good,' Millie informs her regretfully. 'He stopped me. I kissed him and he pushed me away.'

Her mouth dropping open in surprise, Ingrid blinks at her. 'But … are you sure?'

'Yes, I'm sure,' Millie snaps. 'It's hard to mix up someone kissing you back with someone physically recoiling.'

'That doesn't make any sense,' Ingrid mumbles, her forehead creasing. 'You two are meant to be together.'

'Obviously not.' Millie's eyes fall to her hands in her lap. 'I feel like such an idiot.'

'You're *not* an idiot,' Ingrid says firmly. 'Everyone knows you two are a great match. Well … James and I know that, anyway. Maybe he didn't want to kiss you because you had had a few drinks. He was being responsible. He didn't want to take advantage.'

Millie sighs. 'I don't think so. He's not exactly responsible the rest of the time, is he.'

'With you it's different. You mean a lot to him. And he's changed. He is much more grown up now, I think.'

'I don't know,' Millie says thoughtfully. 'Either way, I don't think I can face him today.'

'Yes, you can.' Ingrid jumps up determinedly. 'You are going to get up, shower, get dressed and look nice, and then we are going to have a fun day out in Lisbon before we get to go VIP to the Grand Final of Eurovision tonight. We are not letting Noah ruin your weekend.'

Millie bites her lip. 'But how do I act around him?'

'Perfectly normal, like everything is exactly as you planned,' Ingrid directs. 'He will realise his mistake. Now, up you get. The shower is waiting.'

Not taking no for an answer, Ingrid ushers Millie out of bed and across the room to the bathroom, where she leans across the bath to turn on the shower for her, pulls the curtain across the rail, and then steps back, checking her watch.

'You've got about ten minutes in there. I'll knock when you need to get out.'

Unable to protest, Millie nods, before nervously asking, 'Is this how scary you are when you're stage manager?'

'Oh, trust me, I'm even worse. Ten minutes before curtain's up,' Ingrid grins, marching out and shutting the bathroom door behind her.

* * *

Noah's message doesn't make any sense. *We're downstairs waiting in the hotel lobby.*

Ingrid thinks it must be a typo.

'Or maybe he met James and Mark on the way?' Millie wonders aloud, before carefully applying lipstick.

'The museum they went to is in the opposite direction,' Ingrid says. 'It would make no sense for them to come back this way before going to brunch. He must have typed "we" by mistake.'

Millie has a bad feeling about this. Is Noah so embarrassed by her actions last night that he's invited a bunch of random strangers to join them for the day so he doesn't have to risk being alone in her company? That wouldn't be so out of character. He makes friends easily – he used to have a new crew in every city he landed in.

She really hopes that he isn't making a big deal of this. Ingrid has reassured her enough the last few minutes while she's been getting ready that it was one of those silly drunken moments that are forgotten about. Millie wasn't so sure, but then she thought back to the time that he tried to kiss her in Vienna. That had been brushed over by both of them, so why couldn't this?

And she doesn't want to get her hopes up, but there might be something in what Ingrid said about Noah not wanting to take advantage of her. She knows there's a spark between them. Ingrid and James have both claimed to witness it,

213

and Mark was right about knowing when to trust your gut. Millie can't have made everything up – she and Noah have something special. When he was at the lowest point in his life, he turned to her. That's got to mean something.

It was wrong of her to lunge at him last night. He might have thought she was doing it flippantly and would regret it in the morning. She needs to be sober and in control when she tells him how she feels, so that he knows she means it. And she needs to explain to him that she understands it's scary for both of them to admit how they really feel, especially when it puts their friendship at risk, but they have to take the chance. She wants to do this properly. It was never supposed to be a drunken kiss on a rooftop bar.

Ultimately, she's glad he stopped her.

Sort of.

'Are you ready?' Ingrid asks.

'Yes,' she replies, checking her reflection one last time. 'I'm ready.'

Feeling the need to look particularly good today, she's wearing a red off-the-shoulder summer day dress with ankle boots, and natural make-up with just a touch of mascara, some bronzer and a nude lipstick, leaving her hair down. She's grown it long again, her dark curls falling over her shoulders. With a last spritz of perfume and balancing her sunglasses on the top of her head, she follows Ingrid out of the room and down the corridor.

Millie's room is on the first floor, so they pass the lifts and head straight for the stairs that lead down into reception. When they get to the top, they find Noah is waiting at the bottom for them. He looks up at her. His eyes widen, the corners of his mouth lifting into a smile. With Ingrid at her side, she begins to descend the staircase towards him.

'Hi,' he says softly, when she reaches the bottom.

'Hi,' she replies, gazing up at him.

'Oh my god, the *state* of this reception.' A clipped British voice cries shrilly nearby. 'There is so much dust! I can *literally* see it on the floor. I would not like to stay in a place like this. Your friends should complain.'

Millie turns to see a beautiful statuesque blonde woman with delicate features and plump lips approaching them in a white mini dress, towering shoes and a wide-brimmed sunhat. She stops next to Noah before taking his hand and looking at him expectantly.

'Aren't you going to introduce us?' she prompts.

'Yes, sorry,' Noah replies, flustered. 'Millie and Ingrid, I'd like you to meet Victoria. She flew in this morning. She's … my girlfriend.'

Millie thought the nausea from this morning had disappeared, but suddenly she feels like she might just throw up all over Victoria's immaculate designer heels.

CHAPTER SIXTEEN

Noah had so many opportunities to mention Victoria to Millie.

There was the time Millie came to see him in London for drinks, by which point he'd been on several dates with Victoria. He and Millie chatted for hours about each other's lives. He could have brought her up then. Or he could have said something the weekend he travelled to Brighton and he and Millie sat on the pebbled beach drinking wine out of paper cups and eating ice cream. Victoria and Noah had been officially in a relationship for months by that stage.

He and Millie messaged often, too. She asked him how he was on a weekly basis, what he'd been up to, how his week was looking, what he was doing at the weekend. He'd had countless opportunities to tell her he was in a serious relationship.

But he hadn't been able to do it.

He'd given himself many excuses as to why, but when he saw the look on her face as he introduced Victoria as his girlfriend, none of them seemed near good enough. He had really fucked up. Millie looked shocked. Mortified. Betrayed.

He hates himself for springing this on her.

Although, technically, it's not like she should care. For all he knows, she doesn't. Maybe he misread her emotions at the hotel and she was just surprised that he had invited someone else on their Eurovision weekend without telling any of them. She might even be happy for him, for all he knows.

When she appeared at the top of those stairs, he couldn't take his eyes off her. It's the dress she's wearing today, the way it shows off her bare shoulders and collar bones – it threw him for a moment. And as she descended the steps, there was something about the way she was looking at him that made him nervous, his heart beating a little bit quicker, his breath catching in his throat. It took him a moment before he remembered that this was Millie, his *friend*. He had a girlfriend.

He really likes Victoria. She's great. She's good for him. Perfect for him, really. She's beautiful and smart and elegant, but she also motivates him to be better and healthier, more in control of his life – something he hasn't felt before.

Victoria works on the social media team for an influencer marketing agency and gets up a couple of hours before she goes to the office to go to the gym every morning for a workout with her personal fitness instructor, encouraging Noah to get up at the same time to either join her at the gym or go for a run, an activity he's been getting into. Both of their flats are in West London, so it doesn't matter if he's at home or staying at hers, he enjoys a similar run along the Thames, clearing and calming his mind before a long day at work.

Their evenings and weekends are always packed full of events, whether it's dinners with friends at the coolest new restaurants, art gallery openings, charity fundraisers, or occasionally one of Victoria's work events, where an influencer is launching their latest fashion collaboration. Noah doesn't love those evenings and feels like a bit of a spare part, spending a lot of his night trying to dodge out of being in the background of glamorous attendees' selfies, but Victoria is always sure to schedule in at least one 'self-care' evening, where they're not allowed to make any plans and instead stay in and cook together or watch a series cuddled on the sofa.

Noah and Victoria make sense. He's happy; she makes him feel like a better person. Soon, he's going to suggest they move in with each other. She's been dropping quite a few hints along those lines anyway, so he's not too worried about being shot down.

He only wishes he'd been brave enough to tell Millie, so he wasn't in the situation he's in now, sitting across from her at brunch, trying to read her expression, an impossible task with her eyes hidden behind her sunglasses. He should have insisted they ate at a table inside instead, so she'd have to remove them.

'That ball was last month, hosted by a friend of mine, Lady Jemima Russett, who's launching a new swimwear range. We grew up together,' Victoria says, concluding her explanation to Mark's polite question about the kind of events her agency hosts. 'It went very well. It was covered in the *Tatler* society pages; you might have seen it? There was a photo of me and Noah in there. *So* embarrassing.'

'I must have missed that issue,' Millie remarks. 'And did you two meet through a work event?'

'No!' Victoria giggles, surprised that Millie doesn't already know their story. 'We first met in Australia. Christmas 2016. But we didn't get together until Noah moved to England.'

'You met when you were back living in *Australia*?' Millie asks Noah, trying not to sound as bewildered as she feels. 'That long ago?'

Noah doesn't say anything, downing the last few gulps of the Bellini that Victoria ordered on his behalf.

'Do you have family in Australia, too, Victoria?' James asks, wishing he could whisk Millie away from this horrible situation.

'God no!' she says with a wave of her hand. 'I was there for some winter sun. We spent some time in Sydney and then travelled down to Melbourne for a few days before heading to Tasmania. When we were in Melbourne, I met Noah and the rest of the Pearces – we attended a few of the same events. Our families run in the same circles, if you know what I mean,' she adds with a chuckle, as though she's stating the obvious.

'I don't know what you mean,' Ingrid says bluntly.

'Well, my parents own a few boutique hotels in the UK and abroad, and Noah's family have their incredible property development business, of course.' She hesitates, scanning across all of their blank expressions. 'You must know that the Pearce family own a very sizeable portion of Melbourne!'

Exchanging bewildered looks, the group turns to look at Noah. Furiously blushing, he shifts uncomfortably in his seat, and then holds up his glass to a passing waiter, tapping it on the side before addressing the others.

'I don't know about you, but I could use a top-up!' He laughs nervously.

'Your family owns half of Melbourne?' James asks, his jaw practically on the floor.

'No! That's a *huge* exaggeration,' he insists.

'Not that huge,' Victoria mutters into her glass as she takes a sip of her drink.

'As Victoria said, my dad owns a property development company. It's successful, so I guess … I guess my family is quite well known in Australia,' Noah says, attempting to explain it in a way that doesn't make him cringe at every word and very much failing in that task.

'How well known?' James presses. 'Well known like people in property know who you are? Or well known in a you-could-have-your-own-reality-show way?'

'His mum was actually invited to join the Real Housewives franchise!' Victoria reveals excitedly. 'But she turned it down.'

'Of course she turned it down,' Noah grumbles. 'Look, it's not important. It's not … who I am.'

'I can't believe you never told us about this,' Millie says quietly, in a way that makes Noah's heart sink. She'll see him differently now. It's always the same.

'You should have googled him,' Victoria says with a shrug.

'I don't usually feel the need to google my friends,' Millie comments, unable to hide a bitter edge to her tone.

'Seriously? I google everyone I meet!' Victoria leans in conspiratorially. 'You will not believe the kind of shit that's out there on people.'

'Why don't we move on and make a plan for the day ahead, yeah?' Noah says suddenly, accompanied by a clap of his hands that makes Victoria jump. 'We've got a day to explore Lisbon, so we should finish up brunch soon and get going. Lots to fit in!'

'As long as we don't have to do anything that involves Eurovision,' Victoria rules. 'It's bad enough you're dragging me to the Final tonight. It's so *tacky*.' She turns to James apologetically. 'No offence. I know you're, like, into it.'

'Another Bellini for you, sir?' a waiter announces, passing Noah his refill.

'Couldn't have come at a better time,' Noah mutters, thanking him and downing it all in one go. He places the empty glass on the table while Victoria looks on in astonishment.

'Well,' Mark mutters under his breath, gesturing to the waiter for the bill, 'today is going to be interesting.'

* * *

Today was a disaster.

James is so grateful to finally be in the safe haven of the Lisbon Arena reporting on the Grand Final with the excuse of having to work so he doesn't need to talk to anybody. As always, they are in the midst of an exhilarating atmosphere and, here in the Eurovision audience, surrounded by screaming fans waving their flags proudly in the air, he feels like nothing can bring him down, not even the cantankerous moods of his group.

The whole afternoon was *excruciating*. James wishes that he could blame it entirely on the presence of Victoria, but Mark had a part to play in it, too. His boyfriend hadn't missed any opportunity to make a dig about Eurovision, and whenever Victoria had gone off on a tangent about how awful it was, Mark had smiled smugly as though delighted that he wasn't the only one thinking it. He could at least *pretend* to enjoy the trip for James's sake. If he'd have known that Mark was going to be like this, James would rather he hadn't come.

James understands that Eurovision is not everyone's cup of tea, but that's no excuse to ruin it for those who do love it. As he's said to Mark a hundred times, at the core of this event is fun and goodwill. Mocking that just seems mean.

Luckily Mark's sneering at the contest largely went unnoticed by everyone else, eclipsed by Victoria's willingness to offer her belittling opinion on the matter.

'It's so strange how much people love it. The music is awful and don't get me started on those garish costumes,' she drawled, when Ingrid and Millie had insisted they stop to buy a *pastel de nata*, a local custard tart, from a shop that had Eurovision posters and the Portuguese flag draped across the window. 'Why do all the singers go so over the top? They're popstars, aren't they? Don't they have stylists?'

'I think they want to stand out,' Millie countered, carefully peeling the paper wrapping from around the side of her tart. 'It's not a fashion show. It's an excuse to go as loud and brash as you like – it's fun to dazzle up there on the stage. It helps to be memorable, too, when it comes to the voting process. A lot of the most daring costumes have become iconic.'

Victoria snorted. 'Iconic in *some* circles, perhaps. Amazing the lack of taste people can have.'

'Do you want a custard tart?' Noah asked Victoria in an attempt to change the conversation.

She wrinkled her nose, looking at James as he took a large bite of his, custard spilling out onto his plate below. 'No, thank you. God knows what's in that.'

James paused his chewing, stealing a glance at Millie, who rolled her eyes when Victoria wasn't looking and then pointedly took an even bigger bite than he had, making him smile.

Things only got worse as the day dragged on. They'd climbed to the top of the Panteão Nacional church for a view of the city, and Victoria and Noah had a not-so-secret squabble on the way up because she wasn't wearing the right type of footwear and Noah had specifically told her that morning to wear flats.

'I didn't realise we'd be *hiking* on a city break, Noah,' Millie overheard Victoria hiss at him as she wandered past, pretending not to notice.

When they reached the top, Noah was under strict instructions to take a number of photos of Victoria in poses from different angles. When he was finished, he took a moment to enjoy the view while she scrolled through the images and scrutinised them. Finding a couple she liked, she thanked him, kissed him on the lips and then the two of them made their way back down again holding hands.

'I don't think she actually looked at the view,' Ingrid observed to James, Mark and Millie as they watched her totter away.

'She'll be able to admire it later in the background of all those pictures she has of herself,' Mark remarked, causing James to snigger.

But the dire afternoon peaked when they tiredly collapsed into the chairs of a terrace bar in Commerce Square. Just as they were agreeing that they would have liked more time to roam the city, a group of Eurovision fans ambled past them, all of them dressed in multi-coloured sequined body suits with flags draped over their shoulders. They were chatting animatedly, their laughter echoing across the vast square, not afraid to draw attention to themselves.

'They look amazing!' James exclaimed. 'I have to get a photo for my socials.'

He jumped up and rushed over to them, the others looking on as he asked for their permission to get a picture. The group happily agreed, huddling together and holding their flags up in the air, beaming at the camera.

'Ingrid, you're missing them,' Millie said, nudging her as Ingrid typed furiously into her phone. 'Look!'

Ingrid tore her eyes away from her emails to glance up briefly. She smiled and then got back to her work, explaining that a very important prop had gone missing from backstage and the whole company was panicking about it. James strolled back to his chair and sat down, scrolling through the photos he'd just taken.

'These are great,' he said smugly.

'Those people look ridiculous,' Victoria sneered, stirring her Aperol spritz. 'They obviously don't own mirrors.'

'Victoria—' Noah began in a warning tone.

'What? Look at them!' She gestured at the group as they made their way across the square, their sequins glinting in the sunlight. 'I mean, it's so … *vulgar*. I don't think I've ever seen so many sequins in my life.'

'Oh, that's nothing. We've seen much worse,' Millie informed her breezily.

'You *are* joking.'

Millie raised her eyebrows at her. 'Wait until tonight. It wouldn't be Eurovision without glitter and sequins. Think about ABBA.'

James gasped. 'Do you remember that woman we saw in the bar in Copenhagen with the sequin dress that had twinkly lights all over it?'

'Yes!' Ingrid cried, snapping her head up. 'It was *amazing*. I'd forgotten about her.'

'I think she must have made it herself, you know,' James mused. 'I can't imagine where you'd find a sequin light-up dress with those fabulous shoulder-pads.'

'It really was something,' Millie recalled, giggling.

'A dress that lights up?' Victoria pretended to stick two fingers down her throat. 'Just when I thought Eurovision couldn't get any tackier, you tell me there are light-up dresses.'

'Victoria, come on,' Noah groaned, rubbing his forehead, obviously noticing the flashes of irritation crossing his friends' features. 'Don't say stuff like that.'

'Like what?'

'You know,' he said sternly. 'That Eurovision is tacky. Just leave it.'

'But it is,' she huffed, affronted by his scolding. 'And I don't know why you're being so precious about it. You told me the other day you don't care about Eurovision.'

'I didn't say that exactly—' Noah protested.

'Yes, you did,' Victoria pointed out, crossing her arms, too annoyed at him to care that she was embarrassing him. 'You agreed it was a load of silly bullshit.'

The table fell into silence.

Noah winced at her words and looked down at his shoes. Millie pursed her lips. Ingrid kept her eyes on her phone, her jaw clenching at the awkwardness of it all. James felt personally stung. Not only was this supposed to be a cherished tradition for their group, it was him who had got everyone tickets for the Grand Final tonight thanks to his website *and* he'd had to get Victoria in last minute since Noah hadn't told anyone about her existence. Noah's alleged disdain for the contest felt a little bit ungrateful.

James ended up excusing himself from the table shortly afterwards, saying he needed to get ready for the Final, and Mark accompanied him back to the hotel.

Mark waited until they were out of earshot to start laughing, remarking that Victoria had been 'hilarious'. James agreed they should laugh it off, but it would have been nice if Mark had been a little more sensitive. When James made a comment about how Victoria was not going to enjoy the long night of Eurovision ahead of her, Mark shrugged and said, 'Yeah, but you can leave whenever you want, right? It's not like people have to stay until the end.'

The way he said it heavily implied his own desires and James was left wondering yet again why Mark had agreed to this trip in the first place.

But now James is here in the audience, he's happy to do his best to forget about the earlier debacle and put all his focus on enjoying the music and the ambiance of the arena. In fact, there's a group of Brits right next to them with Union Jacks painted across their faces, and they're jumping up and down exultantly, singing at the top of their lungs along with the UK's entry SuRie. As she warbles about how storms don't last forever, striking purple lights shimmer behind her. It is a song that's impossible not to dance to, and so James has high hopes for the UK this year. The whole arena seems to be bellowing out that catchy chorus.

He's writing as much on his blog when he gets a tap on his shoulder.

'Hang on, Millie,' he shouts over the music. 'Let me finish this sentence and then I'll be with you.'

'Take your time,' comes the reply.

James freezes. That's not Millie. He spins around to see Zachary right in front of him.

'Oh my god!' James gasps.

'Hi James,' Zachary says with a wide grin.

'Zachary,' James breathes, mirroring his smile, struck by a wave of nerves and excitement. 'Hi. Thanks for your text the other day. I did look out for you at the Semi-Final on Thursday, but I couldn't—'

'We had some issues that I had to help with, so I was running about the place, but I was hopeful I'd be able to track you down tonight.' Zachary pauses. 'It's been a long time. You look great.'

'So do you,' James replies, taking him in. His mop of brown hair has been cut and styled, which suits him much better, and he's clean-shaven now. 'You got rid of the beard.'

'Yeah.' Zachary's hand flies to his chin, stroking it. 'What do you think?'

'It's better. Not that I didn't like the beard. You looked great, but you know … it's nice to …' – James gestures at Zachary's face, trying to work out how to put it without sounding creepy – 'you have cheekbones that are too good to hide.'

Zachary smiles modestly. 'It was too much maintenance, anyway. Hey, congratulations on your website. It's doing so well.'

'I have you to thank for it,' James says, holding up the VIP pass hanging round his neck. 'The blog was all your idea, remember?'

'I knew you could do it,' Zachary beams.

'Yeah.' James hesitates. 'I really appreciate my website's loyal fans.'

'I'm sorry?'

'There are certain people who read my content and often comment on it, and it spurs me on to keep making it better. Some of them have followed my posts right from the start and their encouragement … well, it kept me going,' James concludes, scrutinising Zachary's expression.

Feigning innocence at first, Zachary can't help but allow a mischievous smile.

'NumberOneEuroFan?' James asks quietly.

Zachary nods.

'So I owe even more to you than I thought,' James admits.

'You owe your success to *you*,' Zachary insists. 'Let me ask, obviously the EBU know that it's you behind it, but why do you keep it going anonymously? You should tell the world who you are. I think the fans of your website would enjoy getting to know you.'

'I've been thinking about it,' James admits. 'But it seems … I don't know. Maybe I've built it up too much in my head. I'm scared of what people will think.'

'Don't ever let what other people think get in your way,' Zachary says, reaching out to put his hand on his arm. 'You should be proud of who you are and what you've achieved. Nobody should make you feel anything less.'

James swallows the lump that rises to his throat at Zachary's touch.

'Hey,' Mark says, appearing next to James and putting his hand round his waist. 'Everything OK?'

Zachary drops his hand and steps back.

'Yes,' James squeaks, before clearing his throat to regain control of the pitch of his voice. 'Mark, this is Zachary. He's an old friend. He works for Eurovision.'

'Nice to meet you,' Mark says, holding out his hand.

Zachary shakes it. 'And you.'

'How are things with your other half? Nikolas, is it?' James asks with a fixed smile, feeling the heat rise to his face.

'We broke up,' Zachary says, putting his hands in his pockets.

'Shit. Sorry.'

'It was a while ago now,' Zachary informs him. 'A mutual decision. No hard feelings.'

There's a pause in conversation. James tries to think of something to say, but his brain is suddenly scrambled. Thankfully, Zachary manages to keep his cool.

'So, Mark, are you enjoying your night?'

Mark hesitates. 'Bits of it.'

When Zachary looks confused, James jumps in to explain: 'He's not the biggest fan of Eurovision.'

'Ah, I see.' Zachary nods. 'Hopefully by the end of the show you will have changed your mind. It's a great spectacle and a lot of fun. It wins over even its biggest cynics.'

'Maybe,' Mark replies, but it's obvious he disagrees.

'I should get back to work,' James blurts out.

'Sure. Me too. Anyway, it was good to see you,' Zachary says.

James smiles at him. 'And you.'

'Have a good night,' he concludes, addressing both James and Mark, before turning on his heel and leaving them. James watches him go.

Giving James a kiss on the cheek, Mark returns his attention to the performance up on the stage so that James can get back to his reporting.

James lets his fingers hover over his phone screen as he works out what to write next, desperately trying to convince himself that the butterflies flitting about his stomach have been put into motion by the man standing next to him and not the one walking away.

* * *

Millie had to get out of the arena.

She can't take any more of Victoria's complaining. Ever since they got to the arena tonight, Victoria has been firing off snide comments. Millie can't believe she's about to admit to this, but she's *really* not enjoying Eurovision.

Everything is off. She has no idea where Ingrid is – she got a phone call from the theatre, left to take it outside and hasn't come back. James is too busy live-blogging to enjoy the show with her and keeps telling her 'one minute' whenever she tries to get his attention. Mark is clearly hating every moment, barely saying a word and standing by himself. And Noah and Victoria …

Ugh.

Millie considers leaving and heading to the hotel. She's tired from a big night yesterday and a busy day today, and there's no point in forcing herself to have a good time when she's surrounded by people who don't want to be here. She takes out her phone to look at a map to work out the best way of getting back.

'What are you doing out here?'

She turns round at Noah's voice. She's relieved to see he's alone.

'I needed some air,' she explains, folding her arms.

'I'm sorry about Victoria,' Noah says, his forehead creasing. 'What she said just then—'

'About how she was in a room surrounded by the epitome of bad taste?' Millie raises her eyebrows. 'Or are you talking about the other thing she said, when I told her about how my grandparents met. What was it? Oh yeah, I believe her words were, "oh dear".'

He grimaces. 'She didn't mean it like it sounded.'

'Really? Because it sounded like she thought the way my grandparents met was tragic.'

Noah sighs. 'Sometimes she doesn't think before she speaks. She can be a bit harsh. She knows her own mind.'

Millie gives him a strange look. 'OK.'

They fall into silence.

Noah shouldn't have come out here. He doesn't know what to say.

'Why didn't you tell me about her?' Millie demands to know. She might as well take advantage of the fact they're alone to get some answers. 'We talk all the time and you never mentioned her once.'

'I didn't know how to tell you.'

She baulks. 'What's that supposed to mean? It's not hard to tell someone you have a girlfriend.'

'I know, but I wasn't sure it was serious at first, and then I … I don't know. It never came up. And I was worried you'd judge me,' he adds, fully aware it's a terrible excuse.

'Judge you,' she repeats, aghast. 'For *what*?'

'Look at how you've reacted to her today,' he points out. 'She comes from a certain background and I didn't want you thinking—'

'You didn't tell me about her because she's *posh*?' Millie says in disbelief.

'No! Well, sort of,' Noah says, flushing. 'Because then you might find out about my whole family thing—'

'More secrets,' Millie spits, the anger she's suppressed all day rising through her. 'Why did you never tell us about who you are? I feel like such an idiot.'

'Oh, I'm sorry, Millie, I should have led with "Hi, I'm Noah and I'm rich",' he says sarcastically, agitated by her

231

anger and becoming defensive. 'I don't like shouting about it because people tend to judge you on that sort of thing.'

'I feel like I don't know you at all. I feel like you've been lying to me all year. Pretending to be one person in front of me and another in front of anyone else.'

'What are you talking about?' Noah frowns.

'When we speak you tell me how miserable you are working in real estate, but Victoria told me earlier that you're gunning for a promotion. She says you're going to get it and that when you do, you're going to go to Paris to celebrate.'

'So?'

Millie flings her hands up in the air. 'So, what are you *doing*, Noah? You're not even trying to do what you're genuinely interested in; you're settling for a career that you hate!'

'There is nothing that I'm genuinely interested in,' he claps back.

'That's not true! Photography was—'

'Come on, Millie, that is not realistic,' he insists. 'You don't understand, I could never consider photography seriously as a career!'

'Why not?' she challenges.

'Because my dad would cut me off the moment he found out,' he cries. 'If I don't do what he wants me to do, then I'm out!'

Millie blinks at him. 'But … why would that be so bad?'

'*What?*'

'Why would that be so bad?' she repeats, softening her voice, taking a step towards him. 'You don't need your father's money, Noah. Most people don't. I know you're used to a certain lifestyle, but you could make some changes. You have to make your own way in the world.

You could do what you wanted, rather than relying on your parents' financial support and being stuck in a job you hate. Why are you so afraid to stand on your own two feet?'

Noah's chest is visibly rising up and down as he breathes heavily. His jaw clenches.

'I tried that, remember?' he croaks. 'I tried doing my own thing and enjoying life and I was a mess. Travelling around without any direction—'

'You weren't really trying, then,' Millie interrupts impatiently. 'I'm guessing you managed to do all that travelling thanks to your dad's money, anyway. I'm talking about *really* trying. You could apply for a photography course or get in touch with that photographer who offered you an apprenticeship all that time ago. There are so many options that you—'

'Millie, stop,' he demands, holding up his hands and stepping back from her. 'Just stop. I am never going to be a photographer. I have my life now and I am happy with it. I have a decent-paying job and a girlfriend who loves and supports me.'

Millie lets out a snort.

Noah narrows his eyes at her. '*What?* Come on. Say what you want to say.'

'She's hardly supported you today,' Millie reasons, her face growing hot as she realises she's maybe stepped too far, but she might as well see it out now. 'She's done nothing but bring down you and your friends since she's arrived. Why is she even here if she thinks this is all stupid and doesn't give a shit about Eurovision? Why is she—'

'I don't know, Millie,' Noah snaps. 'Maybe because I don't give a shit about it, either.'

Millie can hardly look at him. He is not the person she thought he was. What an idiot she's been. All day she's thought that Victoria didn't know the real Noah. But it turns out that it's Millie who's been in the dark about him all this time.

'You're right,' she says quietly, a tear falling down her cheek. 'This is stupid. This has always been stupid, whatever this is. For fuck's sake, we made a pact eight years ago. Why are we still sticking to it when so much has changed? When *we've* changed. We're too old for this. Ingrid is too busy, James has to work through it, you've never wanted to be here. And now, here I am at Eurovision with a VIP ticket for the Grand Final, and *I* don't want to be here. Why do we bother putting ourselves through it?'

'Millie—' Noah begins gently, looking pained at seeing her cry.

'Whatever this group is, whatever we had, it's run its course,' she states firmly. 'I declare our pact officially void. Goodbye, Noah.'

Wiping her cheek with the back of her hand, she turns and walks away.

'Millie!' Noah calls out. 'Millie, wait!'

But she doesn't look back.

CHAPTER SEVENTEEN

Tel Aviv, Israel

2019

Saturday 18 May

'Thank you, Duncan Laurence!' James exclaims, beaming into the selfie camera of his phone as the singer is ushered away from James's side to take his place with the rest of The Netherlands team. 'Once again, that was Duncan Laurence of The Netherlands, fresh from his powerhouse performance of his song, "Arcade", at the Eurovision Grand Final. And you know what? I'm going to call it now – I have a strong feeling that I may have just interviewed the winner. You heard it here first. Time now for Greece's act, the wonderful Katerine Duska, who will be singing "Better Love", so I'm going to go catch the show. Hope wherever you are, you're having the best time celebrating Eurovision and remember to keep checking in for more live streams of exclusive interviews from backstage at Expo Tel Aviv. See you soon and remember: dare to dream!'

James finishes the live recording and lowers his phone, wiping his brow. He always gets hot with the nerves and adrenaline when he's doing any filming, and his silver glitter shirt isn't the most breathable of materials.

Picking up the water bottle he'd placed at his feet for the interview, he takes a moment to have a breather, stepping out of the way of the crew rushing around him, and finding a quiet spot in a corner where no one looks twice at him. He takes a few swigs of water and screws the lid back on the bottle, observing the numerous people bustling past him, all of the unsung heroes who are running the show from back here.

He smiles to himself, thinking of Ingrid. This must be her world on a daily basis. *How does she do it?* James isn't even involved in any of it and he feels stressed just watching the inner workings of how the show comes together.

He still cannot quite get his head around the fact that he's backstage at the Eurovision Grand Final. His VIP pass hanging on a lanyard round his neck, this year he's been given access to every nation's artists and crews, interviewing them for his social media channels and website, as well as providing his usual live updates of the contest itself.

Ever since he removed the anonymity of his identity from the website, it's gone stratospheric. Now able to provide video content and commentary, he's gained a huge increase in followers and subscribers, and can proudly say that he heads up one of the most popular Eurovision fan websites in the world. The EBU love him, providing him with brilliant material and content in the lead-up to the contest. He didn't have to pay a penny for his trip out here to Israel, it was all covered.

James's magazine colleagues have been nothing but supportive and impressed by the whole thing. If anything, Errol was annoyed that he hadn't told them sooner and has dedicated a new small section of the website to Eurovision headed up by James, allowing him to include links to his website.

'We can support each other,' Errol claimed cheerily. 'I've got a soft spot for Eurovision. Always a fun watch.'

James had found that hard to believe.

'What?' Errol frowned at him, noticing his surprised expression.

'Nothing! I wouldn't have figured you for a fan, that's all.'

Errol raised his eyebrows at him haughtily. 'Just because a man loves The Velvet Underground, he can't enjoy a bit of Eurovision? It has a lot of appeal. And I think, for me, a touch of comfort and nostalgia. I grew up watching it with my parents.' A hint of sadness crossed his expression. 'It's the sort of thing that you should watch with others.'

James knew exactly what he meant.

I can't believe this is my life, James thinks, moving from his little haven in the corner to the side of the stage where he can watch the next act and hopefully catch her after her performance for a few quick words.

He's disappointed that he's here in Israel alone. It doesn't seem right that he's not flanked by Millie, Noah and Ingrid. He has to get used to it – it's unlikely that they'll ever be at Eurovision as a group again. He supposes that he should be grateful they managed to stick to the pact for as long as they did. It was amazing that they met in the first place, but then to have all made the commitment to get to the Grand Final each year, wherever it was on the continent, was nothing short of incredible. He wishes that they could have kept it going forever, but that's hardly realistic. They've all moved on, now, busy with their lives.

Although, James would rather be alone than have to put up with reluctant companions, like last year. Victoria was truly awful and Mark ... well, he tried. Sort of.

Every now and then James thinks about Mark and he misses him. They've only recently been in touch again – after the break-up in June last year, Mark said it was sensible to cut contact altogether. It was horrible, but in the end, James thinks he was right. They'd said all they could possibly say; they'd talked about why it wasn't working any more; they'd cried together; they'd held and comforted each other. They had to break contact so they had a chance at moving on.

So they blocked each other's numbers. James moved out of Mark's flat and into his mum's. He knew the break-up was the right decision. They didn't excite each other any more and, more telling than that, neither of them seemed willing to try to get the spark back. They'd settled into a routine that was safe and comfortable, but they also got on each other's nerves a lot. The differences between them that used to be adorable and interesting became exasperating and annoying, causing vast gaping holes in their relationship. They fought all the time. Mark grew more silent and introverted. James found excuses to go out more, avoiding returning home.

When they found the courage to address their problems, they both suddenly felt distraught because they knew what was coming. Saying it out loud made it real. Neither of them wanted to lose the other one and neither felt they'd done anything wrong. It didn't seem fair that it wasn't working.

Breaking up was the right thing to do.

But that didn't make it easy.

It's coming up to your favourite time of year! Mark messaged him last week. *Have a happy Eurovision. Will be thinking of you x*

James had smiled reading the message and replied to thank him straight away. It was lovely that Mark would have that connection to Eurovision from now on because of his relationship with James. He could try to deny it all he liked, but James reckons that a tiny part of Mark enjoyed the merriment of it all.

A *teeny* tiny part.

James is here in Israel for his website, but there is another reason he wouldn't have missed it. A reason that makes him feel dizzy with nerves and hope. It's appropriate that this year, the theme for the song contest is 'Dare to Dream'. On every bit of Eurovision publicity material, the tagline has been there in bold letters as though speaking to him directly: *Dare to dream, James. Dare to dream.*

James believes that in 1974, Tom and Julie saw each other at the Eurovision Grand Final in Brighton, England, and fell in love at first sight. And he also believes that in Düsseldorf, Germany, in 2011, a man spilt coffee all over James and he looked up and fell in love, too.

James is here for Zachary.

It's ridiculous. The whole idea is absurd. It would be difficult to make it work – Zachary lives in Switzerland, James in the UK. They've only met a handful of times. Zachary might not feel the same way as James.

What kind of naïve idiot confesses their love to someone they barely know? James knows he has to be prepared for heartbreak.

Dare to dream, James.

He'll wait until the end of the show and then he'll look for him. James wishes he could find him now – he's got to be here somewhere – and tell him how he feels, but between blogging and interviewing, he doesn't have time, so the end of the show it is. At least if Zachary turns him down he can leave straight away without the humiliation of having to carry on working.

But fate has other plans.

A little later, while nodding his head along to the beat of 'Spirit in the Sky', the electronic pop offering from Norway's Keiino, James glances to his right to see Zachary standing awkwardly nearby. He straightens, his face lighting up. Zachary smiles shyly and gives him a wave. James responds by striding right over to him, everything else going on around him fading into the background.

'I was going to look for you,' James gushes, as soon as he reaches him.

'I saw some of your interviews, so I knew where you'd be,' Zachary confesses.

The two of them look at each other. James may be reading into things, but Zachary seems as nervous as he feels.

'Your boyfriend …' Zachary says apprehensively, his voice going up at the end, making it sound like a question.

James shakes his head. 'I don't have a boyfriend.'

Zachary's eyes light up. 'Oh. I … oh.' He bites his lip.

James takes a deep breath. Sod waiting until the end of the show. It's now or never.

'Zachary, a long time ago, you told me that we didn't have a chance,' James begins, his voice wavering as his mouth turns dry. 'But in the spirit of Eurovision, I don't believe that different countries should keep us apart. I've never met anyone like you. From the moment we met, when I had a terrible hangover and looked like shit, and you spilt all that coffee and looked absolutely perfect, I knew that you were special. I think we were meant to meet that day. Because no matter what happens in life, no matter where I go or what I do, every gut feeling, every instinct brings me back to you. So, I don't care how hard it is, how many planes I'll have to catch – I want to be with you.'

James pauses, taking a moment to breathe, having been rambling much too fast, the words spilling out of his mouth before he could stop himself.

'I came here today to tell you that,' he continues. 'I mean, I'm also here for Eurovision, but I've spent all week wondering when I should find you to tell you how I really feel, and I suppose the night of the Grand Final is the most appropriate. And if you're not on board, if you have a boyfriend or if I've completely misread everything, if you're convinced that this is never going to work because it's just too difficult, then that's absolutely fi—'

James doesn't have a chance to finish his sentence. Zachary has taken a step forwards and kissed him.

The song on stage comes to an end and the audience beyond the curtain erupts.

'It's not difficult,' Zachary says with a smile, as he breaks away from James momentarily. 'I'm all in.'

* * *

Berlin, Germany

'I heard a rumour.'

Ingrid looks up from her notes to find actor Matthias looming over her in full baroque costume, complete with curly white wig, cravat, richly embellished coat and the perfectly placed beauty spot drawn above the corner of his lip.

'You've just finished the show, Matthias. You should be getting out of costume and on your way home to rest that beautiful voice of yours,' she instructs.

'Is it true? The rumour?'

'What rumour?'

Matthias checks that no one around them is listening before turning back to her and lowering his voice. 'That *someone* is in talks for a huge upcoming production at the Friedrichstadt-Palast.'

Damn it. How did he find out about that? She knows that gossip runs quickly through the theatre world, but she only had that meeting yesterday. How is it already on people's radars?

She stands up, altering her headset, making it a little more comfortable around her ear, and then starts making her way off set, Matthias hot on her heels.

'It's true, then?' he squeaks excitedly. 'Our Ingrid running the show at Friedrichstadt-Palast! You really are conquering the world.'

'I haven't said anything,' she reminds him, marching as quickly as she can down the steps off stage and through the double doors to the corridor. 'And if there were some truth to those rumours, don't think I don't know what you're doing.'

'What do you mean?' he says, scurrying along behind her, dodging out the way of one of the crew members rushing past with a large flower vase that needs to be set on stage for Act I tomorrow.

'You're trying to get on my good side,' Ingrid deduces. 'May I remind you, Matthias, that stage managers have nothing to do with casting.'

'That's not true, is it. You have something to do with everything that goes on here. We all know you're really the one in charge. You're the one with the sway,' Matthias insists.

'I don't know what you're talking about, *and*' – she pushes open the doors to the prop department – 'I don't know anything about these rumours.'

'But—'

'Another great show everyone,' Ingrid announces to the prop crew, who are carefully checking items are in the right order for the next run. 'How's everything looking for tomorrow? All of this intact?'

The prop department assure her they're all set for tomorrow. She ticks them off her list and then heads towards the costume department, stopped on the way by one of the musicians, who asks her if she's seen his oboe case. Helping him locate it by remembering he used it in the green room to catch a spider earlier, she continues on to costume, Matthias still pestering her.

'Let's say *hypothetically* that you are being wooed by the team at Friedrichstadt-Palace which wouldn't surprise me since you are the best stage manager in Germany, who has completely transformed this production with all those creative risks you pitched—'

'Get to your point, Matthias.'

'I am a very versatile actor, not to mention dedicated and always on time.'

Ingrid stops in the corridor and faces him. 'Matthias, even if *hypothetically* I was in talks to manage a production at Friedrichstadt-Palace—'

'The biggest stage in the world,' he notes as an aside.

'Yes. Even if that were happening, I have no sway over the casting.'

He sighs heavily and puts his hands on his hips. 'You can't blame a guy for trying.'

'I admire your persistence. Now, go get changed and give your things back to the costume staff before you get in trouble.'

'I meant it, by the way, about you being the best stage manager in Germany,' he says, shuffling past her through the door. 'Whether you get me a role in your next production or not.'

She smiles, shaking her head at him as he swans away. Her phone buzzes in her pocket. She opens the message to see it's from James: a photo of him with Zachary, backstage at the Eurovision Grand Final.

She gets a pang that she's not there. It doesn't seem right. It's always been her favourite time of year and no matter what she was going through, she made it to Eurovision. She should be there. The four of them should be there: her, James, Noah and Millie. She can't believe the pact has finally been broken.

A voice comes through on her headset: the director asking for her to come up to the sound and lighting box. He wants her opinion on some new ideas he's had.

She tells him she's on her way, hurrying in that direction.

No time to dwell on the past.

* * *

Brighton, UK

Millie thinks she's seen this episode of *Midsomer Murders* before. Yes, she definitely has; she can remember

244

who the murderer is. But she doesn't say that out loud, because otherwise Julie will make a big fuss of finding something else to watch and it's taken them long enough to land on this.

Her phone pings with a message and she puts down her mug of hot chocolate to grab it from where it's sitting on the coffee table. It's from James. She opens it eagerly to see he's sent a selfie of him and Zachary – they're backstage and James is beaming at the camera while Zachary has his arms round his waist and is kissing him on the cheek. James has accompanied the picture with a heart emoji.

Millie grins.

'That has to be a message from a boy,' Julie declares from the other end of the sofa. 'Look at that smile on your face! You look deliriously happy.'

'You're right, it is from a boy and I *am* deliriously happy.'

Millie turns her screen towards her grandma so she can see the picture.

Julie peers at it, then gasps, her eyes widening in delight. 'Is that James and Zachary?'

'Looks like Eurovision worked its magic again.'

'Oh, how wonderful. Something to do with a room full of sequins, I'm telling you!' Julie exclaims, making Millie laugh. 'James so deserves to be happy.'

'He does.'

Millie can feel Julie's eyes on her as she goes back to watching TV, and eventually she can't keep ignoring her.

'Yes, Grandma? Can I help you?'

'Nothing! Nothing,' she replies innocently. 'I was only going to say that you really don't have to stay in with me tonight. I'm absolutely fine! It's a Saturday. You should be out having fun with your friends.'

'I've told you, I want to be here with you! It's nice to have a chilled one. My course is so intense at the moment with second-year exams coming up. I needed a night off.'

'You should be at a Eurovision party or something,' Julie remarks, sadness clouding her features. 'I'm bringing you down. Just because *I* find it hard to watch, doesn't mean that you should have to miss out.'

'You're *not*,' Millie insists, shuffling down the sofa to be close to her. She takes her hand. 'I promise you, Grandma, I really did want to have a quiet weekend. I'd much rather be here watching *Midsomer Murders* with you than at some party. I'm tired, honestly.'

'If you say so,' Julie sighs. 'Did you speak to your mum today?'

Millie nods. 'Sorry, I meant to say she rang earlier when you were outside chasing that squirrel away from the bird-feeder—'

'Bloody nuisance those squirrels,' Julie mutters under her breath.

'She's coming to visit next weekend with – get this – her *boyfriend*.'

Julie looks at her in wonder. 'Your mum is dating someone?'

'She says it's early days, but he sounds quite cool. He's a screenwriter.'

'Goodness!' Julie seems impressed. 'A creative.'

'Opposites attract.'

'Quite.' Julie smiles. 'You know, I think it's been *years* since your mum dated. She's never allowed herself any fun, so I'm really pleased she's found someone. It must be going well if she wants to introduce him to us.'

'That's what I thought.'

Julie yawns and squeezes Millie's hand, pushing herself up off the sofa. 'Right, I'm off to bed.'

'Already? But you don't know who the murderer is,' Millie points out.

'I do, actually. I've seen this one before,' Julie confesses. 'It's a good episode, though; you won't guess who it is.'

Millie slumps back into the cushions, muttering, 'Wanna bet?'

'Oh, before I go,' Julie says, turning back to Millie in the doorway, 'I thought I saw a picture of that boy you and James know from Eurovision. He's in those celebrity and society gossip pages.' She points at the stack of glossy magazines sitting in the corner of the coffee table. 'I think he's in that top one, there.'

'Really?' Millie keeps her eyes fixed on the TV screen.

'I think it's him anyway. Handsome boy.'

'Thanks. I'll have a look.'

'Goodnight, darling.'

'Night, Grandma. Sleep well.'

Millie waits until she hears Julie's footsteps at the top of the stairs before reaching out and picking up the top magazine. She flicks through it, landing on a page filled with photos of guests at the opening of an art exhibition in Chelsea.

She studies the photo of Noah and Victoria. The caption beneath them reads, 'Noah Pearce and Victoria Dalton: engagement rumours are swirling around this society couple'.

Good for them, she thinks, before shutting the magazine and tossing it to the side, trying to ignore how much her heart aches from missing him.

* * *

London, UK

Noah grimaces as he reads the comment beneath his photo. He closes the magazine and slides it away from him across the kitchen island. He hopes his mum doesn't see that. She's already pestering him about when he's going to pop the question and nonsense like this only fuels the flames.

He hears the sound of Victoria's heels clacking across the hallway floor before she looms into sight, tottering into the kitchen, her eyes glued to her phone. She looks up to see him perched on the breakfast stool at the island, eating a bowl of cereal, and makes a face.

'You do know what time it is,' she says disapprovingly.

He shrugs.

She rolls her eyes. 'It's the evening. That is breakfast food.'

'I don't think you have to eat cereal at a specific time,' he points out. 'There are no rules stating that on the box.'

She frowns. 'It's also full of sugar. I've told you, I don't like having that kind of thing in the house.'

'No problem, it won't be here for long. I've almost finished the box.'

She purses her lips and inhales deeply through her nose. Noah has noticed she's been doing this calming mechanism of hers a lot more around him recently.

Once she's exhaled, the muscles on her face relax.

'What do you think?' she asks, doing a twirl. 'You like the dress?'

He dutifully runs his eyes up and down her pink fitted outfit. It looks almost identical to the dress she wore to a party yesterday.

'Love it,' he replies, much to her satisfaction. 'You look amazing.'

'It's new. I bought it today.'

'Very nice. And you've done something cool with your hair.'

'Curled it,' she explains, looking back down at her phone. 'And pinned it to one side to show off the highlighter on my collar bones.'

'Cool,' he says with no idea what she's talking about, although now he peers at her, he can see that her skin on show does look all shimmery when it catches the light.

'We have a really big week ahead of us, Noah,' she announces, her eyes widening as she studies her phone calendar. 'Something on every night and then we have Laurita's birthday bash on Friday night. It's going to be so good.'

'Something every night?' Noah groans. 'Can I get out of any of them?'

She looks insulted. 'Why are you so antisocial?'

'I'm not! But you have to agree that going out every night this week is a bit excessive. And why are we going to Laurita's birthday party? I thought you didn't like her.'

Victoria shrugs. 'I don't.'

'So my question still stands: why would we go to her party?'

'Because it's a *very* elite guest list, Noah,' she says, looking irked, as though she shouldn't have to explain such an obvious answer. 'It's at an exclusive venue. If we stop going to these events just because we don't like the people hosting them, then we'll stop being invited to them altogether!'

He blinks at her. 'Wouldn't that be … a good thing?'

She chuckles, shaking her head, like he's made a joke. She returns her attention to her phone and Noah is left staring at her, baffled.

'My Uber is here,' she announces, grabbing her clutch bag from the island and checking she has all the right things in it. 'Are you sure you don't want to come to Andrew's dinner tonight? I don't understand why you'd rather sit here on your own with nothing else to do. It's embarrassing; I have to make up an excuse as to why you can't come.'

'Last time I saw your friend Andrew, he called me Nigel,' Noah reminds her with a deadpan expression. 'I don't think I'll be very much missed.'

'Suit yourself.' She squeezes her clutch bag closed until it makes a satisfying click. 'Don't wait up. Love you.'

'You too.'

He watches her saunter out the kitchen and gets back to his cereal, hearing the front door swing open and then shut behind her, leaving him in silence. Crunching his mouthful, he stares around at the minimalist blank walls of their home. He thinks it might look less sparse in here with a bit of colour somewhere. He wonders if he should broach the subject with her. Although last time he tried to have any input in the matter of their interior design, it turned into a fight, so maybe he'll let it be. It's not worth it. It never is.

His phone vibrates and he checks it, thinking Victoria might have forgotten something and will need him to run out with it.

But it's not from her, it's from James. It's a photo of him and Zachary at Eurovision this year in Tel Aviv. Noah smiles at the picture.

Picking up his cereal bowl, he slides off his stool and moves over to the sofa, finding the remote and turning on his giant flat screen. He searches the channels until he finds the Eurovision broadcast and settles back to watch the remaining acts.

Just a few minutes in, he realises that it's the sort of show you should really watch with others. Or, for him at least, it's a show he should watch with one person in particular.

I wonder what Millie is doing right now, he thinks.

Pained, he turns the TV off.

The room falls into silence again. His mind racing, he pushes himself up from the sofa and starts looking for his trainers. He'll go for a run.

He needs to shake all thoughts of her from his head.

CHAPTER EIGHTEEN

Saturday 19 March 2022

WhatsApp Group Chat

EUROVISION CREW

> **Ingrid**
> Hi everyone! Wow, it's been a long time since we used this group!! How are you all? It has been a tough couple of years with Covid-19 and I hope you and your families are OK. It has been horrible for theatres here in Berlin but getting back to normal now!

> I have a big favour to ask … PLEASE can you come to Eurovision in Italy this year??

> I miss you and it will be amazing to all be together again!!! It has been too long. I promise it will be worth it. It is a lot to ask but it would mean SO MUCH to me if we could make this happen.

> Please, please will you promise to come??

> Eurovision, Turin, Italy … SEE YOU THERE???

* * *

Somerset, UK

Noah quickly raises the Nikon D850 camera hanging around his neck and, using a wide lens, he gets the shot: having taken their seat at the table for the wedding breakfast, after a loud, exuberant entrance into the dining hall, the bride and groom are looking into each other's eyes and sharing a secret smile when no one else is looking. Noah captures it just before the two of them break eye contact to involve themselves in the conversations of the others on their table.

He checks the picture on the screen and already feels excited about the couple seeing that one when he sends the final selection over in a few weeks' time. There's nothing posed or forced about that photo – two people on show all day sharing a brief moment that no one else is a part of. These are the shots that mean the most to Noah and give him the greatest satisfaction – recording a moment in time that the couple themselves don't necessarily notice as one of the memories they'll cherish the most.

'Excuse me,' a polite voice says behind him and he realises he's blocking the path of a waiter coming out to serve the first course.

Noah jumps out of the way, weaving his way around the tables and shuffling back into a corner while a line of staff file into the dining hall carrying small plates of rye bread and smoked salmon. As they make their way to the top table, the catering manager standing by the door that leads to the kitchen waves Noah over.

'We've put your meal aside for you, if you'd like to come eat,' she informs him.

'Perfect, I'll be there in a minute,' Noah replies gratefully. 'Thank you so much.'

Careful to stay out of the way of her waiting staff, he hangs around a little bit longer to get a few more pictures of the jovial guests and then slips out without notice. Taking the plate of food set out for him on the side of the counter of the kitchen, he ducks out the room and goes outside, sitting down at a wooden table and a bench in the small courtyard at the back of the venue. This is always a calm part of the day for him, when he has a break before he'll be needed for the speeches. He's been on his feet a long time and there's still a lot of action to come: the cake cutting, first dance and the guests hitting the dance floor.

He already knows he's going to get some entertaining photos tonight. This is a big wedding and the wine is flowing freely. By the time the band takes to the stage, the guests will be raring to go and one of the best parts of Noah's job is blending in towards the end of the night, bobbing through the throng of people on the dance floor and capturing those completely uninhabited flashes of elation that only a truly great song can incite. It's been a gorgeous wedding so far – which comes as no surprise when the couple has been so lovely and easy to work with in the lead-up to the day – and Noah is looking forward to the rest of it.

Taking a bite of his bread and smoked salmon, deliciously seasoned with salt, pepper and a drizzle of lemon, Noah gazes out at the peaceful surrounding Somerset countryside, vast fields stretching out for miles in front of him. He's never been to this estate before, but it's a grand country pile, perfect for weddings. The bride and groom got lucky with the weather. A March wedding can be a gamble, but it's one of those stunning cold sunny days where the air is crisp and Noah knows the sun going down will wash the landscape in a soft pink-orange hue. He'll keep an eye on it to make sure he gets some good sunset photos of the happy couple.

Noah isn't quite yet a seasoned wedding photographer – it's been just nine months since he had his first gig – but he's loving it. He was concerned it wouldn't be an easy time to launch a career in it and build up a portfolio when Covid-19 was still threatening the wedding industry in the summer of 2021, but in the end he needn't have worried. There was such a huge backlog of couples scrambling to get their weddings in the diary after postponing them several times from 2020 that he got booked up fairly fast, and his diary this year is already filling, especially the summer months.

When he was furloughed during the 2020 pandemic, he suddenly had a lot of time on his hands and, during a long-overdue clear-out, came across his old camera. It sparked a feeling in him that he couldn't shake off, and so, with nothing better to do, he researched the latest camera models, bought one and took up his old hobby.

It opened Noah's eyes to the fact that he'd been numb to what he really wanted from life for some time. He had floated through the past few years. He'd subconsciously given up and he dreaded to think what would have happened if he hadn't been forced into an enclosed space with himself for company. He didn't like what he'd become. He would sometimes think back on that horrible fight with Millie outside the arena in Lisbon when she demanded to know why he was so afraid to stand on his own two feet.

It was time to make a change.

Many years too late, he enrolled on a photography course. When the world began to open up again, he went back to work, but it didn't seem so painful now that he had something else to focus on in his spare time. He scrolled through social media to admire the work of established photographers and liked the thought of wedding photography, which concentrated on people, rather than things. He emailed a wedding photographer, Marina, whose style he liked, with some of his work and asked if he could shadow and assist her at one of her weddings free of charge. She kindly agreed, happy to show him the ropes of the business. Further lockdowns stalled his progress, but eventually weddings were allowed again and he acted as Marina's second shooter for several events, the first unpaid, but after impressing her with his work and enthusiasm, she began paying him to assist.

Thanks to Marina, he's been able to build up a portfolio and he set up an Instagram account dedicated to his photography. An acquaintance reached out and asked if he'd photograph their wedding – they were having a very low-key event with just thirty guests in London, the reception to be held at a private space in a gastro pub in Dulwich. It was his first ever gig on his own and it went as brilliantly as he could have hoped. They were thrilled with the photos, raved about him, and recommended him to their friends. Their glowing testimonial focused on his candid, authentic style of photography, capturing real moments instead of forcing any.

Other requests began to come in, so he decided to make a go of it. He quit his real estate career and launched his wedding photography business in August 2021. As he gained more experience, he drew in more clients and was able to increase his rates. He's lucky to find fulfilment in his job – something he told his parents over a video call. His mum said she thought he was brave. Charlotte wondered why it had taken him so long. His dad thought he had made a risky and stupid move.

He'd expected that reaction from his father, so he didn't let it affect him. He didn't need his dad's money any more, he was making his own and he'd live the lifestyle that his own work allowed him. He was hugely embarrassed that it had taken him until he was thirty to do so. And he was determined to change his dad's mind, anyway, and show him he could make a success of this.

There are already glimpses that his father isn't as averse to it as he made out.

'What are you doing the week of 20th June?' Charlotte asked Noah the other day when they spoke on the phone. 'Specifically the Tuesday of that week.'

'Hang on.' He put her on speaker and checked his phone. 'I have a wedding lined up for that weekend, but I'm around. Why? Are you coming to London for work?'

'Yes, I am.'

'Great! It will be so good to see you.'

'Sure, but I'm also speaking to you in a professional capacity,' she told him. 'I'm hosting an event to advertise our property portfolio expansion in Europe and I'd like to hire a photographer for the event. I know you special-ise in weddings, but I wondered if you also cover corporate events?'

He was stunned into silence.

'Noah? Have I lost you?' she prompted.

'No! I'm here. You … you want to hire me?'

'Yes. I've been through your portfolio and I like the style,' she said matter-of-factly. 'Are you happy to do it?'

'Yeah! Yes. That's … I'd love to.'

'We can negotiate rates.'

He chuckled. 'Nice try. I'll tell you my rates and you can accept.'

'We can discuss it,' she retorted and he could hear her smiling down the phone. 'Oh, and Noah, don't tell anyone I told you this, but when I said that we should document the event for our website, it wasn't my idea to hire you to photograph it.'

'Mum put you up to it, did she?'

'Not Mum,' Charlotte said, her voice softening. 'It was Dad.'

Gazing out across the Somerset countryside, Noah can't quite believe his luck that he's where he is today. He had to find the courage to admit what he really wanted and try for it. It took him a while, but he got there eventually.

Finishing his plate, he gets out his phone to check his emails. It's been on silent, so he sees there are some WhatsApp messages waiting for him. His brow wrinkles with curiosity when he sees that one of them is from Ingrid on the Eurovision group.

He opens it and begins to read: *Hi everyone! Wow, it's been a long time …*

He scans the message a couple of times before lowering his phone. It's very out of the blue for her to get in touch this year and ask them to gather once again. It would be expensive to get to Italy for the Eurovision weekend and it's been so long since they all spoke, would it really be worth going? Is there much point?

But he's kidding himself.

He knew his answer as soon as he read Ingrid's question the first time round.

If there's a chance of seeing Millie, he'll be there.

He's addressed everything else in his life. It's about time he took notice of his heart.

* * *

London, UK

'I'm going to make a toast,' Millie announces, lifting her glass.

James, Zachary and Aggie follow suit, looking at her expectantly. They're in a lovely French restaurant that Aggie picked in Shepherd Market, a small square tucked away near Piccadilly, and have just ordered their starters and mains. Already blushing from the attention on her – despite it only being three people – Millie clears her throat.

'I would like to raise a glass to my best friend' – she looks at James, who smiles gratefully back at her – 'who has made me extremely happy by returning to live here in the UK with his wonderful boyfriend, even if you have given up your Brighton roots for a glamorous London life' – cue a chuckle from James and Zachary, and a wink from Aggie to James who whispers he's made the right choice. 'I missed you so much when you followed your heart to Switzerland last year and stayed there as a freelance writer, and I could not be more grateful to one of the biggest music magazines in the world, *Stage Dive UK*, for luring you back to home soil with an amazing job as News Editor.'

Zachary whoops, rubbing James's arm proudly.

'And Zachary,' Millie continues, turning her attention to him, 'I know it can't have been easy saying goodbye to EBU after years of working there, but I have no doubt that you are going to be incredibly successful in your new entertainment marketing role for the O2 Arena. England is lucky to have you and so are we.'

Zachary places a hand on his heart, his eyes glistening.

'Cheers!' Millie concludes.

'Cheers!' the other three chorus, knocking their glasses against each other above the centre of the table.

'That was very sweet, Millie, thank you,' James says, blowing her a kiss across the table. He would get up to give her a hug, but the restaurant is so intimate that the tables are all in quite close vicinity, and squeezing himself around their table to get to her would cause a bit of a hassle.

'I have something to add to that toast,' Aggie declares, having taken a large gulp of the expensive wine she insisted on ordering for the dinner. She's already informed them that she's getting the bill, so the 'cheap plonk' that Millie suggested – Aggie's description, not Millie's – didn't fly with her. 'I am really glad that we organised this meal tonight, because it is such a pleasure for me to see my daughter, and you, James, of course, and also to meet you, Zachary.' She pauses, looking a little uneasy for a moment but collecting herself and carrying on. 'I know I don't say this often, but Millie, I'm proud of you for being such a great primary school teacher, especially after surviving the hell of being one through the pandemic.'

'Hear, hear!' James cries.

'I will certainly drink to that,' Millie laughs, staying true to her word and taking a large glug from her glass.

Millie's patience and confidence has been tested many times in the past two years, but now that things have calmed down, she can claim to be a popular teacher among both the children *and* the parents – a difficult balance to strike.

She lives in the same flat, but since Tina left to live with her boyfriend, Millie now shares it with another teacher at a different local school, the lovely Jessica. They've grown to be close friends, spending many evenings together drinking red wine and complaining about the government's dismal treatment of teachers and how school budgets are greatly lacking.

She checks in on Julie a couple of times a week and is almost always told off for making Julie feel old by asking her questions like whether she needs help with the food shop and implying that Julie should take it easy after long afternoons spent gardening.

'I'll have you know that I've never felt more nimble,' Julie scolded last week, waving her secateurs in Millie's face after she was instructed to sit down and put her feet up for a bit while Millie made her a cup of tea. 'Tonight, I have my salsa class!'

Millie stared at her, stunned. 'You're learning to *salsa*?'

'Oh honey, I'm not learning,' Julie replied haughtily as Millie giggled at her shaking her hips. 'I show them how it's done.'

'I see! And who do you attend salsa class with? Do you have a ... dance partner?'

'We swap around during the class, all dancing with each other,' Julie said, before eyeing her up suspiciously. 'And if you're stealthily trying to find out whether I have a special gentleman friend, then you are wasting your time. I remain a one-man woman, thank you very much.'

'I wasn't trying anything!' Millie claimed innocently.

Julie folded her arms. 'And what about you? Are there any "dance partners" on the scene?'

'I'm not sure I have the hips for salsa.'

'Everyone has the hips for salsa,' Julie counters, 'and don't try to avoid the question, you know what I meant. Anyone special?'

Millie shook her head. 'No one, Grandma. Not at the moment.'

It had been the same answer for a while now. Millie's dating life took a hit during the pandemic and she was yet to find the energy to reignite it. Last August, she was encouraged by James over a video call to get on the dating apps, but nothing had come of them. She'd been on a couple of dates, but they were hugely unsuccessful.

There was a guy named Oliver, who seemed perfectly pleasant in his messages, but in person had a voice so booming that it made her cringe. He kept asking her who she banked with, before informing her that she was being 'swindled' and monologuing about why she needed to switch accounts – a speech the whole restaurant was treated to thanks to his lack of volume control.

Another memorable date was with Pete, a personal trainer, who spent more of the evening talking to the very pretty waitress than to Millie. When Millie couldn't help but mention that observation towards the end of the night, he admitted that he felt he and Millie didn't have any chemistry and proceeded to get up to go ask the waitress for her number. Millie paid her half of the bill at the till and left before he returned to the table.

She is content being on her own. She feels in control of her life and her future and, now that James is back in England, there's nothing she feels like she's missing.

Apart from him.

No. She doesn't let herself think about him. Everyone has moved on.

'Here come our starters,' James says eagerly, straightening in his seat as a waiter approaches their table and places steaming bowls of mussels in front of Aggie and Zachary. 'Those look good.'

'Don't worry, you'll get one or two,' Zachary promises him, sliding the napkin out from under his cutlery to lay it out on his lap.

James and Millie both receive a message at the same time, quickly checking their phones before their plates are put down in front of them. James's eyes light up as he reads Ingrid's message.

'Zachary, look at these two on their phones at dinner,' Aggie sighs, gesturing to James and Millie. 'Anyone would think we're boring them.'

Zachary tuts. 'They won't get any mussels at this rate.'

'It's about Eurovision,' James reveals, while Millie puts her phone back in her pocket, her brow furrowed in deep thought. 'Ingrid wants us all to go this year. She seems desperate for us to be together again. You know, the four of us who made the pact.'

'I thought you didn't do that any more,' Aggie comments.

'It fizzled out,' James acknowledges, noting Millie's silence. 'Obviously, Zachary and I are going this year—'

'James is a Eurovision celebrity now,' Zachary interjects proudly.

'But it really would be amazing if the four of us could reunite in Turin. It sounds as though Ingrid has a good reason for wanting us to be there, so maybe we could all make the effort to go ...' James says hopefully, trailing off.

'I'm not sure it's a good idea,' Millie admits quietly. 'A lot has changed. It's really expensive to go when I can just watch it at home and—'

'You should go,' Aggie says.

The others stare at her in surprise. Millie's mouth drops open. Is she hearing things or did her mum just *encourage* her to go to Eurovision.

'*What?*' Millie says, swivelling to face her properly.

'You should go,' Aggie repeats breezily. Noticing James and Millie's equally astounded expressions, she rolls her eyes. 'Yes, I know, that might seem a little strange coming from me—'

'A *little* strange,' Millie repeats, aghast. 'You hate Eurovision! You think it's the worst thing ever, a complete waste of time!'

'I've never said it's the *worst thing ever*,' Aggie asserts loftily. 'But, OK, fine, I'll admit it's not my favourite event of the year. However, having had some time to reflect, I'm not sure it's that bad after all.'

James lifts the bottle of wine out of its bucket to inspect the liquid level. 'How much of this have you had?'

'Look,' Aggie sighs, as James lowers the bottle again, 'the way I see it, if the pandemic proved anything, it was that we shouldn't take things we enjoy for granted. And, as much as I don't … love the Eurovision Song Contest, I can appreciate how important it is for others. And you know what? I would give so much to see my mum light up at the thought of Eurovision again. She has come on a long way since Dad died, but there's still a part of her that's missing, in my opinion. And I know that Dad would want her to find her way back to her love of that ridiculous show.'

James and Millie share a look of disbelief, neither of them sure they're hearing her correctly.

'My point is, if you go to Turin this year, Millie, maybe I can persuade Mum to tune into Eurovision again,' Aggie continues. 'You could make it on TV, hanging out with a Eurovision celebrity' – she nods to James – 'and so I could say to Mum that there might be a chance of spotting you somewhere in the crowd. It's been a while since Dad died – maybe this could be our chance to remind her of all the joy it's brought to her over the years. It might not work, but it's worth trying. You never know what might happen.'

Millie bites her lip.

'You have to admit, it's a compelling argument,' James says.

She feels torn. As baffling as it is, Aggie has made a good point. Julie has come on leaps and bounds. Maybe she would consider watching Eurovision if she thought Millie might pop up on her TV screen. It would be wonderful for Julie to rediscover her love of something that was once so important to her.

But if Millie did agree to go – if all of them ended up at the Grand Final this year – then she'd have to see Noah again. The thought both thrills and terrifies her. After all these years, he still has the power to scramble her brain and make her heart somersault.

'Come on, Millie,' James says with a knowing smile. 'Take a chance.'

CHAPTER NINETEEN

Turin, Italy

2022

Saturday 14 May

Ingrid is being very mysterious. Having successfully gathered the group in Turin for the Eurovision Grand Final, she hasn't disclosed an exact time she'll meet them yet, instead messaging an apology for being so disorganised but saying that she'll let them know details as soon as possible.

Thanks to James, Millie has an incredible view of the stage in the Palasport Olimpico Arena, and she's happy to remain in the audience until she's given her orders of where to go. It is a little unnerving having a row of three empty seats next to her, and she's aware that others around her must think she's been ditched by her friends, but this is Eurovision – within moments of arriving at her seat on her own, the group of Armenian fans to the other side of her struck up conversation and, on finding out she was British, congratulated her on what they'd heard was a very strong entry from the UK this year.

Despite requesting four seats in the audience, James has already confessed he'll have to spend a lot of the contest backstage live streaming and landing interviews with the artists and crew members, and Zachary apologetically told Millie he'd be accompanying James, as several of his old colleagues are roaming about back there and he hasn't been able to catch all of them this week. The two of them have been here in Turin since Monday, soaking up the atmosphere, enjoying the Semi-Finals, and witnessing all the goings-on behind the scenes in the lead-up to tonight, all of which has been recorded on James's website, which Millie has been logging onto every day, feeling more and more apprehensive about the trip.

She arrived in Turin this morning, unable to come out any earlier because of school, but has had a wonderful day sightseeing thanks to Zachary, who was organised enough to work out an itinerary of the best things to do in the city if you only have one day to enjoy it. They had the most delicious cup of fresh coffee in Piazza Castello, the city's central square, before wandering into the Royal Palace of Turin, marvelling at the magnificent building and its lavishly decorated rooms filled with tapestries and paintings. Millie gasped on entering the ballroom, in awe of the grand columns and sparkling crystal chandeliers, while Zachary got a great photo of James dancing in the middle of the polished floor to post on his Eurovision social media channels. Leaving the palace, they strolled leisurely to the remarkable Palatine Gate and then went in search of the best chocolatiers in the city, exploiting any tasters on offer and buying a lot more chocolate than they needed.

'What? It's for *Grandma*,' Millie explained defensively after James gave her a surprised look, catching her making yet another purchase at the third chocolatier they visited.

By the time she arrived for the Grand Final that night, Millie was exhausted, but as soon as she stepped inside the arena and got a taster of the Eurovision excitement in the air, anticipation fizzed through her whole body, and she felt raring to go.

Noah has been in her head all day.

If she's being honest with herself, he's been there since Ingrid sent that message in March. He was the first to reply to Ingrid on the WhatsApp group agreeing to come, which took Millie by surprise. She figured that once she and James confirmed they'd make the trip, Noah might be more inclined to agree, too, feeling a responsibility to complete the group. She hadn't expected him to respond so quickly and with such enthusiasm before she or James had replied. After all, the last time they spoke he admitted that he didn't give a shit about Eurovision.

Noah mentioned that he'd be arriving in Turin late in the afternoon, so would have to meet them at the arena, but so far there hasn't been any word from him. Currently manning the empty seats by herself, Millie is pleased that he's yet to arrive and hopes that by the time he rocks up, Zachary or James will have come to join her in the audience. She has no idea what she'd say to him after all this time.

The lights go down on the audience, the countdown to the live show begins, and Millie is caught out by her own emotional response to being here. She'd forgotten how it can make you feel; how thunderous applause filling an enormous arena can make your breath catch as it hits you just how momentous an occasion this is. This year, the opening act is particularly moving. Millie chokes up as the arena is lit in a blue wash and filled with the voices of the thousands of people in the audience chanting John Lennon's 'Give Peace a Chance' in chorus.

Dazzled by the show of lights and dancers up on the stage during the flag display, Millie cheers loudly along with her new friends for Armenia's announcement and they do the same for the United Kingdom's. When the hosts walk on for the introduction, Millie checks her phone, doing a quick scroll of Instagram to see James has just uploaded some selfies of him with several of this year's acts. He's already got thousands of likes.

It kicks off with the Czech Republic and Millie is about to sit down to enjoy the performance when her phone vibrates in her hand with a message from Ingrid. She's asking them to meet by a backstage door in fifteen minutes. Considering how big the arena is and how she has no idea where this door might be, Millie sets off in search of it straight away, shuffling down her row and out of an exit nearby.

A helpful member of staff points her in the right direction and she makes it to the correct door with a couple of minutes to spare, lingering nearby and hoping that James or Ingrid will appear soon. While she waits, a couple of British teenagers wearing matching Union Jack bucket hats approach the security guard standing by the door. She watches with interest, moving closer to listen to their conversation.

'We must have left our backstage passes at our hotel,' one of them is saying, letting out an exasperated sigh. 'I can't believe we did that!'

'So stupid of us,' the other replies, nodding in sympathy with her friend. 'We really don't want to go *all* the way back there, so' – she turns to the doorman with a hopeful look – 'if you wouldn't mind letting us through just this once.'

'You can't come in without a pass,' the doorman replies tiredly.

'We're not trying our luck, honestly!' she insists. 'We're here with the UK team. Ask Sam Ryder, he'll tell you!'

'Although might be best not to disturb him, because he'll be getting in the zone before his performance,' the other says quickly. 'But if you let us in, we will be able to prove that we're part of the UK team. They're going to be really angry that we're being held up.'

'No entry without a pass,' the doorman states.

'Please! We have passes, they're just not on us! If you could—'

A voice at Millie's ear says quietly, 'Remind you of anyone?'

She jumps, spinning round to see Noah standing there wearing a bemused expression as he looks over at the teenagers continuing to do everything they can to persuade the doorman to let them through.

'Yeah,' she replies, 'there's a definite sense of *déjà vu*.'

He chuckles, putting his hands in his pockets, and she feels her heart lurch at his familiar stance, the heat rising to her face, her cheeks flushing deeply as he gazes down at her, taking her in.

He looks different. Good different. He's cut and styled his hair short, so that it no longer needs to be constantly swept back from his face, and has grown designer stubble over his defined jaw. His whole demeanour has changed, too. He seems so much more relaxed and at ease in himself than when they last met, his easy-going smile and soft laugh reflecting the warm, mellow nature that had charmed Millie, and countless others, from the moment they stepped in his vicinity.

Noah is happy. Finally. She can see that.

'It's good to see you, Millie,' he says, his eyes twinkling at her.

'Good to see you, too,' she croaks. 'How ... how are you?'

'I'm great.' He hesitates, adding, 'I'm a photographer now.'

'Really?' She beams at him. 'Noah, that's *brilliant*.'

'Thanks,' he says, looking down at the ground modestly.

'I knew you could do it,' she says, lifting her chin proudly. 'You were always so talented.'

He shakes his head. 'I had a lot to learn – I still do. But I love it. I started my own business. I photograph weddings, mostly.'

'That makes sense.'

'Yeah?'

'You were never that interested in beautiful views, or any of the cool landmarks and buildings we'd see over the Eurovision weekends. You'd just photograph people.'

'Exactly,' he says, looking astounded by her observation.

'I think you once told me that you liked to capture connections, and how people were full of complexities.'

He grimaces. 'God, sorry. Sounds like I was being a pretentious idiot. Probably boring you to death.'

'You never bored me,' she says without thinking, before quickly trying to gloss over her earnestness. 'I mean, I found the photography stuff interesting, because I know nothing about art or anything. Anyway, good for you. I'm really pleased you're doing what you love.'

'What about you? Are you teaching?' he asks. 'I think last time I saw you, you were doing your degree.'

'Yeah, I'm a primary school teacher.'

'That's great. In Brighton?'

She nods. 'Are you in London still?'

'Yeah.'

They fall into silence. Noah opens his mouth and looks as though he might be about to say something, but he's interrupted by the sound of James's voice floating across to them from the backstage door.

'Noah! Millie!'

They both turn to see him standing next to the doorman, waving them over. The teenagers have disappeared.

She's been so engrossed in her conversation with Noah, Millie doesn't know whether the teenagers managed to get in in the end or if they were sent away. She hopes that it's the latter – meeting Eurovision performers would be fun, but she imagines they'll likely meet some much more interesting people in the city somewhere. Perhaps they'll go to a random bar and sing karaoke with strangers, and embark on the most unlikely and extraordinary of friendships. Guess she'll never know.

As she and Noah hurry over, James holds open the door for them, thanks the security guy, and then opens his arms wide to pull Noah into a hug.

'So good to see you,' James gushes.

'And you. Congratulations on your website,' Noah says, pulling away and patting him on the arm. 'You've smashed it.'

'Wait until you hear about his new job,' Millie adds. 'You're looking at the News Editor of *Stage Dive UK*.'

Noah's eyes widen in amazement. 'Whoa! That's great!'

'I'm waiting for them to tell me there's been a mistake,' James admits. 'It doesn't seem real. I feel like I'm an imposter.'

'Nah, you deserve it, mate. You have paid your dues,' Noah assures him. 'Remember how many articles about seagulls you wrote?'

James bursts out laughing. 'Who knew a bird could generate so many stories? I'm surprised you remember those articles.'

'Hey, is Zachary back here?' Noah asks, moving aside as someone wearing all black and a headset squeezes past them impatiently.

'I think he may have gone back to our seats,' James says, checking his phone. 'I've told him that you'll join him there once we've seen Ingrid. Speaking of whom, where is she? We've got the right door, haven't we?'

'Maybe we're meant to be on the other side of it,' Millie suggests, frowning. 'Why would she be backstage?'

'That's true,' James realises. 'She never specified that we needed to—'

The squeal of excitement they suddenly hear confirms that they are in the right place. Following the sound of her scream, they turn to see Ingrid rushing towards them, her arms outstretched. She launches herself at James, engrossing him in a hug so tight, he suspects his ribs might be cracked, before she gives Millie and Noah the same greeting.

'I can't believe you came!' she cries, her eyes twinkling as she stands back to take them in. 'Look at us! We're all here! Together again at Eurovision. Exactly how it should be.'

'We answered your call,' Noah says.

'Yes, you did. And I'm so happy, because I had to show you this.'

She holds up the pass hanging from the lanyard round her neck. James takes it in his fingers to examine it closely, before gasping and letting it drop as he clasps a hand round his mouth.

'What does it say?' Millie asks eagerly.

'That Ingrid is on the German Eurovision team!' James announces.

'WHAT?' Millie cries, while Noah stares at her in disbelief.

Ingrid laughs, clapping her hands together. 'You see now why I had to make you all promise to be here? I had to make sure I saw your faces when I told you. They are priceless!'

'Just like you always wanted,' Millie breathes.

'I didn't exactly get here in the way I expected,' she reveals with a sly smile. 'But I still got here. I'm the stage manager for the German Eurovision team.'

'That's amazing! How did it happen?' Millie asks eagerly.

'After working on a few big theatre productions, I ended up taking the job to manage the touring production for a German popstar,' Ingrid explains. 'It was very different to the theatre world, but a lot of fun. When that ended I was approached by the Eurovision team, who asked me if I'd be interested. I said yes before the act had even been selected.'

'Of course you did,' Millie says, feeling like she might burst with happiness for her friend. 'It's fate. Everything that happened led to where you were supposed to be.'

'Ingrid, that is so … so … COOL!' James exclaims, throwing his arms around her for another hug. 'I am so unbelievably proud of you! You did it.'

'I don't have long as we need to prepare for our performance, but I'm so happy to see you three,' she gushes, her eyes gleaming with tears as she looks from Noah to Millie to James. 'Thank you so much for coming here today and I'm sorry I couldn't tell you more, but I wanted it to be a surprise! And you all took a leap of faith anyway, coming to Turin without really knowing why.'

'It sounded important to you that we should be here, so here we are,' Noah says with a shrug, prompting Millie to look up at him in admiration.

She couldn't have put it any better.

'Who knew that a spontaneous pact would forge very real friendships?' James remarks quietly, looking overcome with the sentimental charge of the moment. 'So much has changed, but it also feels like nothing has.'

'That's because no matter what, we always have Eurovision,' Ingrid states. She sniffs, shakes her head and starts fanning her eyes with her hands. 'Argh, I don't have time to get emotional! Group hug and then I have to go!'

Wrapping her arms around the three of them as they huddle together, Ingrid breaks away, blows them all air kisses and then demands that they go to their seats to enjoy the show. She'll find them later so they can celebrate.

As she dashes off, speaking rapid German into her headset as she goes, James checks his phone to find several messages waiting for him from Zachary.

'Apparently he's having a lovely time with some fun Armenians,' James reports, scrolling through, 'but he thinks we're missing out by being backstage.'

'I agree. Our seats are amazing – thank you, James – we shouldn't let them go to waste,' Millie comments.

James looks torn. 'Backstage I get access to the artists, though.'

'You'll be able to speak to them later, though, right?' Noah assumes. 'You're going to be invited to every afterparty going. Plus it looks like you'll be getting a pretty cool interview with the stage manager of the German team. I think you can come enjoy the performances with us for a bit.'

'I guess you're right,' James says, linking his arm through Noah's as they make their way to the backstage exit. 'And we do have a lot of catching up to do. Tell me, are you still Australia's sixth hottest bachelor?'

Noah gives him a look.

'What? I did some googling,' James shrugs.

'I'm sorry to disappoint, but my move to England and then my disappearance from London's social scene has taken its toll on my rating over the last couple of years,' Noah admits with a mock-disappointed sigh.

'Don't tell me you're out of the top ten!' James gasps dramatically.

'It's worse than that,' Noah reveals. 'This year, I didn't even make the top thirty.'

'Oh dear.' James tuts. 'Is that partly because you're off the market?'

Noah shakes his head. 'Nope. I'm single.'

'Oh! So you and Victoria—'

'Let's just say being forced to stay at home together during the pandemic didn't go so well for us,' Noah explains, grimacing at the memories. 'It turned out I wasn't the perfect society boyfriend she was looking for. As soon as it was allowed, I moved out. I have my own place now in Battersea.'

'I see,' James nods. 'So, you really have no excuse not to be listed in the top thirty bachelors.'

Noah laughs. 'I'm happy to say I've simply dropped off the radar.'

'Not *everyone's* radar, I'm sure,' James says so quietly that Noah doesn't hear.

Millie does, though. She rolls her eyes, ignoring James's mischievous smile.

But her heart soars.

* * *

James is having so much fun dancing to 'Space Man', the dazzling song being performed by the UK's Sam Ryder, that he doesn't notice straight away that Zachary has got down on one knee. Millie does, though. She claps a hand round her mouth and grabs Noah's arm to alert him, too. Noah's eyes widen in amazement and they both wait for James to pay attention. It's only when James feels a tug on his sleeve and spins around that he realises what's going on. Zachary is holding up a small black box. He opens the lid to reveal a silver ring nestled in the velvet cushion interior.

'Eleven years ago, I met the love of my life at Eurovision,' Zachary begins, as James stands before him, frozen in shock. 'That's why it felt like the perfect place to propose. So, here it goes' – he takes a deep breath, his voice shaking – 'James, will you marry me?'

Through uncontrollable sobs of joy, James gives him his answer. They embrace as the song comes to an end and the thousands-strong audience erupts around them. James doesn't let him go for a long time, burying his head in Zachary's neck, his cheeks wet with tears. Squealing with excitement, Millie gives them a respectful moment or two before she can't hold back any longer, leaping forwards and wrapping her arms around both of them. James breaks away to give her a proper hug, while Noah claps Zachary on the back and congratulates him.

'We need Champagne!' Millie declares, wiping tears from her eyes. 'Immediately!'

'I meant to bring some,' Zachary admits apologetically, linking his fingers through James's. 'But I was so nervous, I forgot.'

'It's on me,' Noah offers.

'I'll come with you,' Millie declares, before turning to James and Zachary, who are holding each other, huge smiles across their faces. 'We'll be back in a minute! You two just enjoy this perfect, perfect moment. Oh my god, this is the *best day*!'

She hears Noah laugh at her excitement, as she practically skips to the exit, pushing her way through the doors and making her way to the nearest bar.

'A Eurovision proposal,' Noah says, after Millie has ordered a bottle of pink Champagne. 'That was incredible.'

'I know,' Millie breathes, pushing her hair away from her face. 'It's the perfect place for Zachary to ask James. It's like my grandparents always said, there's always love in the air at Eurovision.'

Noah raises his eyebrows. 'They said that?'

'Grandma thinks it has something to do with all the sequins.'

'Makes sense to me,' he laughs.

The two of them smile at each other, not wanting to look away. Millie notices Noah's throat bob. 'Millie,' he begins, 'I—'

A loud pop makes both of them jump as the barman pops the cork of their Champagne.

'Here you go!' The barman places the bottle on the bar in between them and rings it through the till. 'How many glasses would you like?'

'Four please,' Noah says, reaching for his wallet. 'I'll get this.'

'I'm happy to get it,' Millie offers.

'No, it's on me,' he insists, paying and then picking up the bottle and two of the glasses, as Millie grabs the other two.

'Were you about to say something back there?' Millie asks, following him back to the door nearest their seats.

He shakes his head. 'It was nothing.'

They return to celebrate with James and Zachary – and the Armenians, who are just as excited about the proposal as the four of them – and by the time Estonia, the final act, take to the stage, Millie's head is feeling a little lighter thanks to the bubbles and her heart full from the pure joy and happiness of tonight.

She's dancing when Noah gets her attention and clears his throat, leaning closer to her so she can hear him over the music.

'I lied before; I *was* actually about to say something to you back at the bar,' he admits.

'What is it?' she asks.

'I wanted to apologise for what happened in Lisbon.'

'Oh, don't worry about that,' she assures him. 'Water under the bridge! It was a long time ago, Noah. Let's enjoy tonight and not think about something that happened in the past.'

'I want to think about it though, because I need ... I need to explain something,' he continues boldly. 'Do you remember during the argument, I told you that I didn't give a shit about Eurovision?'

'Yeah,' Millie says, 'but you were angry and we all say things that we don't—'

'I meant it,' he states.

'W-what?'

'I meant it,' he repeats.

Millie can't hide her crushing disappointment. She's always known he wasn't as invested as the rest of the group, but the idea of him hating Eurovision all this time takes something away from the precious memories she has of them sharing it together for all those years.

'Noah, why would you bring this up now?' she bristles, gesturing to James and Zachary, who are slow dancing together behind her. 'Tonight is so special and you shouldn't—'

'Exactly,' he interrupts. 'Tonight is special. That's why I want to explain it properly to you, so that you know exactly what I meant by that comment.'

She frowns in confusion, looking down at the ground. 'OK. What did you mean?'

'I never cared that much about Eurovision. What I really cared about was you,' he says, his voice soft and earnest. 'It took me a long time to realise it, but you were always the driving force to me being there, Millie. That's why I stuck to the pact, why I came back to Eurovision every year. It wasn't for the contest. It was for you.'

Millie brings her eyes up to meet his. He gazes back at her.

Neither of them notice the camera pointing their way.

* * *

Brighton, UK

'Oh my god!' Aggie cries, perched on the edge of the sofa, pointing at the TV screen. 'There's Millie and Noah! They don't realise they're on live TV!'

Julie watches in wonder as the camera zooms in on her granddaughter and the man standing next to her, looking into her eyes, nothing short of besotted.

The shot switches and a different group of Eurovision fans going absolutely wild fills the screen. Aggie sighs, shaking her head.

'What a shame they didn't notice the camera on them,' she remarks. 'They would have given us a wave, Mum.'

Julie doesn't say anything. Instead, she allows herself a secretive smile.

She remembers when someone looked at her the way she just witnessed Noah gazing at Millie, back in 1974, just after ABBA finished their performance of 'Waterloo' in the Brighton Dome.

It's the kind of look that changes your life forever.

EPILOGUE

Liverpool, UK

2023

Saturday 13 May

Ingrid presses her index finger against the ear of her headset and turns her head away for a moment to speak into the microphone.

'I will be there *in a minute*,' she says, abruptly interrupting the assistant firing questions at her on the other end. 'Nobody needs to panic. This is not a big problem. And don't speak to the lighting technician until I get there. He's sensitive and I don't need anyone accidentally insulting him right before the Grand Final, is that clear? Leave it with me.'

With a weary sigh, she turns back to Julie.

'I'm so sorry, I have to go,' she says regretfully. 'Apparently our team's director has had a minor disagreement with one of the lighting designers, and now he's threatening to demand a change to the hue of yellow for a spotlight – just what you need when everything has already programmed.'

'I'm sure you'll sort it out in no time,' Julie smiles warmly.

'It's easy to solve: I tell both of them they're brilliant and under no circumstances will any changes be made because the show is starting in a few minutes. Sorted.' She shrugs.

'When I see you later I'll tell you about the time one of the lead actors of a show I was working on quit six minutes before the curtain went up on opening night. Now *that* was a big problem.'

Julie's eyes widen in horror. 'You talked them back onto the stage?'

'With a minute to spare.'

Julie chuckles. 'You really are something. Best of luck for tonight, Ingrid. We will be cheering Germany on.'

'Thank you. Good luck to the UK, too,' Ingrid replies, squeezing her hand. 'And after the show, you'll tell me all about Eurovision in the 1970s and the '80s, right?'

'Oh, we had some wild times,' Julie chuckles, giving her a wink. 'I can certainly tell you plenty of stories.'

'*Mum*,' Aggie says in a warning tone, rolling her eyes.

'I can't wait,' Ingrid grins, before addressing the rest of the group. 'I have to get backstage, but I'll see you all later. James, are you coming with me?'

'I'm going to stay in the audience to watch the opening act,' he says, looking up from his phone, 'but then will be coming back there. I've still got the first exclusive interview with Germany after the performance, yes?'

'Yes, but *after* the performance, James,' she tells him sternly. 'I need my artists focused before, so no trying to get some questions in beforehand.'

He holds up his hands. 'I wouldn't dare.'

She acknowledges his answer with a sharp nod, before turning on her heel and marching away towards the exit. Watching her go, Aggie looks impressed.

'I can see why her shows run so smoothly,' she comments.

'I know, right?' James chuckles, getting back to typing into his phone.

He's been busier than ever in the lead-up to this year's Euro-vision. With the UK acting as the host country on behalf of Ukraine, James was offered the most amazing opportunities to get involved with and document the preparations as they got underway in Liverpool. His website this year has been unrivalled and he's had to stay on top of Eurovision news updates, fresh blog posts, filming interviews and subse-quent editing, as well as regular content for his social media accounts that have been gaining swathes of new followers as nationwide excitement for the contest grew more and more feverish the closer it got to today's Grand Final.

He's had to manage all of that around his news editor job, which hasn't exactly been chilled recently, considering it's Glastonbury next month and he's leading the charge on all of the festival coverage.

Oh, and he's planning his wedding this summer.

He hasn't slept in a few days.

It's all worth it, of course – he's never been happier. And if he needed any further reassurance that all this hard work means something, he only needs to take a glance around the people he's been able to invite along to join him tonight, all of whom are in their element right now, jittering with excitement about the show they're about to experience. They even persuaded Aggie to come, and she may pretend otherwise, but he can tell she's excited to be here. Maybe after tonight, she'll have the Eurovision bug.

Most importantly, thanks to him, Julie has one of the best seats in the house. Securing that for her is worth every minute of rushing around the country and writing into the night to meet deadlines.

In the middle of constructing a caption for an Instagram post as Ingrid leaves to head backstage, James is once more interrupted by his fiancé, who wants to ask him a question about buttonholes.

'Zachary, you made a promise, remember?' James reminds him. 'There's a ban on wedding chat tonight. We're only allowed to talk about Eurovision. I have to focus on my work. Also, the Grand Final is about to start in just a few minutes! What are you doing worrying about *buttonholes* right now?'

'Your mum messaged me,' Zachary explains. 'She's creating a Pinterest board for our colour scheme and wants to know if we want the buttonholes to complement the rest of the floral arrangements or if we'd like something different.'

James narrows his eyes at him. 'Tell her that wedding chat is banned tonight. She shouldn't be on Pinterest right now, she should be watching Eurovision.'

'I think she's doing both,' Zachary says.

Mumbling something about interfering mothers under his breath, James returns his attention to his work. Zachary smiles to himself, knowing very well that James loves how invested his mum is in the wedding, which is due to be held this July at a stunning lakeside venue in Engadin, Switzerland. She's been a great help and Zachary feels lucky that he has such a good bond with his mother-in-law. He can't wait for her to meet all of his family.

When he asked for her permission to propose to her son last year before they travelled to Turin, she hugged him so tight for so long he was a little concerned she might never let go, and when she finally did, she looked him in the eye and said, 'You and my son have the spark. He never had it with anyone else. It's so wonderful when you find it, you must never let it go.'

Zachary doesn't intend to.

Careful to keep his voice down so James can't overhear, Zachary leans towards Noah and asks him his opinion on matching or clashing buttonholes.

'What do you mean?' Noah asks, frowning.

'You're in the wedding business,' Zachary reasons, 'so you must have an opinion. Do you think the buttonholes should match with the other floral arrangements or do you think a colour clash might be quite fun?'

Noah stares at him, bamboozled. Millie bursts out laughing.

'I'm afraid that while Noah may be a successful wedding photographer, Zachary, that doesn't mean he's able to offer a valuable opinion on buttonholes,' she explains regretfully. 'However, if you need any advice on booking a DJ for the wedding, he might be able to link you up with a famous Ibiza resident.'

As Zachary takes his question to Aggie next, Noah turns to look at Millie with raised eyebrows.

'Were you just *mocking* me?' he asks.

'Never,' Millie claims innocently. 'I've always had the greatest respect for your Ibiza DJ tales. They were very entertaining.'

'Laugh all you want, but I was a master of those decks,' Noah asserts. 'The DJ world lost a true talent the day I hung up my headphones.'

'I bet they still talk about you now. Noah Pearce – the one that got away.'

Chuckling, he moves to stand behind her and wrap his arms around her waist, kissing her on the cheek and resting his chin on her shoulder.

While they've only technically been dating for a year, for Millie and Noah – and for everyone who knows them – it feels like they've been together much longer.

Noah wasted no time in asking Millie out on a date the week they got back to the UK from Turin – and she wasted no time in saying yes. He offered to come to Brighton, but she liked the idea of a night out in London, so they had countless cocktails in a bar overlooking the river and the conversation didn't stop flowing once.

They had held hands walking home along the South Bank, in the dim light of the old-fashioned street lamps that line the pathway, and then he'd stopped to pull her towards him, dipping his head to kiss her on the lips. She wrapped her hands round his neck and he dropped his to her waist, and the kiss that started slow and lingering at first became more urgent and passionate.

A cyclist zipping past told them in a disgusted voice to 'get a room', causing them to break away as they both burst out laughing.

It was, in Noah's opinion, the perfect first kiss, as he told her after they'd been dating a few weeks. Millie corrected him, reminding him of the time they kissed in Lisbon, but he declared that one didn't count. The way he saw it, the South Bank kiss was officially the first because they had both known in that moment that it was the start of something.

Millie couldn't argue with that.

It took no time at all for them to settle into their relationship; it was so natural and easy that it didn't seem fast for Noah to give up his flat in London and move to Brighton to live with Millie in a new place within four months of that first date.

They flew to Australia for two weeks over Christmas and Noah introduced her to his family. Giving Millie the warmest of welcomes, Charlotte was pleased they finally 'got over themselves' and realised they were meant for each other, something she'd picked up on in the first two minutes of watching them interact in Sweden. Noah's mum instantly took to Millie and fussed over her the entire time they stayed. She made Millie promise to encourage Noah to keep visiting home, because she really did miss her son and video calls just weren't the same – Millie did promise and, now that there had been some movement on their property developments in London, she voiced her hope that Noah's family would come visit them in the UK soon, too.

Things between Noah and his dad may not be perfect, but they've thawed significantly. He's impressed by Noah's photography business and, as Noah suspected he would be, he was charmed by Millie. As he gave Noah a slightly awkward hug at the airport, he'd even said he was proud of him. Noah knew that he didn't need his dad's approval any more, but it meant a lot all the same.

On the flight back to the UK, as Millie pulled on her eye mask and rested her head against his shoulder, it struck Noah that it was the first time Australia had ever felt like home, and that was because Millie had been there, by his side. Wherever Millie was, he wanted to be. And that's why he's booked a surprise weekend for her in Oslo, Norway, this August, a couple of weeks after James and Zachary's wedding, and before school starts again. The city where they first met feels like the right place to ask her to spend the rest of her life with him. He revealed his plan to Julie and Aggie just the other day.

Julie gave him her engagement ring.

'Noah,' Millie whispers excitedly, as the lights go down in Liverpool Arena and the audience joins together in chorus to count down to the Eurovision Grand Final 2023. 'It's all about to begin!'

'Yeah,' he replies with a smile, tightening his arms around her waist. 'It is.'

Acknowledgements

A huge thank you to Olivia, Kim and the wonderful team at Hodder. It was such a privilege to work with you on this book and I hope I have done your fabulous story idea justice. Thank you for trusting me with it! And thank you to the amazingly talented Lucy and the design team for such a beautiful cover that brings the story and the characters to life.

As ever, special thanks to Paul, Justine, Lauren and the team at Bell Lomax Moreton for all your wisdom and guidance.

Thank you to Sam Ryder for Space Man at Eurovision 2022, an incredible performance that made the whole country proud.

Finally, to the readers – myself, Olivia and the Hodder team wanted to create a book that celebrates what Eurovision is all about: love, joy, diversity and unity. I very much hope you will find all of that within these pages and I hope this story, which was ridiculously fun to write, will bring some cheer to your day . . . and inspire you to throw on those sequins and hit up the dance floor.